HITCHHIKE TO MURDER.

Chapter One

The Seeds Are Sown

'I'll be getting it tomorrow,' shouted Barry to his sister Anne, referring to the Elvis Monthly magazine. He worked at the local WH Smith's store with responsibility for the news and magazine department and would be the first to see it.

'Oh great!' said Anne. 'Will you please bring it home when you come for your lunch so I can have a good look at it before you finish work?'

They were both huge fans of the King. In fact, Barry believed his sister was an even bigger Elvis fan than himself!

'Yes, all right ..... if I remember,' replied Barry.

'Oh, don't forget please! Otherwise it will be an age before I get a chance to see it. You'll keep it for days!' pleaded Anne.

The latest issue had just been published and it was earmarked for delivery to the shop that day. He hated having to get up early each morning but, being responsible for the news department meant it was his job to sort all the newspapers and magazines before the shop opened.

The year was 1967 and Barry was an unassuming, happy go lucky, 18 year old lad, somewhat shy but a chatterbox when with his friends. At 5' 11" tall, of a gangly appearance due to his thin build, with short cropped hair and a fresh complexion, he possessed a long nose and a mole on his left cheek. His hazel eyes gave him a rather handsome look but he didn't think he looked anything special - just an ordinary teenager, no different to any others of the time.

He lived on Warwick Place in his home town of Penrith, with his parents, four younger sisters and an older brother. The girls slept upstairs in one large bedroom which occupied the whole of the rear of the property. Barry and his brother Paul shared a second bedroom which looked out over the front of the house ; his parents slept in a smaller bedroom adjacent to the brothers. The bathroom and toilet were downstairs, below the girls bedroom at the rear of the property as was the kitchen. The large living room was to the front of this end-terraced house, looking onto the street where their father, George's car could be seen. Barry's mother was called Iris and the only other residents were the family pets, a dog called Butch - a Labrador -and a cat called Smokey, who kept the far larger dog in check!

The morning dawned bright and crisp which was a relief after the previous day's snow flurries. A cup of coffee and a piece of toast were all he had time for, then off to work. Being a smoker, he lit his first cigarette of the day as he left the house, before making his way through the estate onto Castlegate. He walked quickly down onto Cornmarket where the shop was situated. On his way, he kept humming his current favourite record, 'The Letter' by the Box Tops, unusual in that it wasn't by Elvis.

Barry was a deep thinker who was prone to self criticism, often dwelling on the negatives in his character, which resulted in a lack of self-confidence. He wasn't much of a talker and when this was added to his acute shyness in female company, it meant his relationships with the opposite sex didn't last long. He was sure they liked him but believed they found him boring. He was also lazy when it came to his appearance, only doing the minimum necessary to pass scrutiny. He wasn't a fashion guru, his wardrobe being particularly sparse. This, however, was exacerbated by his love of the horses. His gambling habit was costing him a large chunk of his wages, leaving little for clothes. He knew he should quit but on every pay day he found himself asking to the bookies.

As Barry approached the shop, he realised it was time to stop daydreaming and get to work. Being the only early starter, he had a key to the side entrance. The day's newspapers and magazines were supposed to be piled up outside but there was no sign of them. He opened the door which revealed a dark corridor, at the beginning of which was a hatch through which Barry was supposed to drop the newspapers, to the cellar below. He was now feeling fed up. This would delay him. He needn't have got up so early, he thought, as he went along to the staff room to make himself a cup of tea while he waited for the delivery. He would hear the van as it pulled up outside so he enjoyed another cigarette with his brew. Time passed with still no sign of the vehicle, so he wandered out onto the shop floor for something to do while he was waiting. He walked slowly towards the shop entrance which was at the far end, making his way passed the small sales island which had a glass display front showcasing fountain pens with designs by Parker and Schaefer. To his right was a carousel of cheap 'Music for Pleasure' albums which were also Barry's responsibility. The magazine and news counter was further along on the right, near the main shop entrance. Opposite was a large display of paperback books.

As he approached the entrance he could see something outside under the porch. As he got closer he realised what it was. 'Oh no! For fucks sake! It's the papers! Why the hell did they leave them there? They *know* they are supposed to leave them at the side entrance! How much time have I wasted already? I'm going to be rushed to get them all sorted in time for the shop to open now and I'll get the blame if they are not on the counter ready for the customers! For god's sake!' This was said out loud in frustration while he ran to the office for the keys needed to open the shop door.

Once opened, he had to drag the bundles all the way through the shop before he could drop them down the hatch. He was exhausted by the time he had done so. Breathing heavily after that effort, he remembered to go back to the shop door and secure it before making his way down to the cellar where a gnarled, worn and dusty wooden bench greeted him. It looked like it had been there for centuries and commanded the whole length of the cellar which was illuminated by two small bulbs giving just enough light to see by. Barry thought it was a bit spooky, especially when he was in the building on his own. He hated it but thankfully he had a portable radio which he turned on and tuned in to Radio Caroline, the pirate radio station which was all the rage at the time. Tony Blackburn was on air and currently playing 'Hole in my Shoe' by Traffic. Barry liked this song. It cheered him a bit and he started singing along to the record whilst sorting the magazines. Amongst them he found the one he was looking for, the Elvis Monthly.

'Yeeeeessss, brilliant!' cried Barry, to himself. Anne will be pleased when she sees it, he thought. It was the November '67 issue and the shop had orders for six copies, one of which was his, but he didn't have time to look at it. He glanced at his watch - time was getting on. He quickly sorted the papers and magazines into two piles, those which were customer's orders and those which were destined for the sales counter. As he was finishing, Tony Blackburn was introducing The Monkeys latest release, 'Daydream Believer', which was soon to become another favourite of Barry's and destined to be a chart topper. Grumbling to himself, he didn't have time to listen to is so he switched the radio off but carried on humming the tune as he took the customer orders upstairs ready for opening time.

He placed them in their respective folders and hurriedly returned to the cellar to collect the remaining newsprint which he arranged on the news counter for general sale. He had just finished doing this when two other staff members arrived at the shop entrance. Phew! Just in time, thought Barry. He knew Joan wouldn't be happy if he hadn't got them sorted by opening time and would accuse him of having been late to work, something which had happened in the past when he slept through his alarm.

'Morning both,' said Barry, trying to look relaxed as Joan used her key to open the door.

'Morning Barry,' said Joan, in her usual off-hand way.

'Morning Barry,' replied Margaret, sounding rather chirpy.

Joan and Margaret were like chalk and cheese, both in appearance and character. Joan was 33 years old, about 5'6" tall, slim with long auburn hair, a freckly face and turned up but pretty nose and rather thin but elegant lips. She had lovely blue eyes, but there was a coldness about them, thought Barry. She was classed as a bit of a looker but had no boyfriend and nobody could remember her having one for some time, although she was not believed to be a lesbian. Her attitude towards men was very stand-offish which is probably the reason she had never had a marriage proposal off anyone.

Margaret, on the other hand, was 30 years old, short and tubby with short but thick curly black hair. She wore spectacles and, unlike Joan, was of quite a cheery nature, always with a smile on her face. She also didn't have a boyfriend but she didn't let it bother her. Every time she looked in the mirror she thought she could see why and had given up any hope of finding one, but didn't let this prospect dampen her positive outlook on life. Margaret was always ready to give a good word of encouragement to Barry who, although he had been working there for over a year, was the junior member of an otherwise all-female staff, the elderly male manager, Gerry Attrick notwithstanding.

After changing into her blue uniform, Margaret came out of the staff room first and asked Barry if his magazine had arrived, referring to his Elvis Monthly. He said it had and showed her his copy.

'Have you heard of the Elvis Convention thing they've announced for next year? I think they said it's in Leicester,' asked Margaret, excitedly, whilst thumbing through the magazine.

'No, I haven't. Do you know when?' replied Barry, now all ears.

'I'm not sure' said Margaret. 'I think they said July. It was just a quick news item on the radio. I wasn't taking a lot of notice. I thought you, being the biggest fan of his I know, would already know about it'

'No. I haven't heard a thing. I will have to have a look at that. It's something I would love to go to but I can't see that happening. I can't see me ever having the king of money I would need to be able to afford it'

Joan, who had emerged from the staff room, heard most of this conversation.

'Call yourself a big Elvis fan?' she began, 'you of *all* people should be thinking of going. It shouldn't be *that* difficult!' This was said in her usual snotty manner towards Barry. He thought, what a nasty condescending old woman she is, old before her time! No wonder she hasn't got a male partner with that attitude!

'How am I going to get down there anyway? It would mean an overnight stay at least. With what little spare cash I have from the crap wages I get here, I'll never be able to save enough to afford it!'

'Don't make me laugh!' sneered Joan. 'If you stopped wasting all your money on betting on horses you would be able to afford it in no time. It's not until the middle of next year so what's the problem?'

It so happened Barry was going to the bookies far too often. He was loath to admit it but she had a point. Being told by this condescending bitch didn't go down well with him though.

'Why don't you take your girlfriend?' Joan added.

'Because I don't have one' said Barry dejectedly.

'I know,' said Joan with the sound of glee in her voice.

Barry was getting angry. He didn't like Joan's remarks. None of the staff in the shop had ever seen him angry. He thought he had managed to hold his temper but then he replied, sarcastically, 'Well I can't go by myself. I need somebody to go with. How about you? You said I haven't got a girlfriend and everybody knows you've NEVER had a boyfriend. I could see us both having a great time!' he said.

The slap on his face wasn't seen coming until it was too late. He could feel his face reddening almost immediately. When Joan's hand struck, Margaret looked on in total shock. Her face turned red with embarrassment before she dissolved into half suppressed giggles while Joan marched off to the other end of the shop with her head thrown back as if to say, 'that showed you!'

The first customer of the day had just walked into the shop and it was difficult to tell from his appearance if he had seen any of this incident or even noticed the reddening to Barry's face. It was one of his regular customers and he wanted his copy of the Daily Mirror.

'Morning, Mr. Borrowdale, here's your paper,' said Barry, rubbing the red mark on his face.

When he had finished serving Mr Borrowdale, he got on with his day's work, pushing what had just occurred to the back of his mind. Being the person that he was, it didn't take long for him to cheer up, having a chuckle to himself about it later. For the rest of the morning and afternoon he kept thinking of the Elvis convention, trying to work out how he could possibly get there. Wouldn't it be great to be able to put Joan's face out of joint, he dreamt.

Being Saturday morning, however, he was too busy to come up with any ideas. He remembered to take the magazine home during his lunch break so that Anne could have a good read, otherwise she would be constantly on his back until he handed it over. On his return to work, he was unable to think of any way he could get to the convention. The steady stream of customers kept interrupting his thoughts. By closing time, he was still at a loss of what to do about it. He left the shop to make his way home and by now he was feeling a little depressed. No convention for him next year, he thought.

After tea, Barry tried to give some more thought to the Elvis convention but couldn't think of any way he would be able to go so he reluctantly gave up the idea. He imagined it would be too expensive so he tried to put the possibility of going to Leicester out of his mind.

This darkened his mood for a while so he tried to cheer himself up by making a start on his latest book. He had borrowed a copy of James Clavell's 'Tai Pan' from the shop. It had been the subject of a big advertising promotion by WH Smith's the year before, but he had only just got round to reading it. He was glad the manager allowed staff to borrow books. He said it made us more informative and could help customers but all Barry was interested in was reading. Before he had completed one page there was a knock on the door. Alice, another of his sisters, answered it.

Barry, it's your mate Ian for you. Should I send him up?'

'Tell him I'm coming down. I want to go out,' replied Barry.

He put his book down, hoping he would have time for a read in bed later. He grabbed his coat and left the house with his mate. At one year younger than Barry, Ian Barnes was slightly shorter with a round swarthy face, thick eyebrows and short light brown hair. As you will see he tends to repeat his words. They went for an evening stroll around the estate as was there want when they had nothing better to do. The little heat the sun had possessed on this November day was now replaced by an icy easterly breeze, making them both shiver a little. Barry hated winters. Roll on Summer, he thought.

They lived in a typical council estate of the time, this one being near the town's castle where they often spent some of their evenings, but more so in the summer months. They walked along the cut at the rear of the houses until they reached a road which ran downhill to the left, towards the town centre and uphill to the right, towards a feature known locally as the 'planny'. This was a plantation of shrubs and small trees, hence the nickname and it formed a square with houses on the other three sides. The road on reaching the plantation, split to the left and right, forming the fourth side. This was Castle Terrace. Approximately 50 yards to the right was the entrance to the local park where the castle could be found. Up the hill they walked at a slow, leisurely pace. As they approached the 'planny', Barry said, 'Have you heard of the Elvis convention being held in Leicester next year, Ian?'

'No! You're joking, aren't you?' replied Ian.

'No, I'm not joking. I think it's in July. At least that's what Margaret at work said. I would love to go but I don't see how,' said Barry, trying not to let his friend know how fed up he was at the thought.

'It would be great if we could go though, eh?' said Ian. 'It's just getting there! It would cost a fortune 'cos neither of us can drive and it would mean, like, staying overnight at least. Aye, overnight.'

'No, your'e right. It would be too expensive,' moaned Barry.

He gave a shiver and held his coat tighter round himself as if to gain some extra protection from the

6

cold night air. The wind, although light, was particularly biting that night and Mick wondered what the hell they were doing outside. A minute or two passed with both lads deep in thought before Barry added, 'Apparently, it's something that happens every year but I've never heard of it before now.'

'What does?' asked Ian.

'This convention thing, you dibbo!' shouted Barry in frustration.

Just then a figure came around the corner. It was Rosemary, a girl who seemed to appear as if by accident whenever these two lads were out and about. It was obvious she had feelings for Ian and he for her. It was a pain when they were trying to discuss something but Barry didn't really mind. Rosemary was rather petite with long black hair and rosy red cheeks and a smile which showed her perfect white teeth. She was intelligent, and mature for her 17 years and lived on the Castletown estate which was not too far from the castle itself, hence the name. She was wearing a thick grey coat to protect her from the cold night air.

After initial greetings, the threesome strolled along Castle Terrace towards the park entrance. Up the steps and into the park they walked, turning left and up to the main footpath through the area. They headed towards two buildings which housed a toilet block and a larger structure which contained a small cafe and room for the local bowls team to store their gear. As it was nearly time for the park to be closed up for the night, both buildings were already shut and locked but that didn't matter as the friends had other things on their minds, Barry and Ian being deep in thought.

They walked on with Rosemary chatting about nothing in particular and were now on a path which ran parallel to the town's castle ruin which was to their right. Made of sandstone and surrounded by a deep moat, it loomed up through the gloom and cold of the evening, the sight of it making the group shiver once more. The two lads had been hardly listening to Rosemary's chatter. Eventually they mentioned their predicament to her.

She stopped walking with a quizzical look on her face before shouting excitedly, 'Why don't you hitch-hike down? You could set off a few days earlier if you managed to get some camping gear. I'm sure there will be people who would lend you what you need!' She was now in full flow and continued, 'You could make a holiday of it and if you got there early you could find somewhere to pitch a tent and stay there until after the concert before making your way back home. It would be something to think of and good fun for you!'

'Hmm, I don't know,' said Barry. 'It's an idea but let's chew on it for a day or two. We've still got plenty of time before we need to make a decision.'

This was said without any real enthusiasm for the idea. Ian echoed his agreement and the friends walked on to the war memorial which formed part of the vehicle access to the park. The railway station was opposite and as they were exiting the park a noisy steam train was departing. Commuters were hurrying out of the station into the cold evening air but Barry and his companions took no notice. Turning right, they walked down the main road which skirted the boundary of the park until they reached another entrance to it, at the top of Castlegate where Barry said his goodbyes, stating he was too cold and would make his way back home, through the park. He knew the two lovebirds would like some time on their own so Rosemary and Ian walked over the hill leaving Barry alone.

On re-entering the park he looked over to the castle, which was still on his right hand side. Their wandering meant they had circled it. There was a grey wooden bridge which had been slung across the moat some years ago - he couldn't remember when - to enable easy access for tourists to the castle which was now in darkness. The still cold night air added to it's eerie appearance and the breeze which was picking up made Barry pull his coat tighter around himself once again. He wished he had a girlfriend to keep him warm but, alas, this was something which was lacking in his life at that moment in time. Again, feeling a bit down, he continued his journey home, exiting the park at the same point the three friends had entered it.

Passing the 'planny' and going down the hill, he arrived back home where he spoke to his mother about the convention and how he and Ian would love to go. He told her that he didn't think there was any chance. He also mentioned how Rosemary had suggested hitching but he was yet to drum up any enthusiasm for travelling that way. Muttering to himself he made his way to bed.

His mother, Iris, was 43 years old. She was petite with black hair and had a generally happy-go-lucky attitude to life which Barry had inherited, despite his current morbidity. She was also a smoker and lit a cigarette while she thought over what Barry had said. She could tell that he was not his normal cheery self so she decided she would see if there was anything she could do to help him realise his dream. She knew that Barry and Ian were big Elvis fans and although she would be worried about them hitching all that way, if that was their only means of travelling, she resolved to see if there was anything she could do to help. She spent the rest of the evening deep in thought.

The following day she was speaking to Mrs Simpson from number 19 who knew a neighbour who had some old rucksacks. Within a few hours, Iris had the rucksacks and couldn't wait to show them to Barry when he came home. That evening, he finished work and his mother was waiting for him to arrive. She saw him coming up the road towards the house and when he entered, he noticed a big smile on her face. Like a genie, she picked up the rucksacks and waved them at him.

'What are they!' asked Barry. Before she could say any more, the penny dropped. 'Are those for what I think they are, mam?'

'They are. I think you should think harder about this hitchhiking thing to Leicester,' she said. 'I am sure if everybody mucked in we could get all the stuff you would need to take. I managed to get hold of these for starters!' she said, with a smile on her face, putting them back on the floor.

As Barry looked at them the realisation came over him that all was not lost and they could possibly make it to the convention after all! It would be a dream come true!

He said, 'You know, mam, I think you may just be right!'

He went over to her and gave her a big hug. His smile was back. His mother beamed. She was so pleased that she had acquired the rucksacks. It was not like Barry to be miserable like this.

That evening he went out with Ian as usual. Not being sure what his mate would think about hitch-hiking, he explained what his mother had done and carefully said, 'I think we just might be able to do this after all. If your'e interested, of course! What do you think?'

Ian, even when keen on something, always took his time before making any kind of decision and this was one of those times. He thought hard. Barry knew how his mind worked and kept quiet, knowing Ian would eventually come to a decision. Ian was pacing around, deep in thought until eventually, with excitement in his voice, he said, 'Yes, let's give it a go. Let's see what other goodies we can lay our hands on before we say for definite, of course, but let's give it a go, eh!'

Yessss !' replied Barry. 'Thats great news! Let's go for it !'

He went home that night with a spring in his step and feeling a lot more positive about the convention.

Chapter Two

The Camping Equipment is Gathered

A couple of weeks later and its December. Although still cold, there was no snow but there had been no further progress regarding their trip. Ian thought it was about time they sorted something out about the tickets otherwise they may as well forget all about it, so when he and Barry next met he mentioned this to him.

'If we are really going, we need to get them, eh? They may be sold out.....you know ....aye, sold out! he said. 'Then we won't be able to go. Do you know how to go about getting them?'

'I'll have a look at the latest Elvis Monthly,' said Barry. 'I think I saw details about it somewhere in there if my memory serves me well.'

He dashed upstairs and returned with the last two issues. Sure enough, he found an article about the convention with details of how to purchase tickets. They would cost them 12s 6d each.

'I can give you my 12s 6d tomorrow. Look! It says they accept Postal Orders so if you can get them and send them off, we will really be going to Leicester, won't we,'said Ian, 'aye, really going.'

'OK Ian, I'll do that at lunchtime tomorrow,' replied Barry.

The next day he bought the Postal Orders and sent them off. He told Ian that evening and his mate was only too pleased to hand over his money.

'So it's defo on then, eh! Brilliant! It's defo on!' said Ian. He was wearing a grin which seemed to be fixed to his face. 'When do you think the tickets will arrive, Barry? Next week?' he asked.

'I don't know. It didn't give a timescale. I should imagine by the end of next week but we have plenty of time,' replied Barry, 'but let's just hope we haven't left it too late sending off for them, eh, Ian!'

'Don't say that, Barry!' replied Ian with real concern in his voice.

Our heroes spent the next few days anxiously awaiting their arrival. In fact it was an agonising two weeks wait until the postman finally paid a visit to the house. Amongst the mail was one addressed to Barry. He hurriedly opened it and sure enough the tickets were inside. Well, thats goo, he thought. They hadn't been too late after all! The only other paperwork was a confirmation of the date and location.

It was now Friday night and Barry couldn't wait to tell his friend. Ian came round as usual and Barry ushered him inside. Before Ian could say a word, Barry said, 'They're here Ian! It's definitely taking place. It's on the 21st July at a place called the De Montford Hall!' As he said this his face was one big smile. He handed Ian the tickets to look at. grabbed hold of them and took a good look.

'That's fantastic, eh? We are defo going, we are defo going!' sang Ian and started to dance around the room. He was elated.

Iris asked if she could have a look at the tickets and was pleased they had managed to acquire them. After a while, she said, 'Where's De Montford Hall? I thought you were going to Leicester?'

Barry laughed and said, 'We are mam. It's a place in Leicester. It sounds like an old stately home which has been done up so that it can host events like this one, but it is in Leicester.'

'Oh .... well I didn't know. I'm not intelligent like you two.'

Barry suppressed a giggle. Ian sat himself down opposite his mate and said, 'We'll have to start getting our things together and making plans, eh? Yeh, making plans.'

'At least mam got us the rucksacks, Ian. That's a start.'

'Yes but we haven't got much else,'he replied.

'Well, we will need a tent for starters,'said Barry, 'and some sleeping bags or blankets and cooking things,' he continued.

'Yeh, some cooking things,' repeated Ian, now deep in thought.

There was a pause. Both friends were now thinking hard and every now and then one or the other would mention something they thought they should consider taking. Barry, who was the recognised organiser of the pair, started taking notes. After about half an hour they looked at the list. Barry frowned. The list was long, perhaps too long and it almost outfaced him. How would they be able to carry it all? Some items would have to be removed so they set about streamlining their needs until they were fairly satisfied that they would be physically capable of carrying all the things they thought they should take, but it would all depend on acquiring a light enough tent.

'Hey Mother, you don't happen to know of anyone who has a tent, do you?' asked Barry.

'As light as possible, eh!' interjected Ian, 'yeh, as light as possible.'

'How the hell do I know!' snapped Barry's mother, disinterestedly. She was watching Coronation Street on TV and they had distracted her. She quickly saw the look on their faces and added, 'I'll ask your Dad when he comes in. He's bound to know someone. He'll be home soon. Don't bother me while Corrie is on though, it's my favourite.'

She lit another cigarette and got back to watching her favourite programme. Our two heroes continued to make plans and dream of their adventure. Coronation Street was just finishing when Barry's dad, George, returned home from the local Post Office where he worked. During the 2nd World War he had been in the RAF and on leaving had wanted to become a policeman but he was an inch too short so he applied for and got a job in the GPO. He was 10 years older than Barry's mother and wore his hair slicked back and sported a thin moustache. Iris still thought him a very handsome man. Before he had time to take off his coat, Barry enquired if he knew of anyone who had a tent, a light tent, big enough for two.

George thought for a moment before saying, 'I don't know. I'll ask around at work.'

The words had no sooner been spoken when he had a thought, 'Hey mam, doesn't Bernie Nichols have a tent?'

Iris thought for a moment or two then said, 'Oh yes. Wasn't he talking about what a good holiday they had in it last year? I presume he still has it. I'll ask Ada tomorrow. I'm going there for a coffee in the morning anyway.' Iris loved her coffee meetings with Ada, Bernie's wife, who lived in a lovely house on Neville Avenue.

'Oh that's great, mam. Let's hope they can help,' shouted Barry.

'Yeh, that's great Mrs Davidson. That will be our biggest problem out of the way, like. Yeh, our biggest problem!' said Ian, irritating everyone with his repetitions which got worse when he was excited.

'I'm not promising anything,' said Iris. 'He might have got rid of it.'

'Oh mother! You certainly know how to worry us!' groaned Barry.

'I'm only joking. Stop worrying, you two,' laughed Iris.

With nothing further to be discussed, Ian made his way home and Barry went to bed that night more hopeful that they would make it after all. He would have great pleasure telling Joan at work in the morning. He thought it was sure to put her nose out of joint.

Saturday dawned and Barry's mother did as she promised and went for coffee with Mrs Nichols who confirmed they still owned a tent.

'Of course they can borrow it, Iris,' she said immediately, pouring her friend a coffee. 'I'm sure Bernie will be only too happy to let them use it. We go camping a lot as you know so we have a lot of other camping gear they might want to borrow - sleeping bags, pots, pans - and we even have a portable gas cooker they can use, if they want!'. She handed Iris her mug of coffee and sat down beside her.

'Oh, that's wonderful, Ada! They will be ever so pleased!' said Iris.

'Just send them round and they can see what we have that might be useful to them. I think we have just about everything they could want'

'I can't wait to tell them. They'll be over the moon. And you're right. With what you're saying they will have everything they need, apart from food that is,' added a happy Iris, drinking her coffee.

'Well then, tell them to come round tomorrow afternoon when Bernie will be back from his allotment,' said Ada.

'I will,' said Iris, lighting another cigarette and passing one to Ada. 'They will be so pleased.'

———————

While this conversation was taking place, Barry was at work. He only got one Saturday off in six as did the rest of the staff. Joan was also in work that day. Barry was glad because he hadn't mentioned anything further to her since way back in November when they had their first altercation about the trip. He hadn't forgotten the slap he received that time. Hew was keen to update her just to see her reaction. However, Joan beat him to it and was the first to broach the subject.

'What's going on with this Elvis Convention thing Barry? Am I correct in saying it has died a death, that you're incapable of organising anything? If you carry on like this, life will just pass you by.'

Barry waved to Margaret to join them before saying, 'It just so happens that our tickets arrived yesterday so stick that up your pipe and smoke it. We are definitely going, so there!' Barry continued to sort the magazines before continuing, 'We're gonna make a hitchhiking holiday of it and set off a few days earlier. I've already booked time off with Gerry, so you see, it's all organised and life isn't going to pass me by as you think!' This was said with a triumphant snarl in his voice.

He continued to keep himself busy, waiting for any reply Joan might have. Margaret beat her to it and congratulated him. Although she was his friend, she also didn't think he was capable of organising such an undertaking. The big surprise for Barry was Joan's response.

'Oh, well done Barry!' began Joan with surprise in her voice. 'I'm really pleased for you. I know I didn't think you would do it which is only what a lot of other people thought but well done you! You have shown me a side of you I didn't believe existed.' While saying this she came over to him and gave him a hug and showed him a beaming smile which he realised was genuine!

'Blimey, thanks Joan. I'm taken aback. You've surprised me!'

'Yes, I know,' said Joan. 'The last time we spoke about it I was having a few problems at home. My mother wasn't well and Dad was too busy on the farm to give her the attention she needed so it was all down to me. I couldn't get the time off I needed to help her so I was knackered and that turned me into a miserable person to know.'

'Oh dear! I am sorry to hear that. How is she now?'

'Thankfully she is well on the road to recovery ..... so you are going to hitchhike are you?' said Joan, getting back to the subject.

'Yes, it's the only realistic option for us. And for your info, I haven't been to the bookies since we last spoke either.'

'That is really good news, Barry. Keep it up. It's a mugs game. The only real winners are the bookies. I hope you enjoy your trip. If you find there is something you can't get hold of, let me know. Crotchety old me might be able to help.' She smiled and then went to serve a customer at the other end of the shop.

Barry whispered to Margaret, 'I can't believe it! Joan being nice to me! That's a first! I'm not saying I am not pleased but that was totally unexpected. Maybe things will be different between us now.'

Margaret replied that she too was gobsmacked even though she knew about her mother being ill. It just wasn't Joan in spite of this. They both suggested that maybe there was some good news in her love-life for a change!

— — — — — —

That evening, Iris took great pleasure in telling Barry about her visit to Ada. She told him about the tent and other items they could borrow and as she guessed, he was ecstatic and couldn't wait to tell Ian. He went straight round to his house and told him his mother's news.

'All that stuff? I wish we could go round now, eh!'said Ian. 'Aye, I wish we could go round now. I'm itching to see what they've got.'

'Things are starting to come together, Ian. Exciting times!' said Barry.

'Yeh, you're right there, Barry! Exciting times!' chirped up Ian.

Barry also told him of what happened at work with Joan and he agreed something strange must have happened for her to change her attitude. It definitely wasn't like her.The pair decided to go for their usual stroll outside. No sooner had they reached the 'planny' when Rosemary turned up, out of the blue as usual. The lads immediately told her their news. She jumped up and clapped her hands. She was so happy she hugged them both, particularly her boyfriend Ian.

'I know you still have a lot of time yet but I think you should be having a think of what sort of food you're going to take. Tinned stuff and biscuit's and things like that would be best. I wouldn't take too much water because it's heavy and you can get water anywhere. Don't forget you still have to think of weight,' said Rosemary. She was in full flow now and continued, 'It would be a good idea once you get this stuff, to pack it all in your rucksacks and try them on to see what it feels like to carry to make sure they aren't too heavy.'

'Yes, yes, ok Rosemary, let's wait and see what we get before we get too far ahead of ourselves. We're already aware of the weight implications. I'm sure we will be able to sort it,' said Barry.

'Ok, I'm just saying!' scowled Rosemary, obviously upset at Barry's response.

'Now now you two, calm down, eh? We should be looking forward to it, not falling out, yeh, putting our heads together to sort it,' said Ian.

'Sorry Rosemary,' said Barry. 'I didn't mean anything.'

'Yes, I know you didn't. Don't worry about it Barry. I was getting carried away. I shouldn't be getting involved. I should be leaving it to you two,' replied Rosemary in an equally conciliatory tone.

'No, no,' said Barry, smiling at her. 'You have some good ideas. Put in your two pennyworth whenever you want. You have some good ideas'

They continued to chat excitely for another half an hour before the cold air curtailed their enthusiasm for any more discussion. Barry said his goodbye's and as usual left Ian and his girlfriend to spend some time on their own while he returned home.

On Sunday Barry collected Ian and they went to Bernie and Ada's to check out the camping equipment. They knocked on the door which was soon answered by Bernie. He tugged at his braces which were holding his grey flannels up and said, 'Come in lads. Wipe yer feet and go through to the kitchen. No need to take yer shoes off in our house. We ain't particular folk.'

The Nichol's were a short, dumpy couple who seemed to have permanent smiles on their faces. They loved children. Although they were not blessed with any of their own, everyone said that if they had been, they would have been the luckiest kids on the estate. No need to take yer shoes off, Mr Nichol had said.

'Oh no, we'll take them off,' replied Barry.

Ian was going to walk through without removing his but Barry stopped him. 'Take your shoes off Ian,' he whispered with some firmness in his voice. 'Show some respect to people's property, mate!'

'Oh, OK,' groaned Ian. 'But I've got a hole in one of my socks, yeh a bloody hole and I'm embarrassed!' he whispered back.

Barry was taking off one of his shoes as Ian was speaking. 'Don't worry about it Ian. Snap ! So have I!'

He laughed and Ian chuckled back.

'What's garn on there did you two now?' shouted Bernie.

'Nothing,' replied Barry. 'We're just taking our shoes off. Coming through now!' he shouted, with a suppressed giggle.

They both walked into the kitchen where they were greeted with what to them was a veritable Aladdins cave. The Nichol's had erected their tent just outside the kitchen window and dotted around the kitchen were pots, pans, a calor gas cooker and other useful pieces of equipment. There was a torch complete with spare batteries, a Swiss Army knife, an alarm clock, a set of knives and forks and metal dinner plates. There was even a portable radio for them. The lads were speechless!

15

'What d'yer think then lads?' asked Bernie. 'D'yer think any of it will be of any good use fer yers?' He could see by their reaction that they were more than pleased with what they could see in front of them.

Eventually, when Barry got over his surprise, he said, 'How did you manage to get the tent up in such a small space outside your kitchen?'

'When you lads 'ave put this 'ere tent up as many times as me and Ada 'ave, yer'd manage it. There isn't much space for ought else out there. Thats why we used the kitchen. Yer can see everythin' else we have fer yer in 'ere.' replied Bernie, proudly.

Ada said, 'Choose what you want lads. We know you will be hitchhiking so you won't be able to carry everything but as well as the tent I would suggest you take the cooker, these pots and pans.....'

Ada pointed to each item as she mentioned them. As she was speaking, Barry took a pen and piece of paper out of his pocket which contained a list of items they thought they would need - a shopping list for their trip - and began crossing things off .

Ada was 3 years older than Bernie, at 53 and, as previously mentioned, was rather rotund, mirroring her husband's figure. At barely 5 feet tall, she had thick curly greying hair and wore spectacles as did her husband. She was wearing a pinny over a skirt and thick denier stockings. She was old before her time but had a jolly appearance, always smiling and welcoming. When she had finished speaking, she noticed the lads looked overwhelmed at what they saw. She could tell they were mentally checking out everything they had prepared for them and she could also see that they were pleased.

The lads worked out that between them they could carry all the items she mentioned. Once they got over their shock they couldn't stop thanking the Nichol's. They said that all the items they mentioned would suit them perfectly and started, with the Nichol's permission, to gather this veritable bounty. Bernie and Ada were so pleased that they were able to help them in their quest. They looked at each other and just smiled. Once they had collected all the camping gear, Bernie showed them the tent and how to take it down and pack it up. He told them he would come round some day to make sure they were able to erect it, despite the lads saying they would be able to manage. Bernie insisted, saying that it would need to be properly aired anyway. Barry and Ian put their shoes back on over their wholly socks and left with their haul. As they walked out, they kept thanking the Nichol's who found it so funny they couldn't help but giggle. Both Barry and Ian made a mental note to check their socks and invest in some new pairs!

The decision was made to leave their haul at Ian's house until it was time to pack for their trip because he had more space in his bedroom. Now all they had to do was take on board Rosemary's ideas for the food they should take and to continue saving money.

'We need to plan our route to Leicester, eh! and decide when we need to set off 'cos we will need to give ourselves time to get there, don't you think?,' suggested Ian, 'yeh, time to make our way there.'

'Aye. I'll have a think about it. We have plenty of time yet though. Let's see what we can come up with. One thing we will need is some sort of map to get us down there. We sell maps at work. There's bound to be one suitable for what we need,' said Barry. 'I'll suss it out.'

After dropping the stuff off at Ian's, Barry went home and his mate went out to meet Rosemary to tell her about the gear the Nichol's had produced for them, from the tent to all the utensils they would need.

For the next few weeks Barry tried to save as much money as he could but although he managed to keep away from the bookies, he still hadn't amassed much. One ray of good news was that his boss, Gerry, chose a suitable map and gave it to Barry free of charge....well, Gerry paid for it himself to be exact. He thought the trip would be good for his confidence. With his finances in a poor state, Barry had a very quiet Christmas. The same could be said for the first few weeks of the new year as he strove to boost his funds but he was still a long way short of what he felt he needed to take to Leicester.

One day, he came home from work as usual and greeted his mother. While taking his coat off, she said, 'I spoke to Ada today. She said Bernie would like to come over on Sunday afternoon to show you the best way to put the tent up. I said that would be OK,' said his mother, who was preparing the family's evening meal - roast leg of lamb - one of Barry's favourites.

'Aye, I suppose so. I'm sure we can put it up all right but seeing as we are borrowing it from him we better keep him happy,' said Barry.

'That's good,' said his mother, lighting another cigarette. 'It's best to keep on the right side of him. As you say you have borrowed a lot of stuff from them. He's such a nice man. He'll do anything for you, you know.'

'Yes he is and I don't mind. It might be a good idea after all, to make sure we can do it right,' said Barry.

Chapter Three

The Storm

Sunday afternoon arrived and Bernie turned up just as the lads were taking the tent out of it's packing but it was soon put back.

'There's a helluva storm coming tonight so ah think it's best if we don't bother today lads. Ah'll cuback on Tuesday night if thats aw reet wid yer and we'll do it then,' said Bernie.

'A storm?' said Ian. 'I haven't seen the news so I didn't know. I bet it's nowt when it comes, eh! But Tuesday's OK by me, yeh, Tuesday's OK.'

'Aye, that'll be fine Mr Nichol,' said Barry. 'And the rest of the stuff you've lent us is brilliant. Thanks very much for all you've done, you and Ada,' he added.

'Eeh, nay problem Barry, lad. Ah just wish ah was coming wid yer both. Could do wid another bit of an adventure, ah could,'

'I'm sure you'll get away again Mr Nichol. We will look after your stuff when we are away, you can count on that,' said Barry.

'Aye, I know yer will lads. See yer both Tuesday,' and off he went, leaving the lads to complete the repacking of the tent.

Once they were done, they went for a walk and bumped into Rosemary who arrived at the 'planny' at the same time.

'I was just coming down to your place, Ian , to have a look at the tent. I thought you were putting it up tonight,' she said.

'Hiya, Rosemary. We've had to cancel it tonight 'cos there's this big storm coming, eh! We were planning on leaving it up all night to air it out and that, but Bernie said about this storm, so we are going to do it on Tuesday instead,' said Ian, 'aye, Tuesday.'

'Oh yes, it was on the news earlier,' said Rosemary who always seemed to be in the know. 'They've been talking about it on the news for a few days. It's set to be the worst storm this winter! It's what's left of that hurricane which caused all that damage in America and their's lots of damage expected in this country,' continued Rosemary with some excitement in her voice and added, 'It's set to hit tonight. It's starting to get a bit windy now isn't it?'

'Yes, it is a bit and it's bloody cold with it. I think I'll go home and leave you love birds to it,' said Barry.

'OK, see ya Barry,' said an embarrassed Ian and Rosemary in unison.

Sure enough, the storm arrived in all its ferocity and Barry found it hard to get to sleep because of the howling of the wind and especially the noise of the rain which rattled in with the sudden violent gusts. It sounded like machine gun bullet's hitting the windows! Someone's rubbish bin could be heard being blown down the street and the creeks and groans of a couple of nearby trees were frightening. Barry's brother, Paul, seemed to sleep right through it. Barry wondered how he managed it!

In the morning, being Monday and Barry's day at work, he got up with a groan after such a disturbing night. Wiping the sleep out of his eyes he made his way downstairs, had a quick wash and forced himself to make some toast. The rest of the household was still asleep, Barry, as usual, being the only one who needed to get up this early. He was envious of their extra hour in bed, especially this morning because the storm had ruined his sleep. It left him in no mood to go to work. He switched on the radio and listened to the news while he ate his toast and drank his tea. The newscaster was already reporting on the overnight storm.

'In one of the worst gales ever to hit the North of England, wind speeds of up to 134 mph were registered in the early hours, at the Board of Trade's radio station, 2,800 ft up on Great Dun Fell in the Westmorland Pennines. It was the highest speed ever recorded in........'

'Bloody hell!' said Barry to himself. 'No wonder I could hardly sleep! It WAS bad then!'

There were still some powerful gusts as he set off for work but the winds had otherwise eased down. There were signs of how violent it had been. Barry's eyes were met with a trail of devastation. The rain had stopped, at least for the moment, but the dark, angry looking clouds gave the impression that it could start again at any moment and he thought that if it was anywhere near as ferocious as earlier, he would be soaked by the time he got to work so he kept his fingers crossed. The dustbin Barry could hear during the night was still in the street, but it was in a battered state, wedged in the railings of a property further down. Barry was sure that if it hadn't been wedged there, it would have been blown completely away. Rubbish was strewn everywhere and there were a number of large tree branches which had smashed through some garden fences and were now partly obscuring the road. He had to pick his way passed them. Here and there were some roof tiles which had been blown off. He was glad he hadn't been outside when they came down. He passed a greenhouse which had more smashed glass panels than undamaged ones.

On arrival at work there was more bad news to greet him. No sign of the newspapers or magazines! Because past experiences, he checked the front entrance straight away but they were conspicuous by their absence.

'Oh no,' groaned Barry out loud to himself. 'This is going to be a long morning.' He let himself into the shop and made his way to the office where he picked up the phone to call Menzies, the wholesaler, but the phone was dead. 'Thats all I need. The lines must be down. At least we still have electricity,' he said, to nobody there

Menzies was down King Street, not far away, so Barry decided he better have a walk down to see what the situation was. He gave a big sigh, put his coat back on and went outside, making sure to secure the shop before continuing. The wind was still howling and he had to shield his eyes from the rubbish and dust which kept blowing into his face. The news wasn't good at the wholesalers. The papers hadn't turned up. They had made some enquiries with the police only to be told that some vehicles had been blown over on the A6 which had blocked the road completely. When asked, they didn't know if one of the vehicles involved was their delivery van so all Barry could do was go back to the shop and hope they turned up sooner rather than later.

The storm had caused chaos throughout the north of England and in southern parts of Scotland and it was now chaos in the shop. Customers were demanding their morning papers and some of them couldn't understand why they couldn't have them .... as if it was Barry's fault! Needless to say, he spent a fraught morning at work. The papers were eventually delivered at 2 in the afternoon. Barry mumbled and groaned whilst sorting them because he rightly guessed nobody would want a newspaper this late in the day. 99% of their newspaper sales occur in the mornings. The day limped on and Barry was glad when it was closing time! By then, the weather had just about returned to normal with only a few spots of rain. When he eventually got home, he sank into a chair and breathed a sigh of relief. He was just in time for the news on the TV. The newscaster said that at least 6 people were killed overnight in various parts of the country, three in Scotland when a large tree fell on a car. Huh! thought Barry. People dying and all some can do is complain about not getting their newspaper!

We move on now to Tuesday evening and the expected visit of Mr Nichol. Sure enough, he arrived on time with the ever present smile on his face and showed the lads how to erect the tent which turned out to be as simple as they imagined. At least this kept Mr Nichol happy. Rosemary turned up to watch and was very impressed. As usual she had a few things to say about where best to put things whenever they stopped to camp for the night. Barry let her get on with it. He didn't want to upset her. She was a nice lass who had become one of their crowd and only meant well.

A dry, windless night was expected which was amazing after Sunday night's storm so Mr Nichol agreed that they could leave the tent up. It would probably be a good idea after all, giving it a much needed airing. He knew the lads would have no problems taking it down so, having satisfied himself that they knew what to do, he made his departure. The following evening the lads managed to dismantle and pack the tent without a hitch and as far as that was concerned they were ready to go. All they had left to do was to work out the best route and to acquire their victuals!

The weeks go by and it's now February and Elvis's latest release, 'Guitar Man', is in the charts which pleased the lads. A cold snap had set in and was expected to continue for the next couple of weeks with a number of inches of overnight snow. Barry couldn't be bothered to go out at night in those conditions so instead, he took out the map his boss had given him and began to work out their route to Leicester. It wasn't rocket science. Just take the A66 to Scotch Corner then down the A1 then the A46. Sorted! He also had a street map of the city so that when they arrived in Leicester they would have no problem finding somewhere to camp which was not too far from De Montford Hall. Under normal circumstances, Ian would also have stayed in, but his heart was elsewhere, so, cold or not, he wrapped up well and left his house to meet Rosemary. These two were really happy in each other's company.

During these cold, dark winter nights after work, James Clavell's 'Tai Pan' became Barry's main source of company. He was a slow reader and as he hadn't picked it up for a while, it lasted him for quite some time. The further he got into the book, the more he wanted to continue reading it. A real blockbuster in his view. He dreamed of some day paying a visit to Hong Kong where the novel was set, but he thought the chances of that happening would probably be nil.

As Barry's other love was music and in particular, Elvis Presley songs, on the rare occasions when he had the house to himself he would switch on the record player and concentrate on his idol's latest rendition which, as has been mentioned, was, of course, 'Guitar Man'. He tried to learn the words, a habit he employed with his other favourite Elvis songs and when he felt he knew it, he would continue to play the record again and again while singing along. Obviously this didn't go down well with anyone else who happened to be at home at the time, so he had to snatch these moments whenever the rest of the family were out for the evening.

On one of these evenings, his sister, Anne, came in with her two friends. They were also called Anne. First through the door was Anne Simpson who lived nearby, quickly followed by Anne Wharton who lived on another estate in the town. Barry's sister Anne, was 15 years old, had long black hair, a full mouth, beautiful blue eyes, a typical 'Davidson' nose - protruding but pretty - and a slim figure. She was a quiet, gentle person who always saw the best in people. Barry had never seen her angry. She was his favourite sister and also an avid Elvis fan. It has already been said that she is a bigger fan than Barry! She enjoyed joining in on his sing-a-longs.

The two other Anne's also had long black hair. All three were the same age. Anne Simpson was short in stature with a round, slightly chubby face and brown eyes above a short stubby nose. Anne Wharton was the tallest of the three, with a slim figure although thickening at the waist. She also had brown eyes, with thick eyebrows and a long straight nose. Barry found his sister's friends were as easy to get along with as she was so it wasn't difficult to enjoy their company. They were also Elvis fans but hadn't heard 'Guitar Man' enough to know the words so they could sing along, so they asked him to play 'His Latest Flame' which he obliged.

When that record finished, before any others were suggested, Anne Simpson said, 'Are you looking forward to going to the Elvis Convention thing in Leicester, Barry?'

'Silly question! Of course I am!' he replied. 'I can't wait to get going. It's going to be a real adventure for us!' A big smile came over his face as he thought of the trip and the fun they would have.

'When do you go?' asked Anne Wharton.

'I'm not sure yet. We haven't decided. It all depends on how long we think it will take us to hitch down there. If the worst comes to the worst we could always find a town with a train station or a bus to make sure we get there on time. The show is on a Sunday so we would really need to be in Leicester by Saturday night, but ideally we wont need to do anything other than hitch there. We don't have a lot of money so the less we have to spend on trains or buses the better.'

His sister had put 'Crying in the Chapel' on their Dansette record player, so they all started singing along imagining they were individuals on stage. The noise must have been amusing if there had been anyone nearby to hear them but thankfully there was nobody in the vicinity.

'When is this convention again Barry?' asked one of the girls.

'Blimey, how many times do I have to tell you? It's the 21st of July, a Sunday.'

'That's about five months away,' said one of them.

'Yeh, I know. It feels like forever,' moaned Barry. 'It means I have five months where I can hardly afford to go out. I haven't been able to save as much as I would like. If I could stop smoking that would help but c'est la vie, it's not going to happen, and on top of that I still need to buy some decent clothes for the trip.'

'Yes, five months *is* a long time, Barry. Hopefully you'll be able to manage it. I am sure you will,' said Anne Simpson in an attempt to keep him in a good mood for the rest of the evening.

They listened and sang to a few more Elvis tracks until other members of the family started to arrive home which put an end to their fun for another night. There will be other sessions, thought Barry.

The next would be Sunday so Barry decided he would have a lay-in. To take advantage of this, he took his book to bed and had a good read before sleep took over. He enjoyed his ly-in and was up late the next day relaxing until there was a knock on the door. In walked Ian.

'Hello, it's just me,' he shouted.

'Hi Ian, what brings you around today?' asked Barry.

'I just thought I would pop in to see what you were doing, eh! I haven't seen you for a while because of this bad weather. I heard you had a good sing-a-long last night,' he said, 'aye, a good sing-a-long.'

Yeh, that's right, but who told you?' asked Barry.

'Oh, I went to the shop to get a loaf of bread for mother and I bumped into Anne Simpson, eh! She said she had been round with Anne Wharton and your sister.'

'Yes, it was good, even though they haven't learnt the words to 'Guitar Man' yet so we had a session with some other songs,' replied Barry.

'How's your book coming on?' enquired Ian.

'Great!' said Barry. 'It's brilliant! One of the best books I've read. You would like it. It's a great pity your 'e not into books. You don't know what you're missing. It's set in Hong Kong. I would love to go there.'

'Oh well, maybe one of these days, eh! but I'm just not a book reader, eh.' said Ian, 'No, I can't get into them. I prefer listening to music. Anyway, while I think about it, I've got some good news. My aunt Ivy has given me a lot of tinned food for us to take with us, so that cuts down what we need to get, eh!"

'Oh brilliant! What did she give you?'

'Beans, some soup and some tins of stew. She says the stew will be great with bread. There is enough for about four main courses which is a great start..... yeh four main courses!'

'Tell her thanks from me. That's brilliant!' replied Barry. 'And we still have 5 months to go.'

— — — — — —

Those five months went by without anything occurring of interest to our story other than the decision to set off on the Thursday before the convention. Let's face it, during that time, Barry and Ian didn't have enough money to go out and enjoy themselves much anyway, although it was OK for Ian - he had Rosemary!

We are now only a couple of weeks away from 'Elvis Day' which is what they dubbed the day they would set off. Excitement had been building, not just for our two heroes but the whole street, which was now buzzing as knowledge of their impending trip had become widely known in the immediate area and a number of neighbours had given their three-pennyworth of advice. More food had been donated by some which went down well with the lads.

A couple of weeks to go means we are now in July and Elvis has released a new film in the States called 'Speedway'. It stars Nancy Sinatra and a new single has been released from the film, called 'Your Time Hasn't Come Yet, Baby', just in time for the convention. The lads didn't have much hope of it doing well though. Elvis churns them out too often from the rubbishy films which Colonel Tom Parker, his manager, insists on him doing, but it was Elvis so they tried to learn the words so they could sing it anyway.

'Maybe they will show the film on the day!' said Ian.

'Wow! Yes! That would be good. Let's keep our fingers crossed!' said Barry. 'Nancy Sinatra is Dishy, isn't she?' he added.

'She sure is,' replied Ian. 'She sure is!'

'We only have two weeks to go before we set off. I'm itching to get going, Ian. I think we should pack all the things we've got so we can work out what we still need.' There was a pause before he continued, 'But I think we're just about there, don't you?'

'Yeh, I can't think of anything important that we've forgotten,' replied Ian.

The lads completed their packing and were happy to note that their rucksacks were manageable. Once done, they couldn't think of anything else they might need so it was just a case of waiting impatiently for 'Elvis Day' to arrive. They had decided that if they left Penrith on Thursday morning it would give them time to get to Leicester for the convention and, as they had already said, if the worst came to the worst there was always the train or even a bus.

— — — —-

We now move on to Barry's last day at work before they set off on their trip. As usual, they were having a quiet Wednesday in the shop. Barry was tidying the counter when Joan and Margaret came over.

Joan handed Barry an envelope and said,'We thought you might like this to help you on your trip. We have all contributed including the boss.'

He opened the envelope, feeling a little embarrassed. He didn't like being the centre of attention. Inside there was £5 (a lot of money in those days). Barry didn't earn much over £7 for a week's work!). He couldn't believe it! He just stuttered and stammered for a while, his embarrassment clearly visible and the girls were almost laughing - but in a friendly way. Eventually he managed to compose himself and thanked them for their generosity.

'Just make sure you have a good time and get back safe,' said Joan, giving him a cuddle.

'Thanks Joan,' said Barry who's face got redder, his shyness coming through.

Margaret also gave Barry a hug and said, 'Yes, Barry. Go and have a good time. I can't wait for you to come back and tell us all about it.'

'I will,' replied Barry and he continued to thank them for the money.

Later, when Joan went to the staff room for her afternoon break, Barry noticed Margaret hurrying along to the magazine counter to speak to him. She looked conspiratorial.

She whispered, 'Joan has a new boyfriend!'

'No!' replied Barry in total disbelief.

'Yes, yes!' said Margaret excitedly. 'She was telling me on the way in. It's a farmers son from near where she lives! Yes, she says he's a real hunk! I had a feeling something was going on with the way she was behaving. She sometimes didn't share the same bus home which was strange.'

'How long has this been going on, I mean the bus and things?' asked Barry.

'I think she has been seeing him for a few months now.'

'I wonder if that ties in with her starting to be nice to me?' asked Barry. 'She said it was her mother's illness that made her cranky, but I bet this was the real reason she started being nice,' he continued.

'You're right, Barry. His mother helped out sometimes when Joan's mother was ill and he used to go to collect her to take her home and that's how they got to know each other.'

'Let's hope it lasts!' said Barry and the conversation ended.

On his return home he told his mother what had occurred including the news of Joan's boyfriend. 'Bloody hell! Somebody's finally thawed that heart of ice!' said his mother in a surprised tone. 'But that was good of them anyway ..... and let's hope this boyfriend thing of Joan's lasts.'

'That's what I said when Margaret told me,' said Barry.

After tea, Barry and Ian made their final checks of their things and while doing so Barry also informed Ian of this breaking news, repeating the conversation he had just had with his mother. Ian, like Barry's mother, was gobsmacked.

During their checks, Barry paid particular attention to the convention tickets. It would be disastrous if they turned up without them! They agreed that they would set off about ten in the morning and see how far they could get before they stopped to camp for their first night.

After satisfying himself that everything was in order, Ian left, having nothing further to say and Barry watched a bit of TV. He wasn't really paying much attention to what he was watching - his mind was obviously still on the trip. When he finally made it to bed he tried to have a read of his book but he couldn't concentrate, the excitement of their forthcoming adventure taking over. It would still be there on his return, he thought.

Ian checked in with Rosemary for a final kiss and cuddle. She told him to enjoy himself and again she wished she was going with them but understood it was not possible. It would look bad and although she was sure nothing improper would happen, she didn't want to gain a bad reputation. She also told him to take care and be wary of strangers, aware that neither of our heroes were very streetwise. Ian merely mumbled, said his last goodbye and returned home for what he hoped would be a good night's sleep. However, it was not to be. Their impending journey meant it took both our heroes some time before they fell into an uneasy slumber.

Chapter Four

The Journey Begins!

Thursday morning dawned and the weather couldn't have been better. The sun was shining - not a cloud in the sky - and the forecast for their time away didn't show too much rain apart from Friday night. They were hoping they would be in their tent before any downpour. Both lads were up with the sparrows but their plans to leave early, were scuppered because both their father's had already left for work, planning on returning later to see them before they set off. Ian's mother, Nancy, made sure he had a good breakfast. She was concerned he wouldn't eat properly and made him his first full cooked breakfast that he could remember! A few doors away, Iris was preparing a similar feast for an equally surprised Barry! Breakfast was consumed by both lads while their doting mothers looked on. Barry's siblings came downstairs one by one and all wished Barry the best of luck on his trip and hoped he would keep himself and Ian safe. They weren't going to get a cooked breakfast but knew the reason why Barry was, so they didn't mind.

Gradually, all his siblings left for school or work and Barry was left alone with his mother. After finishing his breakfast, Barry said, 'I'll go and see how Ian is getting on. I bet he is fully packed and raring to go,' he smiled, unable to hide the excitement from his voice.

'OK son, I'll see you later.'

Barry arrived at Ian's house to be told he had gone to the 'planny'. He was obviously meeting Rosemary again even though he had said his goodbyes last night. Having to wait for his father meant he had time to see her again. Sure enough he found Ian and Rosemary there. The three of them had a quick chat until Rosemary realised the lads were wanting to be on their way so she said, 'I hope you have a good time. Make sure you get there by Saturday night or you might struggle to make it in time. Try to find somewhere to camp near the hall,' she continued. 'It's the De Montfort Hall isn't it? I have a friend who lives near there and she said there is a big park not far away and nobody will stop you camping there if you want to. Just make sure that you get up early enough to pack your things on Sunday morning and take them with you to the hall or you might come back and find them all gone!' finished Rosemary in her usual no nonsense way.

'Aye, we will remember that Rosemary. Hopefully we will find it,' said Barry in response.

'Find what?' asked Ian who had been daydreaming.

'The park, dibbo!' laughed Barry who was enjoying the funny side of things.

Ian and Rosemary joined in the laughter. Although he felt a little embarrassed, like Barry, he was a shy lad but had found someone in Rosemary who was happy with him the way he was. He was also the practical one out of our heroes. When he was about 9 years old he got hold of some batteries and experimented with them, joining them together to power a portable fan which resulted in the fan spinning faster than previously. Although not rocket science, this thrilled Ian and was the birth of an enquiring mind where practical matters were concerned. It was bookwork he wasn't keen on. Probably because of his interest in these matters he was first to fathom out how to put the tent up. Also, unlike Barry, he was more particular about his appearance. He always made sure his hair was properly groomed and wouldn't go out until he was satisfied with it and, unlike Barry, he insisted on using deodorant and, on occasion, aftershave. However, like Barry, his wardrobe was not extensive. He, too, couldn't afford a lot, although he earned more as an apprentice Welder than Barry did as shop assistant.

The friends returned to their respective homes and Barry did a cursory check of his packing for something to do. He was restless. He was keen to get going. It was only 10:30 and he was looking for something to pass the time before the off. 'I know', he thought, 'I'll have a read of my book!' He went upstairs and came back down with his latest title. He made himself comfortable on the settee and picked up where he had left off. He was nearing the end of the book and found it so exciting that when he looked at his watch he was surprised to find that an hour had passed by. He became restless once more which was noticed by his mother so she asked him if he would like a cup of tea but he declined. Another half an hour or so went by before his dad turned up for his lunch.

'Why don't you go and see if Ian's ready, Barry? Bring him back here if he is, and tell Nancy to come along as well, will you?' said Iris, realising Barry was impatient to get away.

'Yeh, good idea,' replied Barry.

Off he went and sure enough Ian was also itching to get going. His dad, Henry, hadn't returned home yet but he took his mother to Barry's house as requested. Henry would know where to find them.

'Well, today's the day ..... yes, today's the day!' said Ian, to no one in particular, sporting an embarrassed grin on his face and rubbing his hands together expectantly.

'Yeh, I'm really itching to get going,' replied Barry as a hint to his parents.   As it was a warm day, Barry was wearing just his jeans and a T shirt along with his boots. He had a bomber jacket, which had seen better days, tucked into the straps of his rucksack, thinking, if it turned chilly he could easily put it on. Ian was similarly attired although his jacket was an old leather one.

Iris put the kettle on and said, 'A brew to see you on your way, you two?'

Barry and Ian just wanted to get going but they thought they had better keep her happy, after all she had done for them. They were waiting for Ian's dad to arrive anyway.

'How do you take yours, Ian? The usual for you Nancy?'

'Yes thanks Iris' and 'milk and two' were the replies. Iris nearly spilled the milk, and the sugar seemed to go everywhere as she struggled to control herself. She was worried something bad would happen to her son while they were on their travels. She always hated parting with her children, being very maternal. With a great effort, she managed to control herself, and the tea was served with a biscuit and a forced smile. Nancy wasn't at all bothered! She couldn't imagine that anything terrible would happen. While they were having their tea and biscuit's, Ian's dad, Henry, finally turned up. He had gone to his own house but when he found there was nobody in, he guessed correctly that they would be at Barry's.

He walked in and said 'Hi all, sorry I'm late. I take it the wanderers are ready to go?'

There was a general mutter of ascent as Iris made him a brew. The lads were subject to a barrage of do's and don'ts, particularly from Iris and replied yes and no in, hopefully, the correct places as they were only half listening, their minds being elsewhere.

'OK, time for us to go, Ian,' said Barry when there was a lull in the conversation, and put his cup down. The words were really directed at his mother. It took some time before she took the hint.

'Right then, you two, have a good time and don't forget that if you are near a phone box we are only a phone call away if you need anything,' said Barry's dad.

'Yes we will and we won't forget,' said Barry as he gave his mother a big hug. 'And thanks for all the encouragement you gave us for this trip, mam. Getting those rucksacks was a good start and look at us now! We can make the trip after all!'

The lads picked up their gear and walked out of the house and started down the road with continuous 'goodbyes' and more advice ringing in their ears. With a final wave, round the corner they walked, and out of site. some neighbours were in the street waving at them and wishing them luck and hoping they had a good time on their trip.

'Phew!' said Barry. 'I thought that was gonna go on for ever!'

'Yes, so did I!' said Ian with a great outtake of breath, 'so did I!'

They walked on down West Lane until they reached Crown Square where the Post Office was situated. It was known that some lorries often passed that way so all they had to do was find a driver who was going east and was willing to take them. It would have been impossible to get in a car with all the gear they were carrying, they thought, so a lorry was their aim. They stopped there to gather their thoughts and Barry lit a cigarette. Ian was a none smoker but it didn't bother him. There were one or two people in the street but nobody they knew.

Barry sat on his rucksack and said, 'I wonder how far we will get today, Ian? Do you think we will make Scotch Corner?'

'I dunno,' said Ian. 'I hope we get at least to Scotch Corner, eh? I'd like to think we could get at least some way down the A1 to about the Leeds area even .... yeh, the Leeds area! That would be good wouldn't it?'

'Yeh, that would be good. We'd be well on our way if we got that far. But you never know, we might find somebody who's going nearly all the way! That would be even better!'

'Yeh, true ...... hang on ..... here comes a Border Wagon. They travel all over...... he's stopping at the junction, quick!'

Ian ran over, leaving Barry to grapple with both rucksacks. It was a bit of a struggle but he managed to carry them over to the vehicle. Ian having spoken to the driver, turned back to Barry with disappointment clearly visible on his face.

'He can't take us,' he said. 'He's not going our way but he suggests we go up to the junction with the A66 at the end of Bridge Lane, eh! We should be able to find a lorry going our way from there,' he continued, 'well, *hopefully* going our way.'

'OK, never mind,' said Barry.

He handed Ian his rucksack which he slung over his shoulders. The pair of them were now similarly attired and they walked slowly on, up Bridge Lane with the midday sun now beating down on them. Both were thinking that maybe it wasn't going to be as easy as they thought to hitch all that way, but kept these negative thoughts to themselves. After a few minutes spent in silence they reached Walkers Funeral Directors just in time to be held up by a hearse, complete with coffin and flowers, rolling slowly out of the driveway and onto the main road followed by a procession of five cars, two of which belonged to Walkers, the others being private vehicles carrying members of the bereaved family. Our heroes had to stop while this 'motorcade' drove out.

Barry said, 'I hope that's not an omen for our trip!'

'Eh?' said Ian.

'This funeral!' said Barry, pointing to the vehicles.

'Eh? ....Oh! .... ah, I see what you mean! .... I hope not ..... no, I hope not,' replied Ian.

Once the procession of vehicles had gone by the intrepid two continued on their way, but they weren't destined to get out of town that easily. The next building was Greengarth. It was a one story sprawling prefabricated property which was used as an old folks home. There was a grassed area which covered the front of the property, crossed by a couple of paths beside which were some benches for able-bodied residents to sit on during warm summer days while they admired the flowers and watched the passing traffic and pedestrians. The building itself was designed to have a lot of large windows facing the front so that the less able residents could at least see what was going on outside. Of the benches in the grassed area, one was situated near the main thoroughfare beside the road, along which the lads were walking. At this time an elderly male resident who wore a pair of striped pyjamas and a dressing gown, was making use of it. He had a large beard but was completely bald on top. The only other visible hair was that issuing from his nostrils. As for the beard, it was a wonder the home allowed him to grow it so long! He was smoking a cigarette and as the lads came close by he shouted with a gravelly voice, 'Where are youse two off to wid all that gear, on sek a nice day now?'

He was waving his nicotine stained hands around all the time, which made him look a bit comical.

'We're hitchhiking down to Leicester. We're going to a concert for Elvis Presley which is on Sunday,' explained Barry, making a great effort to enunciate his words in case the old man was a little hard of hearing.

'To see who?'

'Elvis Presley .....yer know! .... the singer ......known as the King..... he won't be there, just his English fans. *He's* still in America.'

'America? Elvis Presley? Do yer know I kinda think 'ave 'erd of him. So how can he have a concert thingy if he's not gonna there, now?' said the old man in a confused manner.

'Because he won't come over here. He doesn't like flying so the local fans thought they would have some sort of a meet up, eh! and they just call it the Elvis Convention, like, even though he isn't gonna be there, you see?' shouted Ian.

'Yes, he's our favourite singer. He has records in the charts all the time,' added Barry.

'Oh, I see, but no need to shout lads. Ah may be old but as not deef, not yit, any road,' said the old timer.

Suddenly a glazed look came over his face. 'Ooh .....ahh ...err ....hmm,' he muttered, while clearing his throat and pulling some strange faces.

The lads didn't understand what was going on until Ian pointed to the old timer's pyjama bottoms and whispered to Barry, 'Look, he's pissing himself!'

As Barry looked on, a damp patch began to grow in the old fellow's nether regions and just got worse until urine started dripping off the bench onto the ground. A grunt was then heard and a great fart issued from his backside and the smell was horrendous. What he had been eating, they shuddered to think, but they realised the man had shit himself!

'Aw, that's awful!' said Barry stepping backward and holding his hands up to his nose.

31

'Barry, I'll nip inside and tell them what's happened, eh! You make sure he doesn't bugger off!' said Ian as he put his rucksack down beside Barry before running off to the building's entrance.

'OK, but make it quick. I don't think I can stand that smell for too long!' said Barry, still holding his nose while keeping an eye on the old timer.

Ian ran inside and found a female dressed in a green uniform similar to a nurse.

'Hello, darling, can I help you?' she asked, with a broad smile on her face. She was in her mid 40's, short and stout and carrying a clipboard stuffed with papers in her left hand and looked to have a lot on her mind, but she gave Ian a smile anyway.

'Sorry to bother you but you see that gent out there?' said Ian, pointing to where the resident was still sitting.

'Yes, that's Mr Buck,' she said, looking out of the window.

'I'm afraid he's peed and shit himself, eh!'

'Oh no,' she said, then turned and shouted down one of the corridors, 'Gladys! Gladys! Are you there, dear?'

A voice from nearby replied, 'Just here Maureen, what's up?'

'Donald is on the bench outside and I'm being told he's messed himself again. Can you go and sort him please, dear.'

'Oh no, not again.' The voice started to get closer as hurrying feet could be heard along the corridor. 'I'm getting fed up with him doing this. He should be-' Just before she could say any more she came round the corner and spotted Ian who was still standing there. 'Ooh, hello!' she said, with an embarrassed smile on her face and fidgeting as if she was nearly caught saying something unkind about Donald.

Gladys looked slightly older than Maureen, with greying hair which she didn't seem to pay much attention to. She had a slim torso but huge thighs and backside which looked as though they belonged to another body. She was wearing a similar uniform to the other female, whom Ian now knew to be Maureen.

'Right, well if you can sort him please Gladys dear. That would be much appreciated. This kind young man has just been in to let us know, haven't you dear,' she said with a smile and a nod at Ian.

'Yeh, we were just walking by when he wanted to chat, like, then it just happened. Yeh, right in front of us! ..... so, I'll be going then,' said Ian, feeling slightly embarrassed, having run out of things to say.

'Thanks for coming in to let us know. That was very good of you,' said Maureen.

'No problem. Cheerio now,' said Ian before turning and leaving them, or should I say, poor Gladys, to it.

Meanwhile, Barry was feeling a little embarrassed outside. He was now far enough away to be just about clear of the stench but close enough to ensure that the elderly gent didn't wander off. He could now see the nurse hurrying to where Donald was, with Ian leading the way. Donald just sat there with a confused look on his face.

Barry said 'It's OK Mr...erm .... it's OK, my mate has gone to get somebody to see to you and she is coming now, look!' and he pointed at Gladys who was muttering and cursing to herself as she hurried along the path.

'What's she coming here for? Is there something wrong?' asked the confused old resident, turning to look at Gladys. By the time he had finished speaking, Ian had returned, with Gladys a couple of yards behind him. She started to speak to Donald so Barry passed Ian his rucksack. He knew the old gent was in safe hands so they began to walk away.

'Bloody hell,' said Ian, taking his rucksack, 'we haven't even left Penrith yet. If things carry on like this we will have enough stories to fill a book before we even reach Appleby, aye, before Appleby!'

'Ha ha!' laughed Barry.

'I wonder if the inmates have a good time in there? I don't think Gladys is as caring as she makes out. I think she was just about to slag the fella off until she saw me with Maureen and just managed to stop herself.'

'Did I hear you say 'Inmates'?' asked Barry.

'It was the striped pyjamas. Made me think of a prison camp ... and the way Gladys was talking it may well be, eh!' chuckled Ian.

Barry also chuckled. He couldn't believe Ian had become the joker.

'The laughable thing is the name of that old fella, Barry. It's Donald Buck!' laughed Ian, 'aye, Donald Buck!'

'What's so funny about that?'

'Donald Buck! Donald Buck! ..... Don't you get it? Donald DUCK !!'

'Oh, yeh, now I get it. Very funny .... not,' sighed Barry.

Ian wasn't wired to be funny, thought Barry. What had got into him today? Maybe it was because he was enjoying the journey they were on.

Chapter Five

Tally Ho!

Our heroes reached the junction with the A66 and sat down on their rucksacks for a breather. Barry lit a cigarette, took a long drag and after a moment or two he started thinking of the hearse and once again he hoped it wasn't an omen. After all, he thought, nobody is going to die on this trip, are they? No, surely not.

The sun was still shining strongly, so Ian reached into his rucksack for a bottle of water which he opened and took a good long swig before passing the bottle to Barry.

'Cheers Ian,' he said and took an equally good drink from it.

Barry was still thinking about what had occurred at Greengarth and although it was Ian who ran in to inform the staff about Donald Buck, he felt that between them they had performed a good deed for the day. This gave him a good feeling inside. He wondered if there would be any other occasions when they would perform good deeds on their trip.

Once fully refreshed it was time to make their move. They stood up and stuck out their thumbs as wagons going east drove passed. They were not as lucky as they would have hoped. They were not experienced at hitchhiking and thought it would be better if they started to walk down the road. All the time, they kept looking over their shoulders at the sound of any approaching vehicle and thumbing when they thought there was a chance of one stopping to offer them a lift. A few hundred yards on, they came to a lay-by which they later learned was called 'Crow Wood' lay-by. There was a mobile snack van set up waiting for customers but none were there when our lads arrived.

'Ah! This looks promising! I bet some wagons stop here!' said Barry.

'There aren't any here at the moment, Barry, but I think you're right,' said Ian. 'Yeh, I think you'll be right!'

The owner of the snack van was leaning over the counter, watching the lads approach. He was ready to receive his next customers, the last vehicle having, apparently, left a few minutes earlier. He had greasy black unkempt curly hair, a black well-trimmed beard and a thin black moustache. He had a swarthy skin and a stubby nose with full thick lips. When he smiled he revealed white teeth but there were a couple of noticeable gaps in them. All in all, he didn't give the impression of being the cleanest, considering the business he was in!

'How ya doin' lads?' he said. His accent wasn't Cumbrian but they couldn't place it.

'All right, thanks,' said Barry.

'All right, thanks,' echoed Ian.

'I was watching you's two coming along and I thought to myself, I thought, number one, I bet these lads aren't coming to me 'cos they wants to buy anything, am I right?' Before either of our heroes could reply, he went on, 'and, I thinks, number two, I bet they intends waiting to see if a lorry driver stops so they can ask for a lift, am I right? and I thinks number three, I bet they wants to know how busy I gets so they might be on their way sooner rather than later. Am I right then lads?'

Making sure the man had stopped speaking and was waiting for a reply, Barry thought he would be clever and reply in a similar manner, 'Number one, yes you are right, we don't want to buy anything off you, number two, your right again, we are hoping to get a lift and as for number three, how busy *do* you get?'

'Hahaha!' laughed the van owner. 'Very good, I like it! To be honest with you's I don't know. I only started pitching here on Monday but don't get me wrong, I've been kept busy so far and today has been OK as well, up till now anyways. So, then lads.' he said, taking a good look at them, each in turn, 'where are you's off to today then?'

'We're off to the Elvis Convention. It's in Leicester on Sunday, so we decided to make it into a holiday and hitchhike down there, eh! We're hoping to get a fair way today but we haven't been lucky with a lift yet, like, so we thought we would walk a bit, and then we saw this lay-by and your snack van, and thought, this would be a good place, eh! Snack vans in lay-bys are usually busy with lorries. They like these sort of places and while they were 'ere we could ask them if we could have a lift, hopefully as far as Scotch Corner at least, aye, as far as Scotch Corner, eh!' said Ian, quite quickly.

'Hold on just a minute there! You said you's are going to Leicester, am I right?'

Barry decided to reply. 'Yes, you're right, we're going to Leicester. There's a big meeting of Elvis Presley fans from all over the country down there on Sunday and we've got tickets to it, but because we haven't got a lot of cash, the only way we could afford to go was if we hitched down so that's what we're doing.'

'Elvis Presley! I used to be a big fan of his but he's spoiled himself with doing all these films, am I right? They are all full of crappy songs and crappy storylines, am I right lads?'

'Yeh, I suppose you're right with a lot of 'em but we still like them, don't we, Ian.'

'Aye, we still like them. Most of them, anyway, eh! The latest isn't too bad. It's called 'Your Time Hasn't Come Yet, Baby' and it's from his latest crappy film as you call it. The film's called 'Speedway'. The good thing is it co-stars Nancy Sinatra and she is *well* fit!' added Ian, 'yeh, *well* fit.'

'It will still be a crappy film. Well you could be in luck if you wait here. The last place I was at I had a few hitchhikers like you's two and none of 'em failed to get a lift.'

'That's good to know,' said Barry.

'What time do you pack up for the day?' asked Ian.

The snack van owner came outside, sat on a stool and lit a cigarette. 'Want a fag lads?'

Barry was happy to take one. 'Thanks,' he said and taking out his lighter he lit the swarthy gents cigarette first, then his own. He took a few drags while the gent went on.

'Let's see, it's 2 o'clock now, I'll probably give it another couple of hours. Don't worry, I'm sure you will be on you's way before I pack up,' he said, and gave them a friendly smile.

Both lads relaxed and sat on their rucksacks. Ian kept looking back up the road, hoping to see a wagon pull into the lay-by.

The van owner finished his cigarette. 'Do you want a brew lads? No charge, I'm having one meself, so I am. I'm thinking you might be ready for one, am I right?'

Ian and Barry looked at each other then back up the road and looked unsure.

'Relax lads, if a wagon pulls in here, he won't be going straight out for a whiles, at least until he has had summat to eat and drink so you's two will have time to sup a cuppa, am I right?'

'Aye, a good point,' said Barry. 'I'll have a brew. Milk and one sugar for me.'

'Yes, two sugars for me,' chirped up Ian.'

'All I'll give you is a mug o' tea. The milks and sugars is there on the counter,' said the man as he got back into his snack van. He reached for the mugs from somewhere under the counter, filled them with hot tea and handed them to the lads who helped themselves to the milk and sugar. They settled down to drink them, once again thanking the man for his generosity.

'No problem lads, it's only a cuppa. It's not gonna do me out of business, am I right?' He gave out a friendly smile, once more revealing the gaps in his teeth.

'Ah, here we go!' he said at last as a lorry turned into the lay-by and parked up nearby.

As the driver approached the snack van he noticed the two lads and immediately said, 'Hi, lads, I don't see another vehicle nearby so I'm guessing your'e after a lift to some place?'

'Bloody hell, is it that obvious? asked Barry, sounding surprised.

'When you've been driving lorries as long as I have, son, you get to know the signs.' He reached into his pocket before saying to the owner of the van, 'A bacon and egg butty and a mug of tea please.' Turning back to the lads he said, 'Where are you off to then?' While waiting for the answer he turned his back on them and put some money down on the counter.

'We're on our way to Leicester. We're looking for somebody to take us to Scotch Corner or even further, if you could do that for us",'said Barry, trying not to sound as if he was pleading, although inside he was!

'I'm going over to the North East, to Middlesbrough', said the lorry driver while picking up his change. After a pause, he said, 'I'll get ya to Scotch Corner but not until after I've had me break,' and turned round with a big smile for the lads.

'Oh, that's really good of you!' said Barry with a smile that matched that of the lorry driver.

'Yes, that's brilliant!' said an equally happy Ian.

The snack van owner gave them a wink.

'I'm Barry and this is Ian, by the way,' said Barry by way of introduction.

'And I'm Tom,' said the lorry driver. 'Tom Bowler.'

Barry guessed that Tom was in his mid 30's. He had very short brown hair, going bald on top. He had a muscly torso which Barry thought must have been gained through hard work in a gym, so unlike that of a lorry driver.

They made small talk while they waited for him to finish his break which took nearly half an hour. Barry and Ian were then allowed to enter the vehicle's passenger side and were safely ensconced there along with their rucksacks. Tom checked his load, climbed into the driver's side and off they went on their journey. Tom said he had been a lorry driver for 10 years and he lived in the village of Bramham which wasn't too far from Scotch Corner. However, he wouldn't be going home until he completed a delivery on Saturday. He thought he was going home after work tomorrow but he had been told that he would have to take another load out early on Saturday morning. He would be getting the rest of the weekend off and wouldn't be back at work until Tuesday so he was looking forward to the break.

It took nearly an hour and a half to travel along the A66 to Scotch Corner, during which time the lads told Tom of their plans and how much they were looking forward to the concert at the De Montford Hall.

Barry once again noticed Tom's physique and said, 'Do you work out, Tom ? You've got some huge muscles on those arms of yours.'

'Ah, you noticed. Yes, I go to the gym as often as I can. Sometimes the job gets in the way but I manage around 3 times a week, sometimes more. I like to keep in shape. This job, sitting on your arse all day, isn't good for you. I've lost a couple of mates who just sat in their cabs and stuffed their faces and put on weight. They ended up having heart attacks. One of them was while he was driving and he took out a car with his wagon, killing a family. I don't want out like that to happen to me and I've got a wife to think of as well,' said Tom.

'I've never been to a gym,' said Barry.

'No sweat? Well I have to be honest, you can tell,' laughed Tom. Ian just sniggered and Barry just smiled. He didn't mind the comment. Working out was not something he did and he knew he was thin.

Tom dropped the friends off at Scotch Corner, all the while receiving their thanks for his help. He gave them a wave and wished them good luck and hoped they enjoyed the concert, before he departed for the company depot in Middlesbrough.

Picking up their gear, they walked to the A1 southbound slip road. It was now well after 4:30pm so the lads were feeling a little peckish but they didn't feel they were in a position to cook anything. They had some bread and margarine with some cheese. A sandwich was all they allowed themselves, fully expecting that they would have something decent to eat when they set up camp later in the evening, wherever that was going to be.

On completion of their frugal feast, they sorted their gear before starting to thumb for a lift again. After about ten minutes and no luck, Ian got impatient and said "Let's go down to the road and thumb. There seems to be a lot of wagons going by down there that we are missing..... yeh, ones that we miss. Look!"

Barry wasn't sure this was a good idea but he could sense Ian's growing irritability and thought he had better amuse him, so against his better judgement, he agreed. Down the slip road and onto the hard shoulder they walked.

Once there, Ian said, 'See ! We were missing all these wagons going by!'

'Yeh,' agreed Barry in reply. They were indeed missing a lot of wagons.

'Yes, all these wagons,' repeated Ian.

They continued walking and putting their thumbs out at the approach of lorries but all that happened was a blast of horns from nearly every wagon that went by. Very strange, they thought.

Another couple of dozen yards were walked when Ian shouted, 'Here, Barry! This one's stopping! I told you we should have come off that useless slip road, it was no good up there!' He had a huge smile on his face.

The lorry driver stopped, opened the passenger door from inside the cab and shouted, 'Get in quickly lads!' he yelled. 'And close the door after you..... hurry up .... hurry up now!'

Once inside, he set off again and after a moment or two Ian said, 'Thanks very much. We are going to Leicester. Will you -'

At this point the driver cut Ian short. 'You're going as far as the next roundabout, that's all you're doing, lads! Not only is it against the law to walk on the hard shoulder, hitching, it's also fucking dangerous!' he said, in a firm voice.

The lads just looked at each other, in total surprise, Ian looking rather sheepish.

'We're coming up to the next roundabout in a minute. I will drop you off at the south slip and you can try your luck there but DON'T go onto the fucking road or the cops will lift you and give you a fucking bollocking, all right?'

'Yeh, sorry about that,' said Barry. 'We didn't know.'

The lorry left the A1 at the next slip road which was signposted 'Catterick' and the driver pulled over to let our heroes out, waved goodbye, then made his way back onto the road and gradually disappeared into the evening.

Barry and Ian picked up their gear and walked onto the roundabout. Time was getting on and although they waited for around half an hour, not one lorry came passed them.

'Sorry,' said Ian.

'What you on about?' replied Barry.

'Getting you to go down to the road. I didn't know we weren't allowed on there.'

'Don't worry about it, Ian, neither did I .... but at least we do now,' said Barry with a friendly smile. Ian was forgiven.

'It's getting late. Why don't we find somewhere to camp for the night and get something decent to eat? What do you think Barry?'

'Yeh, I think that's a good idea, Ian. Let's have a walk down here and see if there is anywhere for the tent.'

The lads walked off down a single track road to the left of the roundabout and soon came across a gate into a field which would take them away from the noisy A1.

'Let's go into this field and see if there is anywhere to pitch the tent,' suggested Ian.

'All right,' said Barry.

Over the gate they climbed and began to walk down the field. Encountering uneven ground and a large number of thistles, they walked on. Not really thinking where they were going they crossed aimlessly into another field, hardly a word passing between them - tiredness and hunger was taking hold. This next field was also very rough and uneven underfoot and gave the impression of having been churned up. Definitely not suitable for a tent! They weren't having much luck. In the night air, a hint of a mist began to form and grow. After a while, the fledgling moon struggled to penetrate it. They continued to walk on in the darkening gloom when gradually, about 30 yards ahead a strange apparition began to take shape. It was big enough to be another hedge but as far as they could tell they were still in the middle of a field. The swirling mist obscured first one part then another of the strange object making it difficult to define what it was.

Our heroes came to a halt as they tried to make sense of it. There was an eerie silence, hardly a breath of wind. A hoot of an owl startled both lads who took a big gulp of air, steadied their nerves and moved gingerly forward but now at a crawl, keeping closer to each other, neither happy to take the lead. Suddenly Barry came to a halt again. He could just make out the object which was about 20 yards long. The mist was still playing mayhem with his vision but finally he noticed that the object rose high into the mist at either end.

The penny dropped and so did Barry. He sank to his knees with his hand on his hips and let out a loud noise. This startled Ian, who jumped what felt like a thousand feet in the air! His heart was racing. He jumped round first looking to his left then his right then behind him, peering into the gloom but he couldn't see anything which could have caused Barry's sudden outburst. He continued looking this way and that with fear in his eyes.

'What is it? What's wrong ? What's happening? Barry! Barry!' he shouted, trembling.

Barry, now giggling, said, 'I know what it is Ian and where we are. When the lorry driver dropped us off, did you notice the sign saying Catterick?'

'I did, but what has all that got to do with anything?"

It's a horse jump, Ian! A horse jump! We are right in the middle of Catterick racecourse! Can't you make it out, the shape of it?

Ian crouched down beside Barry, not daring to leave his side. He was still a little spooked. He looked at the structure as the mist danced along it. Like a jigsaw, he put the pieces he saw together in his mind until he could see what Barry saw. Yes! It *was* a horse jump! They *were* in the middle of Catterick racecourse!

'How the hell did we manage to end up here?' said Ian with a sigh of relief.

'I haven't the foggiest!' said Barry, as amazed and relieved as Ian.

'Hahaha!' laughed Ian 'Foggiest! Get it? Foggiest! Hahaha!'

At first Barry couldn't understand what Ian was on about, thinking his mate had flipped his lid. Then it dawned on him. While laughing out loud, Barry thought 'Foggiest. Yes, all this mist. Ian is continuing to let out wisecracks! Very unusual!'

He clasped his mate on the shoulders and their laughter continued, more in relief than anything else. Their laughter eventually subsided and after regaining their breath and courage, they stood up and looked at it in awe. Neither of them realised horse jumps were as big as this. They looked a lot smaller on TV.

Barry slowly made his way towards it. Ian followed, keeping as close as he could to his friend and continuing to look around him. Although recovering from their fright, they were both still a little spooked. The utter silence, the mist and darkness and the sudden appearance of the horse jump in the night gloom, all continued to play on their minds.

After a cursory inspection of the jump, Barry said, 'Hey Ian, time is getting on and it's already dark. I think we should make a better effort to find a place to pitch our tent so we can get something to eat and a good kip.'

'Yeh, you're right and anyway this place has freaked me out a bit, eh, and I think it has you, too!'

'Aye, you're spot on with that! replied Barry.

They re-traced their steps back and as luck would have it, they ended up back at the gate near the roundabout. Back over it they climbed. Once over the gate, Ian said, 'I'm tired and fed up, Barry. Let's pitch the tent here on the grass verge beside the road.'

'Don't be daft! We are beside a road! We can't stop here!'

'I'm not going any further. I'm knackered. Let's put the tent up here,' said Ian in a firm and bad tempered manner which was unusual for him. He was definitely fatigued and had had enough of the events of the day and just wanted to get into his sleeping bag.

'But cars could go passed and we won't get any sleep and it could be dangerous.'

'I don't care. I'm knackered and I'm not going any further. Anyway, I doubt there will be many vehicles on this out-of-the-way piece of road!' yelled Ian.

Barry understood his mood and acquiesced but he was a bit concerned about pitching a tent by the side of a road no matter how quiet it was.

He said, 'OK. If you can manage the tent, I will make us something to eat and put a brew on, is that all right?'

'OK. That suits me fine,' said Ian.

He's tired, thought Barry and to be fair, we have been through a lot on our first day and I'm feeling knackered as well. I know, I will put the radio on for a bit of music. That will cheer him up along with a good feast. He found the radio and put it on. It didn't matter what station as long as it was music.

It didn't take long for Ian to get the tent up and sort the bedding inside. Thankfully Barry had a brew ready and the smell of some beans heating up in a pan and some spam frying, seemed to cheer Ian up a bit.

'Here Ian, get that down you,' said Barry, handing his mate a brew. 'Grub won't be long.'

Ian took the offered mug and sat down beside Barry, his smile returning as he hungrily sniffed the food. Barry managed to butter a couple of slices of bread each and placed them on their plates. The spam and beans now ready, he loaded the plates with equal portions. Ian happily took his and began to eat. A period of silence followed, apart from the noise of the food being eaten and the radio playing.

'Aah, I was ready for that,' said Ian, putting his now empty plate down. 'Funny how everything tastes great when you're hungry, eh! I really enjoyed that. Well done Barry. Yeh, well done. I'm sorry I was grumpy earlier, it's been a long day.'

'No problem Ian. You're right, it has been a long day and yes, that did taste good, didn't it?'

'Yeh, I feel a lot better after that, eh. Let's get to bed.'

'I'll just have this cigarette,' said Barry. 'I really need it after what we've been through. I haven't had that many today.'

He lit up and took a long satisfying drag. Ian smiled and went inside the tent. Barry didn't take long to finish his cigarette. He stubbed it out in some grass and joined his pal who was already asleep and Barry wasn't far behind him.

Vrooooommmmmmmm !!!!! Peep! Peep!

'Bloody hell!' groaned Barry.

'Eh? ..... wha..... what's up, Barry?'

'A car or something has just gone passed. The driver pipped his horn. I thought he was gonna drive right over us! Talk about scary!'

'What time is it, Barry, what's the time?' asked Ian.

Barry checked his watch. 'One in the morning.'

'I can't imagine any more cars. Not on this small stretch of road at this time of night, so we should be OK now .... yeh, I think we should be OK,' said Ian, trying to sound convincing.

'I hope you're right! It's not funny thinking you're gonna get run over!'

After a while, tiredness prevailed and out heroes were once again sound asleep ...... but not for long! Barely an hour had passed when another vehicle drove by, the driver giving one loud continuous press on his horn. Barry held his head in his arms, expecting any second to be crushed to death under the car wheels. Ian, although a little shaken, pretended not to hear. After all it was his idea to pitch the tent there, ignoring Barry's forebodings. The vehicle continued on its way with a loud whoosh without causing them any physical harm, thankfully failing to damage their tent.

Barry got out of his sleeping bag and crawled outside for a much needed cigarette to calm his now very fraught nerves. Lighting up, he began to think back on what a day they'd had for day one of their travels - the hearses, the incident at Greengarth, hitchhiking on the A1 and the scary apparition that was the horse jump. These memories brought a smile to his face and he began to relax. He was only half way through his cigarette, however, when it started to rain and it quickly became heavy.

'Not my flaming night !' he thought. They weren't expecting any rain until tomorrow night. He hurriedly nicked off the end of his cigarette, making sure it had gone out properly, before putting the remnants back in his packet. Waste not want not was his motto! In the dark, he felt his way back to his sleeping bag, hoping he would finally be allowed to sleep. The rain was now pounding heavily on the canvas. So far, no leaks and for this Barry silently thanked Bernie and Ada Nichols. Although the rain was loud, it had a soothing effect on Barry and he soon managed to get back to the land of nod, hoping this would be 3rd time lucky.

Barry checked his watch. It was 6:30 a.m. before the next vehicle went passed. This time the driver did not toot his horn but just continued on his way. He realised it was now light outside and the rain had abated. Best make a move, he thought. He quietly made his way outside to light the half completed cigarette which the rain had earlier forced him to give up. Looking up at the sky, he saw that the clouds were now light and there were signs of a nice day in front of them so he began to cheer up. He finished the cigarette and decided it was time for a brew. Lighting the gas burner, he soon had the kettle on and their tin mugs sorted ready for the hot water. He had just finished pouring when Ian emerged from the tent, rubbing his eyes and giving out a great yawn.

'Morning Ian,' said Barry.

'Morning Barry,' yawned Ian. 'What time is it?'

'Nearly 20 to 7,' replied Barry, handing Ian his mug.

'Aw, cheers Barry. Just what the doctor ordered,' he said. 'Aye, just what the doctor ordered.'

'Your'e right. I'll make some breakfast in a minute. Are you all right with the tent?' asked Barry.

'Yeh, I'll have this cuppa then crack on with that while you make us some nosh, if that's all right, Barry.'

'Of course it is Ian,' chirped up his mate who switched the radio on before rummaging in his rucksack for something to cook.

It didn't take long for the tent to be packed, breakfast to be had and the washing up completed. Our heroes were now refreshed and back to their happy selves, ready for whatever the day would throw at them.

Chapter Six

Bramham

It's now Friday, and with renewed vigour in their step, our heroes walked back up to the roundabout where the last lift had so unceremoniously dumped them the day before. The sun was now bathing them in its early morning warmth, the clouds having now dispersed to leave a clear sky. On to the slip road they walked and remembered what they had been told. While they waited for the first of the day's wagons to turn up Barry began to sing Elvis's latest song 'Your Time Hasn't Come Yet Baby' and Ian joined in.

Soon, a wagon with the name 'Kerr's' on the side came off the roundabout onto the slip road. The lads stuck out their thumbs and to their surprise the wagon slowed down and stopped. They ran to the passenger side and opened the door and told the driver where they were going.

'I can tek yer to the junction with the A659 'cos I'm off to Collingham. You should be able to get a lift from there. Hop in now!'

A bald fat head attached to an extremely rotund body covered in dirty blue overalls, greeted the lads as they climbed into the cab. The driver put the vehicle back into gear and off they set onto the main road.

'So', said the driver. 'My name is Joe and I own this here truck. I'm tekkin' pallet's to a company in Collingham. It's a regular run a does. They mek roof tiles. They supply 'em to companies all ower the country, the knows.'

'You say your name is Joe?' asked Barry.

'Aye, that's reet. You're sharp is you. You've seen the name on the side of t' wagon and put two and two together! Joe Kerr. Now no laughing. Ive put up with it all me life and I'm not bothered any more, see. My wife says to get me name changed by deed poll but I can't be bothered.'

He lit up a cigarette and offered one to the lads which Barry gratefully accepted. Joe even mentioned, over his CB radio, where he was dropping them off, just in case any other lorry driver was willing to take them further. He didn't get a reply but he said they shouldn't have a problem. They continued with some more small talk until they reached their drop off point where they left the vehicle and thanked Joe for taking them this far. He wished them luck and gave them a wave before continuing on his way.

It was now 9 a.m. so they were making really good time. The sun was still shining and the day was warming up, so they decided to leave the main road and make their way onto a minor one, which ran almost parallel to the A1, the plan being to get back onto it later.

Ian said, 'Fancy getting into a wagon driven by a Joker!' he laughed, 'a joker, hahaha.'

'Hahaha, yeh, hilarious!' laughed Barry with a touch of sarcasm.

Walking on, they noticed a signpost for a village called Bramham which they saw was on the other side of the main road. Ian remembered that Tom Bowler had said he lived there. They wanted to buy some eggs and could do with some other items, especially water so they decided to walk into the village in the hope that it was big enough to have a shop.

They followed a single track road flanked by hedges. Approaching the outskirts of the village Barry felt the need to go to the toilet. He mentioned this to Ian who advised hanging on until they got into the village itself, in the hope it had a public loo. They continued a little further until they rounded a bend and noticed a gate in a low hedge which led into a small well mown field. Barry was now feeling desperate so, armed with a toilet roll, he took his chance and jumped over the gate and made his way to some lovely pruned bushes. He squatted down to do his business and when finished, he let out a great sigh of relief. Just as he started to pull up his jeans, he heard a loud shout from the other side of another hedge further back.

'Oy! What the hell do you think you are doing in my garden? Get him Bruno!'

Barry heard an equally loud 'Woof' and a large dog appeared. It was heading in his direction with an ominous growl. His heart sank. It's a good job he had already finished his bowel movement otherwise he would be doing it right now!

Ian looked on in horror and shouted 'Barry! Run! Run as fast as you can!'

With one hand holding up his unfastened jeans and the other pumping as fast as he could, Barry ran and hopped towards the gate but the dog was easily gaining on him. Ian realised this and found a stone on the ground beside him and decided to throw it at the dog in the hope of slowing it down. It only startled it for a second before it resumed its pursuit, however, it gave Barry time to reach the gate. It was closed. Ian was too busy watching the events unfold and hadn't thought of opening it. Barry had no time to do so, opting to hurdle it instead. Just as his feet were leaving the ground, the animal reached him and with a frightening snarl, it opened its jaws and fastened them on Barry's jeans. There was a ripping sound as the dog shook its head. This disrupted Barry's flight and he fell down. Luckily for him he landed on the other side of the gate, out of harms way. It was probably also lucky for Barry that he hadn't completed putting his jeans on or the damage would have been to more than his clothing! Further luck followed when the dog, which turned out to be a Rottweiler, made no attempt to follow. It concentrated on barking and snarling ferociously, as if waiting further instructions.

Barry had a look of shock on his face. All his colour had drained, but he was otherwise unhurt. The owner of the dog was shouting something but the continued barking had the effect of drowning him out. The lads didn't wait to find out what he was saying, Barry finally fastened his jeans and grabbed his rucksack. He ran after Ian who was already heading down the road and imploring Barry to follow which he did. On they ran, into the village itself. They noticed the barking of the dog receding which they hoped meant they were not being followed.

They continued into Bramham and were now recovering from what had just happened. All of a sudden, Ian stopped and burst into hysterics.

Barry said, 'What's up with you?'

At first Ian couldn't speak. He took a few stuttering breaths and then said, 'I can't believe what has just happened. Look at your jeans! There's a massive chunk out of them! Yeh, a massive chunk!' He continued laughing as pointed at the flap of material revealing part of Barry's backside.

Barry knew his jeans had been torn but hadn't stopped to check how badly. He now looked and felt round his right leg. His heart dropped. The tear was massive but at least the material was still there. This would need some urgent repairs. He was just grateful that he was uninjured!

He unzipped his rucksack and fumbled around inside but didn't find what he was looking for.

'Ian,' he began, 'did you pack a needle and cotton? I can't remember doing so.'

'Ah, come to think of it, I don't think I did...... no, I didn't,' replied Ian.

'Oh no, what the hell am I going to do?'

At that moment, a woman came round the corner and gathered from the way they were looking that something was amiss and asked, 'Is everything alright lads?'

The lads turned round to see who was speaking and saw the woman who was between 30 and 40 years old, about 5'6" tall, with quite a voluptuous figure covered by a low cut top and a mini skirt. She looked 'quite fetching" to say the least.

Ian was the first to speak. 'He's ripped his jeans and we've just realised we haven't got anything to fix it with.'

'Oh dear! You'd better come with me then, lovelies,' and proceeded to put her key in the door to the house they were standing beside.

Our heroes looked at each other, smiled and followed her inside without saying another word.

'Come into the living room, lovelies.'

They followed her in.

'I'll sort them jeans for you. Have you got anything else to wear while I get on with it?'

Barry said, 'Yes, I've got another pair in my rucksack' and proceeded to search inside for his spare pair.

'OK, go into the kitchen and swap them. What the heck have you been up to, to get a tear like that anyway?'

'Barry got attacked by a dog, like eh! We were coming into the village and Barry accidentally went into this guy's garden. We didn't know it was a garden, it was so big! Then this fella came out and shouted at him and set his Rottweiler on him! Barry had to run like hell but the dog took that chunk out of his jeans just as he was leaping over the gate to get away, aye, leaping over the gate,' explained an excited Ian.

'He set his dog on him? That's a bit out of order lovey, not right at all! .....What brings you to Bramham anyway?'

Ian explained the reason for their trip and why they ended up in Bramham. By the time he finished, Barry returned wearing his spare pair of jeans and passed the damaged pair to the woman.

'I'm Barry, by the way, and this is my best mate Ian.'

'And I'm Lucy, Lucy Bowler. My husband's a lorry driver. I'm expecting him home tomorrow.'

Barry and Ian put two and two together and realised that she was the wife of the lorry driver who had given them a lift to Scotch Corner. They kept this to themselves. He had said he lived in Bramham. What a coincidence!

'When was the last time you two had a good wash? These jeans are filthy!'

'Not that long ago,' replied Barry with some indignation in his voice.

'Right. I will mend these jeans for you, lovey, but while I am doing so you can go and have a shower. It's upstairs second on the left.'

Despite Barry's protestations she wouldn't take no for an answer. She took him upstairs and showed him where the shower was and how to use it before returning downstairs with her sewing kit to begin the repair. The only shower Barry had had before this was at the swimming club by the river on the outskirts of Penrith so he was looking forward to it. They didn't have a shower in the bathroom at home. This was a big house, thought Barry as he got in.

'So, where are you two from again?' Lucy asked Ian.

Ian now entered into a conversation with her while she started sewing Barry's jeans. They spoke about what sort of food they had with them and where they planned sleeping. It didn't take her long to finish sewing. She set the repaired jeans down to one side before standing up.

She looked at Ian and said, 'The kitchen is in there, Ian,' pointing in its direction. 'Go and help yourself to a cup of tea. You will easily find where it all is, lovely, and I will be back shortly. Biscuit's are in the tin near the kettle, by the way.'

Meanwhile, Barry was upstairs enjoying his shower when a voice from the hallway asked, 'Would you like your back scrubbed?'

Barry, thinking this was just a joke, replied, 'Yes please.'

He carried on with his shower until suddenly the door opened and Lucy entered, obviously stark naked! She noticed the look of shock on Barry's face and watched as his eyes quickly darted from one part of her body to another.

'Come on then my lovely, pass me the soap and turn round,' said Lucy in a friendly but commanding voice and a suggestive smile on her face as she joined him.

When Lucy had finished with him, Barry was no longer a virgin. He had a massive smile on his face which she was pleased to see.

'How was that then my lovely?'

'Fantastic!' blurted out Barry.

She put her arms around him and gave him the sexiest kiss he had ever experienced.

'So, now you're not a virgin! How does that feel?'

'Like I said, just fantastic!' replied Barry.

Lucy laughed and said, 'Finish your shower and get dressed. I will make you two something to eat in a minute.' She grabbed herself a towel and strode off to her bedroom.

Barry got dressed. He was on cloud nine as he kept thinking back to what had just happened. 'Wow! I'm no longer a virgin! That was unbelievable! Wait till I tell Ian. He won't believe me!'

He left the shower room and as he hurried downstairs he could hear Lucy humming to herself. He found Ian in the kitchen having enjoyed a cup of tea and a biscuit. Barry sat down beside him and whispered, 'You will never believe what just happened!'

'Surprise me. By the look on your face you're gonna tell me that she joined you in the shower, aren't you?' sniggered Ian.

'You got it in one! My first ever time! It was brilliant!'

'Never!' whispered Ian.

Before the could continue, Lucy came down the stairs wearing a shorty dressing gown.

'Ian, I bet you are just as dirty as Barry was, so up you go for a shower, my lovely. Go on, upstairs. You'll find it. If you have any problems turning it on, give me a shout and I will show you.'

As she finished speaking she stared at Barry with a knowing look and a wink.

'I'll be making you something to eat so don't be too long,' she said.

Ian got off his seat and said 'OK' and set off up the stairs to the shower room, wondering if she would follow.

Lucy turned to Barry and said, in a slow sexy drawl, 'Well Barry, how do you feel now?'

'Words can't cut how I feel. I'm floating on air, thanks to you,' beamed Barry.

Lucy went on to tell Barry about her relationship with her husband, Tom and said that they didn't get on very well. He was always accusing her of having affairs. He's right, thought Barry! She went on to say that his jealousy often got the better of him and this led to him beating her every now and then. She would like to leave him but didn't have anywhere else to go so she was stuck with him for the moment. The conversation continued with Lucy recalling various events in her life while she began to prepare some food. Eventually they could hear Ian coming back down the stairs.

'I haven't changed my clothes because I forgot to take my rucksack upstairs, eh! Aye, forgot my rucksack, but never mind, it will do for now,' said Ian when he joined the other two.

'That's good timing, my lovely,' said Lucy. 'I've nearly finished making Spaghetti Bolognese for you. I hope you like it.'

'Never had it before,' said Barry

'Neither have I,' said Ian, 'neither have I.'

'Where have you two been all your life? I thought everybody had had Spag Bol at least once! You're going to try it now anyway my lovelies.'

Turning to Barry, she said, 'Set the table while I get it out. That drawer over there has everything you need. I won't be a minute.'

Barry opened the drawer and got out what he thought would be needed and proceeded to set the table. Lucy brought their food over in Spaghetti bowls. Before sitting down she went back to the drawer to get some spoons. Barry didn't realise they were needed to eat spaghetti. She had great fun teaching them how to eat it and when they eventually finished, our heroes both agreed it was lovely and helped with the washing up.

'We will have to be on our way soon, time is getting on,' said Barry.

'So where are you planning to get to this evening, lovelies?'

'Barry, I think we should head towards Leeds and get a train to Leicester just to make sure we get there for Sunday, eh!' said Ian, 'aye, get there in time, like.'

'Yeh, I think you're right,' said Barry.

'I tell you what, my lovelies, I will take you in my car down to the A64. That's the road to Leeds so it will be your best way of getting there.'

'Are you sure?' asked Barry. 'That would be great. Thanks very much!'

'Aye, that would be great,' echoed Ian.

'Don't mention it. It's the least I can do after today,' said Lucy and winked at Barry.

This is good, thought Barry, we will get to Leeds in no time if she does that. Our heroes set to, getting their gear together and putting on their jackets. It was now late in the afternoon and there were some clouds in the sky. The weather forecast mentioned the possibility of another night of rain so the sooner they got going the better chance they had of reaching Leeds before dark, although another night camping out wouldn't be too much of a disaster.

Lucy ushered them into her car after they put their rucksacks in the boot and very soon they reached the roundabout for the A64. Once they were out of the vehicle she pointed them in the right direction before they said their goodbyes. Barry thanked her for everything and she knew what he meant. Ian said thanks for the tea. It was the first time he had eaten Spaghetti Bolognese and he loved it. Barry concurred. Lucy shouted 'good luck' to our heroes and left with a friendly wave and a toot of her horn.

Chapter Seven

To Roundhay Park

Our heroes got their gear together and began to stride off the roundabout onto the beginning of the A64. There was a signpost for Leeds so they knew they were heading in the right direction, just as Lucy had said. Having learnt from previous mistakes they decided to wait for a vehicle to come off the roundabout before moving on any further. It was quiet for a Friday night so Barry lit a cigarette and used his rucksack as a seat. Ian followed suit, minus the cigarette.

'We are certainly having some interesting times on this holiday, eh Barry!' said Ian.

'Your telling me and I'm no longer a virgin. It was bloody good!' I wonder if either of us will manage it again on this trip?'

'You lucky bugger, Barry! How did you manage that? She didn't come up to see me, aye, she didn't come up while I was in the shower, eh! I wonder why not! You lucky bugger!'

'I suppose it's because I was first in the shower and she only wanted it once. She also told me she likes a drink and that's another thing Tom doesn't like about her. I hope she doesn't get pissed when he gets home tomorrow and tell him what happened! He knows where we are going and she might tell him where she dropped us off and that we are gonna head for Leeds train station. If he is really jealous he might come after us. He's beaten her up before now!'

'Has he? What a bastard!'

'He isn't due home until after his job tomorrow so we should be OK, though. The only time we should worry is when we are at the convention on Sunday. Anyway, she might not tell him anything so I'm probably worrying about nothing.'

'Aye, you're right, Barry, you're worrying about nothing. And I'm glad she didn't follow me upstairs as well. I would feel guilty the next time I saw Rosemary, eh!'

'Yes, she's a good lass is your Rosemary but I haven't got a girlfriend.'

A couple of minutes later a vehicle could be heard on the roundabout. Our heroes hoped it would come off the roundabout where they were and sure enough it did. It was a blue Ford Cortina. As it approached they started to thumb and sure enough the driver stopped and wound down his window.

'Where you going lads?'

'To Leeds,' shouted Ian. 'Aye, to Leeds,' he repeated.

'I'm not going that far but I can get you to Oakwood.'

'Is that near Leeds?' queried Ian

'Not far off. Almost walking distance for 2 fit lads. Besides, you seem to have some camping gear and if you can't get a lift into the city and don't want to walk tonight, you could always camp in Roundhay Park.'

'That sounds great,' said Ian and they got into the vehicle.

When the driver set off he jammed his foot hard on the accelerator, causing the wheels to spin with an awful screech. The sudden burst of speed pinned our heroes into the back of their seats and put a feeling of dread in their hearts. They were beginning to wonder if they had made a mistake accepting a lift from this madman!

A mile or two further on, the driver spoke. 'Where have you come from lads?'

Ian said, 'First of all, let me introduce us, I'm Ian and this is my mate Barry. We're from Penrith in Cumbria but we were given a lift to that roundabout by a woman from Bramham. You see, Barry had a sort of accident in Bramham....' Ian then told the tale the reader is already aware of. He even included the fact that Barry had been seduced by the lady in question. He went on to say it was a great coincidence because it was the wife of a lorry driver who had given them a lift to Scotch Corner the day before and then joked about the lorry driver being called Tom Bowler. The driver of the car laughed as well.

When he had finished the tale they continued on their journey with some small talk. It wasn't long before they reached Oakwood where the driver brought the vehicle to a screeching halt beside the entrance to Roundhay Park which is one of the biggest city parks in Europe, covering more than 700 acres of parkland, lakes, woodland and gardens.

The driver, who had not given his name, began to speak, 'This is the entrance to Roundhay Park. If you can't be bothered to walk any further I would suggest you go in there and camp for the night.' He pointed towards a road leading into the park which formed a wide avenue with trees on either side. 'You're sure to find somewhere to camp for the night. It's a large park and at the far end there is a lake. It's called The Upper Lake and you will find a nice wooded area there if you want to be out of the way. That's where I would go. Tell you what, I'll drive you up the road a bit to save your feet. In the morning you could walk to Leeds railway station. It's only about an hour and a half's walk if you are feeling energetic. Just go down Wetherby Road there, then onto Roundhay Road and just keep going. You will soon pick up signs for the main railway station. Easy walking distance for you two.'

Without waiting to see if that was agreeable, he drove into the park, dropping the lads off, not too far from the lake.

'Keep walking in that direction and you will see signs for the lake. It's not far. Bye!'

Again, without another word and not waiting for any thanks or otherwise, he drove away at speed.

'Bloody hell! He was in a hurry, all of a sudden!'said Barry, picking up his rucksack.

'Your right, Barry. If you ask me, he's a bit of a weirdo, aye, a bit of a weirdo,' said Ian.

Now with their rucksacks on their backs, the two mates slowly made their way along the road towards the wood the driver had indicated. Now that they were in the park the decided they may as well find somewhere suitable to camp for the night. They had all day to get to Leeds tomorrow and it would only be an hour or two to Leicester from there.

— — — — —-

Meanwhile, the driver of the Cortina had arrived at his destination which was only a couple of hundred yards further on from the park entrance. He used his keys to enter a property and immediately made his way to a telephone. He dialled a number which was eventually answered.

'Hello, can I speak to Tom Bowler please ...... oh good ..... yes I'll hold.'

'Hello,' boomed a familiar voice on the other end.

'Tom? It's your brother, Harry.'

'Now then, Harry, you've just caught me. I'm due to go home shortly. My job for tomorrow has been cancelled thank god so I get a good long weekend. I haven't told Lucy yet. I think I will just surprise her.'

'Yeh, I know what will be going through your mind. I know how jealous you get and that's why you want to surprise her. That's the reason I'm calling.'

'Why, what's happened, Harry?'

'You're not gonna like me for telling you this but I have just given two lads a lift. It seems you gave them a lift to Scotch Corner yesterday.'

'Ah yes! Ian and Barry if I remember rightly. On their way to a concert or something in Leicester. What a coincidence! .... what have *they* got to do with anything?'

'Well, I didn't tell them that I was your brother and one of them started talking and to cut a long story short, it looks like they ended up in Bramham. They bumped into Lucy and she invited them in. She allowed them to use the shower apparently and ...... you won't thank me for telling you this, Tom, but one of them had it off with her in the shower. She then made them Spag Bog for them and to cap it all she drove them to the A64 so they could get a lift to Leeds .... and guess who stopped to pick them up?

'No!

'They plan to get a train to Leicester tomorrow so I took them to Roundhay Park and suggested they find somewhere there to kip for the night. I suggested the wood near the lake, you know the one, and go to Leeds train station in the morning. I've just dropped them off now. I thought you might be interested in where they are.'

'Fucking hell! I *knew* she would be up to no good while I was away this time! I had a feeling about it. She seemed too happy to see me go, this week. But I can't believe she had it with one of those two skinny runts!'

Harry could sense the rage rising in Tom and was only too aware of his temper and that he had beaten her before. Although he thought Lucy wasn't good enough for his brother and although he liked to get her into trouble, Tom's reaction was worse than he expected. He was beginning to wish he hadn't phoned him. His reason for calling was that he thought Tom would maybe go and see if he could find the lads in Roundhay Park and give them a bit of a beating. Now he realised he had been a fool and Lucy would be the one to suffer badly at his hands.

He was about to speak again and ask him not to be too hard on her and suggest he takes his anger out on the two lads but he didn't get a chance.

Tom said 'Thanks Harry' and the phone was put back in its cradle.

Harry put his phone down. He hoped Tom wouldn't be too hard on Lucy. Although thought she deserved some sort of punishment, he was beginning to worry. Maybe he would kick her out and end the marriage. About time. He deserved better. He didn't know what else he could do so he decided to dismiss it from his mind and hope nothing terrible happened.

— — — —-

It's now around 6pm and our heroes are deep in Roundhay Park. It had started to rain heavily shortly after they were dropped off and it was difficult to make out exactly where they were. Ian pointed to what appeared to be the wooded area.

'Look,' he said. 'We should be able to find a place to pitch our tent over there and it might give us a bit of a break from all this rain, aye, some shelter. What do you think Barry?'

'Yes Ian. At least it will be better than anywhere else we have seen and I am sick of walking about, getting soaked.'

The wood was about 100 yards away through a thin line of trees. They set off walking towards it when they noticed an old dilapidated building some distance to their right. The lads agreed to head towards it. They could make it out through some trees. It looked like an old overgrown forgotten folly of some sort. Maybe it would provide a nice dry place to camp, they thought.

As they approached, a tall wide blackened doorway, heavy, like church doors, revealed itself. It stood slightly ajar and they could see the hinges were barely holding it up. The heavy cloud allowed only a little light to enter the building. The damp, dull walls rose up to some small battlements overgrown with moss and ivy. A small bell tower encapsulated the nearest portion of the roof. Our heroes could imagine a slow ringing of the bell reverberating on dull dark days. Ashen clouds now hung heavy in the sky, having only a minute ago ceased from their almost relentless torrents of rain which left large pools of water on the path leading up to that door.

Our heroes hesitated at the entrance, neither wanting to be the first to venture inside the uninviting darkness. A crack of thunder sounded above. Barry jumped, his nerves already fraught. At the same time, this gave Ian all the momentum he needed. He moved timidly inside, looking left and right in the heavy, almost impenetrable gloom. Some shafts of light could be made out, penetrating the blackness through some gaps in the badly damaged roof. There had been a fire, some time in the distant past. This allowed them to make their way with care through the building but wherever they walked they were tripping over fallen beams, rubble and all kinds of filth. It soon became clear that it would not be a suitable place to pitch their tent. They would be filthy in no time and it looked dangerous so they decided to leave.

A sudden shriek up above was followed by a hoot and our frightened heroes realised that although there were no humans to worry about, the place was probably populated by wildlife and it would be better if they went to the wood they saw earlier. They both breathed a silent sigh of relief as they exited the building, neither wanting to admit to the other the fear they had felt while inside. They had only walked a few yards, however, when the Barn Owl they had heard earlier came flying out of the building, glided passed them and disappeared near some trees. Although beautiful to see, this was not expected and it nearly freaked out our pair of heroes!

By the time they reached the wooded area, their nerves had recovered. They found a perfect place to pitch their tent. The heavy, leafy canopy above, had kept this part of the wood nice and dry, despite the rain. Ian said he would put it up again if Barry could do the honours with the food like last time. This suited Barry. He lit the storm lantern to give him some light before he got the cooking gear from his rucksack. He was starting to feel jovial again and decided the first thing he would do would be to put the radio on and make a brew to warm them up again. The heavy rain had chilled their bones a little. Some music might just be what they needed to blow away the memory of that stupid dilapidated old building. There was nothing to be frightened of after all, he told himself. 'Baby Come Back' by The Equals, was playing. It was number 1 for the 3rd week running. Both lads hummed away at this record while getting on with setting up the camp. By 9pm the tent was up, a good meal was had and the washing up had been completed.

Ian decided it would be a good idea to have a camp fire so they rummaged round to see if they could find any dry wood. The rain had soaked a lot of the undergrowth near their campsite but they managed to find some they thought might do the trick. As usual, Ian used his ingenuity and eventually managed to get a half decent fire going. When they found something dry to sit on, Barry lit a cigarette and once again, they settled into a conversation about their trip so far and once again they were surprised by how much had happened in such a short a time. While they were chatting, they heard the DJ say, 'The king of rock and roll has hit the charts again with his latest release 'Your Time Hasn't Come Yet, Baby', in at number 20......'

This cheered our heroes up even more and they sang along as the record was played.

'How did we not notice it was in the charts, Ian?' said Barry when the record finished.

'I don't know. We were so busy getting ready for our trip, I suppose, aye, so busy getting ready.'

The pair were back to their normal happy selves now. Another hour passed and the fire petered out. They were both tired so they decided it was time for bed. Ian went first while Barry extinguished the storm lantern and had one last cigarette. There were no stars to see, the cloud cover was too heavy. Never mind, it had stopped raining so he switched the radio off and joined his mate in the tent.

Chapter Eight

Tom Confronts Lucy!

Meanwhile in Bramham, let's return to earlier in the evening and to the problems between Tom and Lucy. Tom still had a few chores to do before he could drive home and all the time he was brooding about what his brother had told him. He couldn't stop thinking about it and the more he thought, the angrier he became. 'Wait till I get home, that bitch is going to pay for this,' he thought. 'This is the last time she does the dirty on me.' Chores completed, he got in his car, slammed the door shut and set off. It would take him an hour to get home, maybe less if his anger kept rising.

Lucy was already back home after dropping the lads off. Once inside she started to think about her life and how much she hated Tom. She was sick of the beatings even if she did give him cause. A man should not hit a woman! When he comes home tomorrow, she thought, she would give him the remains of the Spaghetti Bolognese she had made for the lads. She would take great pleasure in watching him eat it, knowing she had made it specifically for them. It was a good job she was in the habit of batch cooking, making enough for another day. This was a habit which she was glad she had inherited from her mother before she met Tom.

This gave her more time to think so she opened a bottle of Gin and found some Tonic. She slouched down on the sofa with her glass in hand. I should leave him, she thought, but where would I go? Maybe I could find a woman's refuge somewhere. Deep in thought, she had one drink after another.

It's now approximately 7pm and she can hear a noise at her front door. 'Who can that be?' she asked herself. A key could be heard in the lock. What ? Don't tell me he has come home early? He is supposed to be working until at least tomorrow afternoon. Thank god the lads have gone!

Sure enough, in walks Tom. No greeting from him, just a look of thunder on his face. Oh, oh, she thought. He has a problem! I hope he hasn't had a bad time at work. My life won't be worth living this weekend if that's the case.

'Hello!' she said, with the friendliest look she could give him. 'You told me you weren't coming home until tomorrow. I thought you had another delivery to do?'

'I did', said Tom. 'But it got cancelled so I thought I would surprise you.'

He didn't say this with any joviality in his voice. There was nothing in it to suggest that he was happy to get home early to see her. In fact, she detected the opposite from his tone. He sounded decidedly confrontational! What can have put him in this mood? He can't have found out about the lads, that would be impossible, but I better be on my toes all the same, she thought.

'You must be ready for a beer by now, love,' she said, trying to lighten his mood.

'I see you've already started with the Gin. I bet you've had a few already,' he replied with a snarl.

Lucy was getting worried. She decided it was time to get if over with and find out what was irking him. It must be to do with work. She said, 'What's the matter, love? You sound a bit upset.'

'I'm going for a shower and then I want a word with you. I'll tell you no more 'til then,' he said.

His mood still appeared black. Surely he can't have found out what had occurred. That wasn't possible! She was getting increasingly anxious. He had been angry with her on previous occasions but then she knew the reasons why. This time she was completely at a loss for the cause of it. She got the Spaghetti out of the fridge and started to heat it up, hoping one of his favourite meals would lighten his mood. She set the table and prepared to wait for him, all the timer trying to figure out why he was in such a mood. Whatever it was, she was resigned to the fact she was going to have a bad tempered husband for the night and there was no telling where this mood might take him.

Shower completed, Tom dressed and made his way downstairs. Lucy heard him coming and the Spaghetti Bolognese was ready to serve so she placed it on the kitchen table ready for him, a bottle of beer already opened next to the spaghetti bowl. He sat down and ate his meal and drank his beer in silence. Another worrying sign. Lucy decided not to attempt to engage him in conversation as this had in the past brought on a storm and she would rather wait a little longer.

He finished eating. 'Another beer!' he shouted.

Oh dear, here we go, thought Lucy. She quickly produced another bottle and put it in front of him on the table. He took a large swig from it before slamming it back down.

Although worried about the outcome, she once again changed her mind and decided to confront him.

'Come on Tom, you're frightening me. What's the matter with you tonight? You started on me as soon as you came in the house tonight but it can't be anything I've done!' she said, in her friendliest voice.

'So you want to know, do you? Well, let's see. Where do I start. Ah yes! I had a call from Harry this afternoon while I was at work,' he began. 'You'll never guess what he told me! He picked up two young lads who had been hitchhiking.' He paused as he let these words sink in. 'He said he picked them up on the roundabout for the A64 on his way home from work.'

Her heart dropped1 She nearly fainted with shock! Oh my god! she thought. I'm in trouble! He knows!

'You know the one, on the junction with the A1.'

Lucy was now trembling and at a loss of what to say.

'Guess what! What a coincidence! They happened to be two scrawny lads who I gave a lift to yesterday from Penrith. I dropped them off at Scotch Corner,' he continued.

Lucy was trying to keep cool but fear was rising inside her!

Tom continued with his tail, 'They told him something which he thought would be of interest to me,'

He took another swig from his bottle while staring straight at Lucy to see if there was any reaction. And there was! Sweat beads were now visible on Lucy's face as she became increasingly concerned. Oh my god! What could they have told Harry?

'They didn't know he was my brother, so they told him what happened ...... here,' and in an increasingly loud voice he continued, '....... in this house ...... in the SHOWER! ..... where I have just been! ...... you didn't come up to join me! .... like you did those lads!'

He slammed the flat of his hand on the table. The noise made Lucy jump and cry out.

She didn't know what to say. Tom suddenly stood up, obviously in a rage, shoving his chair back with some force. He opened a kitchen cupboard where he knew there was a bottle of whisky. He removed the top and took a large gulp before turning to look at her.

'What have you got to say for yourself this time, you slut?' he bellowed.

'Tom, I don't know what you are talking about!' she spluttered in desperation. 'I haven't done anything wrong. I was just being charitable when I saw -.'

He cut her short. 'Charitable! Well, well, I've heard it called some things in my time but never charity!' he screamed.

'No,' she uttered. 'No, I don't mean that. I mean, well, I felt sorry for them, they'd had a problem so I took them inside and let them get cleaned up. One of them had been bitten by a dog and his jeans were ripped so I said I would fix them for him and then off they went. That's all, Tom! That's all! I promise! she pleaded.

Tom walked up to Lucy and yelled, 'Ha! You've missed a lot out, including giving them a lift to the A64 where Harry found them! They told him it was you who dropped them off there!'

He took another large swig from the whisky bottle. His face was now red and his eyes were staring hard at her. She had seen him in some ferocious moods before but this was far worse than any previously. She was now becoming very afraid, not just for her safety but for her life!

'I'm sorry, Tom, I thought that if I told you I had taken them down to the A64 you would have told me off but nothing else happened that you need to be concerned about, honest Tom! Those lads must be lying. It will be a macho thing to make them feel big in front of a stranger. Honest Tom! Those lads must be lying! It must be a macho thing to make them look big in front of a stranger

Don't believe what they say, I beg of you!'she pleaded, with a look of fear on her face, her hands reaching out in supplication.

He took yet another large swig from the bottle and she realised that tiredness meant the alcohol was having a dangerous affect on him. He seemed to be getting increasingly upset and angry. 'Honest, Tom, Honest Tom! I'll honest Tom you !' he snarled.

He swung his hand which came crashing into the side of her face as he lashed out in his torment. He was physically very strong and was still holding the whiskey bottle. The damage caused by it was immense. A lot worse than he had intended. Blood immediately spurted from ruptured blood vessels in her left temple as she fell heavily to the floor. She cracked the other side of her skull when it came into contact with the edge of the concrete fire hearth, causing further serious damage! Blood now poured from both the left and right temples of Lucy's head as she lay now fatally injured.

Tom was unable to move as the shock of what he had done came home to him. His heart missed a beat as he surveyed the horror in front of him. He stood there, still holding the bottle out from his body, frozen in time at the moment he had struck his wife. He eventually managed to shake himself from his stupor. He looked at the bottle in his hand. In horror at what he had done, he threw it down. It shattered loudly. It shattered loudly on the stone floor.

He gave himself a shake and knelt down beside the body of his wife. Oh my god! he thought. He could tell instantly that she was dead. Her lifeless eyes staring into space told him all he needed to know. They were frozen in the moment of death. He made an effort to find a pulse but as he expected, there was nothing there. He had killed her! He had killed his wife! She had caused him heartache and his jealousy had got the better of him on many occasions but he still loved her. How could he have done this? He didn't mean to, he kept telling himself. It was an accident! He was in deep trouble now, all because of those bloody kids! Why had he let it get to him so easily? Oh yes, because his brother had told him and this time it wasn't suspicious jealousy, it was the truth. But he loved her! He would never have hurt her like that. That bloody whiskey bottle! Those fucking kids!

He stood up, still looking in disbelief at the lifeless body of his wife and sat back heavily into the nearest kitchen chair trying to get his head round what had just taken place. 'What the hell have I just done?' he said in a whisper to himself before crying out in grief. He looked at the shattered remains of the whisky bottle on the floor. 'My god! I am in for it now! I've gone too far this time! The police are already aware of my temper because of the complaint the neighbour made last time.'

He held his head in his hands and felt the warm tears streaming down his face. He tried to shout out but there were no words, just a screech of anger mixed with anguish. 'What am I to do now?' he thought. He made his way to the cupboard and grabbed another bottle of whiskey. Why not? he thought. 'I'm as good as dead anyway.' He walked into the living room and fell into his favourite chair. He opened the bottle and took another large swig, feeling the burn as he swallowed it. One large swig followed another. The tears stung his eyes so he closed them. Without intending to, he fell asleep. The fatigue caused by a hard week away at work, the effects of the whiskey and the drama which had just unfolded, all had their effect.

A number of hours past by before he awoke. It was dark. He checked his watch. It was just after 1a.m. He stood up and went back into the kitchen, half hoping that all was OK, that he had just been the victim of a nightmare. But it wasn't something that happened in his sleep. There, by the hearth, lay the body of his dead wife, surrounded by an immense pool of blood. He broke into further tears of anguish as he saw her there. After pulling himself together he noticed his face in a nearby wall mirror and walked up to it. He was splattered with her blood.

He made his way upstairs and washed the blood away. While up there, his thoughts turned again to the two skinny youths and the coincidences which resulted in him killing his wife. The lift he had given them, how they had ended up in Bramham, how they had met his wife and how his brother had been the one to pick them up on the A64. Maybe this was meant to happen. Well maybe, he thought, we will meet again! The coincidences kept churning around in his brain. Maybe the 'coincidences' are meant to continue, he thought, as his anger towards the lads began to surface again. If he hadn't given them a lift, none of this would have happened. It's their fault, he thought .... and they must pay!

His anger was growing. He quickly dressed in some clean clothes, leaving the blood spattered ones on the floor of the bedroom. The police are bound to turn up at some point. They will know it was him so why bother trying to hide the evidence, he thought. He resolved to admit it anyway but first, those two fucking lads!

It was now nearly 2 a.m. as he secured the house before getting into his car. He drove to the A64 and headed for Roundhay Park. He knew he was well over the limit but he was beyond caring. The whiskey bottle accompanied him and he kept drinking as he arrived at the park. He knew it well, although he thought it might take him a while to find where they were camping if they had indeed stayed there for the night.

Chapter Nine

Back in Roundhay Park

Meanwhile, back in Roundhay Park, Ian decided to pay another visit to the dilapidated 'folly' and have a look inside. Something in his head made him imagine there was something valuable hidden there. He didn't know what but he wanted to check. He left Barry behind as he was sound asleep. Ian had a torch with him and was checking all the dark recesses inside. He carefully made his way towards the far end, the area where earlier they had seen shafts of daylight illuminating some of it.

He almost stumbled over fallen beams and had to negotiate some piles of rubble. He suspected he would be getting filthy but thought it would be worth it, so he continued his search. He heard the hoot of the resident Owl. It must have returned after almost scaring them earlier.

Suddenly, he heard a noise to his left! He froze and listened. Nothing. His heart was racing but he decided to continue. Maybe he had imagined it or maybe it was the Owl. Another couple of paces ......a scratching noise. What was that? He froze again. More scratching to his left. He shone the torch in the direction of the noise. He could just make out something moving about in another pile of rubble. What is it? A cat? Maybe a rat! ..... Or something more sinister! Despite the cool night air, his fear was now evident by the sweat on the palms of his hands and further beads of sweat on his forehead. Wait! More movement! Is that a figure emerging from the rubble? It can't be! It is! Aaahhh! Let me out!

Ian tried to run as fast as he could but he kept falling over the rubbish on the floor of the old building, kicking up dust which got into his eyes. He made it worse by rubbing them which obscured his vision. Where is the door? He couldn't make it out. Is it over there? No, maybe this way! He could hear the apparition moving towards him. It was laughing! The most hideous, deep-throated, terrifying laugh he had ever heard! Ian screamed in terror! At last, he was able to see the door and dashed for it but somehow he never seemed to get any closer! What's happening! What's going on? He fell down ...... then sat up...... in bed!

He was shaking all over and covered in sweat, but he was alive and he was in the tent. He realised that he had just suffered the worst nightmare of his life..... but survived it! He was breathing fast and the sweat was real but he was OK.

As his heart started to beat more easily he heard Barry whimpering. 'No! No! ..... get off me!

Ian realised his best friend was also having a nightmare so he gave him a gentle shake in an attempt to wake him up. Sure enough Barry opened his eyes with a start and a gasp and then realised he was awake. 'God in heaven! I was having a nightmare about that bloody old building, Ian. Thanks for waking me up. I haven't had a nightmare like that before. It was bloody awful!' splurged out Barry. He was also covered in sweat.

'Snap Barry! I was dreaming of it as well. I mean, having a nightmare about it, eh! I think that old place has had an affect on us Barry.'

'It sure has. I don't think I can go to sleep for a while. What time is it?'

Ian looked at his watch. 'It's 3 o'clock.'

'I think I'll make a brew to settle my nerves. That was awful!' said Barry. 'Do you want one, Ian?

'Aye, bloody right I'll have one!' said Ian. 'Bloody right! I don't think I could get back to sleep yet either.'

Barry got dressed and was leaving the tent when Ian said, 'I'll get some more firewood and get another campfire going to keep us warm while we are outside.'

'Do you want me to help you!'

'No. I'll be fine. You make the brew.'

'OK,' said Barry as he lit the storm lantern before putting the kettle on.

— — — — — — —

A few minutes before this conversation, Tom arrived in Roundhay Park and was searching for any possible places the lads might go to set up a tent. Nothing yet but he wasn't giving up. He remembered where his brother had dropped them off. He thought they wouldn't be far away.

— — — — — — —

Barry put some water in the kettle and lit the stove. The cups and teabags etc were within easy reach so he got them ready. Ian remembered he had put some firewood to one side for the morning, so he decided to use it now to get the basics of a campfire going. Satisfied, he used his torch to go in search of some more so they could be comforted by the warmth of a good blaze.

— — — — — — —

Tom was still driving round. He looked over to his right. What's that? He pulled up and had another gulp of whiskey. Is that a light in the woods over there? At first he wasn't sure. The woods were about 100 yards away. The light appeared again. Yes. Two lights! One was brighter than the other. One was stationary. Maybe a lantern. The other was moving further into the wood. A torch! A sliver of moonlight was visible as the clouds started to break up. It illuminated a narrow plume of smoke which was breaking through the canopy of the trees. Tom wondered if the coincidences were continuing. This could be the camp site for the two shit-heads! That smoke could be their fire and the torch and lantern mean they are up. What they would be doing up at this time of night he couldn't imagine.

— — — — — —

A few minutes later, Ian returned with some more firewood and stoked the fire with it. They now had a good warming blaze going. Barry gave Ian his brew and they had a little chat. After a pause in a general conversation, Ian said, 'I need a shit, Barry. Keep the fire going so I know where you are in case I get lost. I know it's only a small wood but it will make me feel better after that nightmare, eh!'

'OK, Ian. I'm gonna have another brew while you're away so no need to rush.'

Ian got some toilet paper and their shovel and off he went, aiming for the far end of this small wood, while Barry put some more fuel on the fire.

— — — — — — —

Meanwhile, Tom found a suitable place to park his car properly before leaving it. He was going to give them both a good hiding and the one who had been in the shower with his wife was going to die! Maybe both of them, he hadn't made his mind up! He didn't bother arming himself with anything. He wanted to use his bare hands. They were two scrawny, weak looking individuals anyway and he was quite powerful and was in no doubt he could take them on, both at the same time. They would be easy pickings.

He found an animal track which led towards the wood so he followed it as silently as he could. Reaching the edge of the wood he almost stumbled into their camp. He wanted to see where each of them was before making his move.

Barry could hear some twigs snapping. The noise startled him at first but as it came from the direction Ian had taken on his way for his 'dump' he relaxed. He looked ahead, expectantly but still wary. To his relief, Ian and his torch appeared through the trees and his mate rejoined him.

Tom remained hidden from view.

'That was a good one Barry. I think I have just got rid of all that Spaghetti Bolognese Lucy made for us!' laughed Ian, taking the brew that Barry handed him.

Barry chuckled. 'I've yet to go. I'm sure it will be the same for me but I think it will be after some more shut-eye though.'

'It was really good, I must admit. I'll have to tell mam about it, eh! Aye, maybe she can find the recipe from somewhere. I bet Tom enjoys it when he gets home tomorrow. She said it's his favourite. Did you see she had made enough for him as well?'

'Aye, Ian, I did. Do you know, I think she really loves him but can't help herself where other fellas are concerned. She was a good lass to take us in like that and do what she did for us and even to take us down to the roundabout. A good egg she is,' said Barry.

'Aye, she is that. I hope he appreciates her as much as we did. What a coincidence to bump into her after getting a lift from him, aye, a lift from her hubby!'

'Yeh, it was. I wonder if it will be a theme for our trip, coincidences that is? Anyway, I think I am ready to go back to bed. How about you?'

'Agreed, Barry. I'll just put this fire out,' said Ian and proceeded to do so while Barry had a pee by a nearby tree.

Tom was listening to what they said. He was close by and could hear everything. He was almost tearful when he heard what they said about his wife. He had loved her in his own way and they were saying that she had loved him. Despite this, he was hoping that they would reveal which one of them had been in the shower with his wife, but they hadn't . Whoever it was, he was going to kill and leave the other to tell the tale, he decided. He would throttle the lad who had done the dirty with his wife and just beat the other one up. He thought of it as getting his revenge and wanted to leave the other one alive to tell the police it was him that committed the killings. He was looking forward to seeing their faces when he told them what he had done.

He took a deep breath then walked into their campsite just as Barry was about to enter the tent. A crack of a twig ushered his arrival. His appearance startled our heroes, throwing them into total shock! When they saw him they couldn't believe their eyes. The moon kept vanishing behind the now thinning clouds, gradually allowing more light to penetrate the wood. They saw Tom was wearing a pair of jeans - Levi's they guessed - and a black plain T-Shirt which was tight to is body, accentuating his muscles. A thick gold necklace was also visible round his neck and on his feet were a pair of Doc Martin boots.

He was near the tent entrance where Barry was standing, Ian being about 10 feet further back next to the fire which he had been in the process of putting out.

'Well, well, well,' began Tom in a slow drawl. 'We meet again!'

'Bloody hell, Tom. What are you doing here? How did you find us? I thought you were working in the morning!' said Barry, unable to hide the fear in his voice.

'I bet you did!' said Tom. 'It looks like you have had quite the adventure since I dropped you off at Scotch Corner, haven't you!'

He was eyeing them both up, working out how to deal with them.

'I hear you even bumped into my wife in Bramham. What a coincidence! ..... and she looked after you ..... *really* looked after you!' he said as he walked around their camp.

Our heroes were speechless, wondering what he was going to come out with.

'Fed you ..... gave you the use of our bathroom ...... and oh how good she was to you!'

His voice was rising along with his temper.

'Even getting in the shower with one of you to give you, well, how should I put it, a good seeing to, maybe? You might call it something else. How kind of her!'

Our heroes are now quaking in their boots. He knows it all! How did he find out? She must have told him!

Tom walked up to Barry. The stench of whiskey on his breath was overwhelming. Tom continued his revelations, 'You see, the coincidences didn't stop there. She gave you a lift to the A64 didn't she, and guess who picked you up?'

Oh no, here we go. It must have been somebody he knows well and we told that driver everything!

'It just happened to be my brother, Harry!' he shouted.

Barry's jaw dropped. He wished he had gone for that dump after all! He was nearly shitting himself where he stood. He felt as though his heart was in his mouth and he gave an inadvertent but audible gulp.

'He knew exactly who you were referring to and when he left you, as soon as he got home he gave me a ring and told me everything, yes, everything you said!'

While he was talking, he was walking around the lad's campsite, getting to know where everything was. He continued walking and the words kept coming.

'The only thing he didn't discover was which one of you was in the shower with my wife so come on, who was it?' screamed Tom.

Silence.

He repeated his question but this time louder and more menacing!

Silence.

Tom kept walking between the two friends, trying to identify guilt on one of their faces, exulting in the fear he saw there.

'I'll tell you something and maybe then you will tell me who it was. My job for Saturday was cancelled so I got home earlier today, or should I say, yesterday now. Can you imagine what I was feeling after what my brother had told me? I was pissed off. VERY pissed off ! So maybe you can understand how it went with me and Lucy. She even had the nerve to serve me the left over Spaghetti Bolognese she made especially for you two! That *really* made my blood boil!'

Tom was still walking around the campsite. Ian noticed a slight stagger in his step and had also detected the strong smell of whiskey. The lads hadn't moved. They were routed to the spot, waiting for further revelations from Tom, which were about to come.

'I got myself a bottle of whiskey. Well, SHE was already on the Gin after dropping you off!'

He was now beside Ian, looking him up and down, the smell of whiskey too strong to ignore. Ian felt as though he was holding his breath. He was terrified. He kept looking around for the quickest way out of the wood. There was a path in front of him which Tom had used to get to them. Despite his fear he managed to keep a mental note of it. If things went really tit's up, which he fully expected, that's where he planned to go.

'Guess what happened, boys! ….. And it's all your fault! ….. I still had the bottle in my hand when I hit her!'

Ian and Barry's mouths were now wide open. Total shock written on their faces! Bowler continued to tell them how she died and included as much of the gory details as he could, just to scare them even more.

'So!' he said, 'Back to my question. Which one of you enjoyed themselves in the shower with my wife?'

Silence.

Bowler continued his parade, walking up to each mate in turn.

'Because which ever one it was is gonna DIE! The other one I will leave alive to tell the police. One of you was the last person to have her and that one is gonna pay for it!'

Silence.

He is now behind Barry. Was it him?

'I smashed her over the head with my whisky bottle and as I said, she is now lying dead in the kitchen where I left her! Yes! As sure as I am standing here, she's still lying there and it's all your fault! If you hadn't gone into Bramham she would be alive now!'

By now he had walked back over to Ian who was still rooted to the spot. The stench of whiskey was still strong, almost making Ian throw up. His face wash ashen. He couldn't believe what he had heard. It was too shocking to comprehend but he understood by the way he spoke that it must be true. They were in deep, deep shit!

While Tom was talking, Ian, always the practical one, was looking round in the dim light for anything he might be able to use as a weapon for when the worst happened. He prayed the whiskey would slow Tom's reactions. Tom was allowing his anger to rise once again. If the whiskey didn't affect him, it didn't look good for at least one of our terrified heroes!

67

'So I go back to my question, which one of you was it that had her? Whichever one it was is gonna die, the other will live to tell the tale to the police. I don't mind. I know I will be going down whatever happens. Just as good for two as for one. So, if you didn't do it (he prodded Ian hard in the chest) then you will live. If you did, you will die here tonight. Think about it, but not for too long or I may have to kill both of you!'

A few more seconds passed as he made his way over to Barry who noticed Tom appeared to be staggering a little.

He spoke up, 'It was me, you drunken bastard!' He could still smell the whiskey on Tom's breath.

'No it wasn't. It was me, aye, ME!' shouted Ian, feeling brave at last, mimicking Tony Curtis in his 'Spartacus' moment. He had spotted a fallen tree branch and decided he would make a grab for it when the time came, as it surely would.

'Don't take any notice of him. It was me. I had your wife and she loved it, oh, and so did I, so there!' shouted Barry.

Tom was still suffering the effects of the whiskey and was struggling to understand what he was hearing.

'I know it wasn't both of you,' said Tom, 'so, which one was it? I will kill both of you if you don't tell me! If you didn't do it you better tell me if you want to live!'

Our heroes went silent again.

Tom's patience had run out. What the hell, both must die! He turned and hit Barry with a glancing left hook. Barry collapsed on the floor, more in shock than the effect of the blow. Tom chuckled as he turned to face Ian, but the whiskey had slowed his movements. Before he could do anything, he felt the weight of a tree branch as it gave him a glancing blow on the side of his head. This made him rock on his feet but, despite the effects of the whiskey, he remained standing. Ian's fear meant his aim was not very good and at the same time he had inadvertently lost his grip on the branch and it fell to the ground. While he was recovering it, Tom shook himself and made a grab for him. However, before he could reach Ian, Barry had recovered from the blow he had received. Not really knowing what he was doing, he lunged at Tom who had his back to him and pushed him forward. Thankfully, the whiskey had taken its toll, enabling Barry to push him into a tree. Tom's head collided with the trunk and he fell to the ground. Our two heroes were still terrified and their only interest was in putting as much distance between them and Bowler as they could. They were sure he would get straight back up and attack them again! Ian set off down the track he had made a mental note of earlier, with Barry hot on his heels!

'Come on, Barry. Follow me!'

Barry didn't need any encouragement! Onto a track and through a field they ran until, gasping for breath, they reached the road. Ian turned left and continued running, heading back the way they had come, that evening. He had no idea why he ran that way. Maybe it was because he thought it was the way out of the park. He just wanted to get as far away from Tom as possible. Barry was right behind him. Where Ian was going, *he* was going! He didn't want to be separated from his brave mate. The two of them together had a better chance facing Tom than on their own.

'I think there are some houses down here, Barry. We should knock on a door and get them to call the police,' panted Ian.

'Yes,' replied an equally out of breath Barry. 'You're right,'

They continued to run down the road. It didn't matter that they were beginning to tire, they kept going as best they could. A house became visible not too far away. They made a beeline for it. Ian was first to the door. He found a bell and rang it. He shouted and also knocked on the door, hoping that the occupants would realise their need was urgent. Barry took sentry post. His eyes were scanning back down the road in case Tom was chasing them but there was no sound and no indication of any movement.

There was no answer at the door despite Ian's persistence. Frustrated, he searched for another property further down the road but saw something else. Was that a telephone box? It may well be!

'Barry, I think there is a phone box further down. Quick!' and he ran off in it's direction.

Barry followed.

Ian reached the box and when Barry saw it, he understood what he was planning to do.

'You keep an eye out in case Tom is following us while I call the police.'

Ian searched for some coins, as he entered the box, before remembering its free to dial 999 which he did. He was put through to the local police control room and proceeded to inform them of all that had happened at their campsite. It took him longer than expected to make them understand what had been going on because he was speaking so fast and getting himself all mixed up due to his terrified state. He eventually managed to pull himself together and got them to understand that this man, Tom, had tried to kill one of them and had claimed to have murdered his own wife.

After a while, a female voice on the other end said, 'OK, Ian, we have officers on their way to you. Now, do you have the address where this Tom lives?' she asked.

'It's somewhere in Bramham, on the Main Street I think. It has a white door with an oval shaped piece of glass in the top of it and a gold coloured letter box half way up, if I remember rightly, but that's all I can remember. She has an old Vauxhall of some sort and its grey in colour which may be parked outside. I can't tell you any more though. Oh, yes, their surname is Bowler, B, O, W, L, E, R, so maybe they are in the phone book or something,' said Barry hoping he was being helpful.

'Do you know if he has a vehicle with him?'

Ian hadn't seen any vehicle and didn't know what make or model he had.

'What is he wearing?' she asked.

Ian described him as best he could.

'Ok Ian, the officers are only a couple of minutes away from you. They will ask you to repeat most of what you've told me. They are heading for the call box you are in. If you believe that this man may be looking for you, find yourselves somewhere to hide nearby and flag the police car down when you see it.'

'But Tom must have a car to have got here. What if it is his car we see coming?'

'Don't worry. You will know the police car when you see it.'

'Ok,' said Ian. 'We will keep a lookout for it. Thanks.' He then hung up.

He exited the phone box and told Barry what he had done and informed him that the police car should be here any minute. Barry hadn't seen any sign of Tom but that didn't mean he was not nearby. A street light was illuminating the phone kiosk so they got themselves behind some bushes on the opposite side of the road. Thankfully, the light didn't reach their chosen hiding place.

It was another five tense minutes before some vehicle lights came into view. Thankfully they recognised it as the police car. They could see the tell-tale blue lights on it's roof. Our brave heroes ran into the road and waved the vehicle down.

'On scene!' said one of the officers over his radio. 'Roger,' replied the operator in the Control Room.

'Now then lads, get in the back and tell us what's been going on,' said the driver, PC 666.

'Shall I tell them? said Barry to Ian.

'Aye, go ahead Barry, you'll be able to explain it in the Queen's English better than me, eh!'

Barry then proceeded to inform the police officers of all that had occurred including how Tom Bowler had given them a lift to Scotch Corner; how they had met his wife and what had occurred in the house; how Tom had found out and followed them to their camp. Barry told them that Tom claimed that he had killed his wife and wanted to kill one of them and that by the skin of their teeth they had managed to fight him off and escape.

'OK, thanks for that. So your Barry and your mate is? asked PC666.

'He's Ian.'

'Well, Barry and Ian, just to let you know, we have some officers on their way to Bramham to make some enquiries. The electoral register is being checked as we speak and hopefully the address will be in there, otherwise they will have to do some door knocking based on the information you have given them. Now, back to you two. Whereabouts is this camp of yours?'

'It's in that wood. You might just be able to make it out over there, aye, those trees over there, eh! But to get to it we will need to go back down this road a bit, passed that house and then there is a track and that takes you to it. That's how we got away from him and I think Tom would have seen which way we left, like, so he could be anywhere around here now!' said Ian, unable to hide the anxiety both he and Barry were feeling.

The officer drove as far as Ian directed then parked up near the path he mentioned.

'You better come with us to be safe. Stay close by. We have some good torches and I reckon if he is still in the area he will recognise two police officers and keep well away,' said the other officer, PC 601.

In the safe hands of the officers who lead the way, the two lads followed close behind until they reached the camp. They checked around but there was no sign of Tom.

'Where did you leave him when you ran off?' asked 666.

'Over there, by that tree,' said Barry, pointing to the spot. 'He banged his head on it when I pushed him but he's not there now.'

'601 to control.'

'Receiving.'

'We are at the lad's campsite but there is no sign of the suspect, repeat, no sign of the suspect. Suggest his vehicle details are obtained and passed out, over.'

'Roger. Will do.'

'Right, lads, I suppose you better get your things together and we will get back to the panda while we work out what is going to happen next,' said PC666.

The policeman could see our heroes were still suffering from their experience, so he thought he would try to take their minds off it by engaging them in conversation.

'Did you say you were on your way to some concert in Leicester?'

'That's right,' said Barry. 'It's an Elvis Presley Convention on Sunday. It happens every year apparently, but it will be the first one we will have been to and I think it might be the first to be held in this country. We were hitchhiking there but then we decided we would get a train from Leeds later today', said Barry, looking at his watch. 'Just to make sure we got there,' he continued.

'You will be looking forward to it then.'

'We were! Ask me again tomorrow!' said Mick.

It didn't take the lads long to pack everything up with the help of the powerful police torches and they were soon on their way with all their gear. They accompanied the officers to the police car where they dumped their gear in the boot and settled back inside.

Chapter Ten

A Grisly Discovery

In Bramham, two police cars arrive.

'Charlie Two Zero to Control.'

'Go ahead.'

'In Bramham. Any luck with that address?'

'Roger. It's Clifford Road,' and the street number was passed.

'Received.'

'Clifford Road now. Stand by.'

A male and female officer exit the first vehicle and two burly male officers exit the second, one of whom is carrying a 'door opener'. One of the burly officers, PC323 from C23 (Charlie Two Three) rang the door bell and hammered on the door.

No answer.

Another attempt.

No answer.

They wait a little more before trying again.

Still no answer.

'Charlie Two Three to Force Control Room Inspector.'

'Force Control Room Inspector speaking. Go ahead.'

'There is no answer at this property. We have a door opener with us. Do we have permission to force entry?'

'Yes, go ahead. Force entry, over.'

'Roger.'

'Ok Geoff, do your worst.' Geoff is PC400 from C23.

Bang! Bang! Bang! The door flies open. The police officers enter 'Police officers! Is here anyone there? Police officers! Is there anyone here!'

No answer. A quick inspection of the living room reveals nothing. They move on in to the kitchen and there, lying where she fell, they discover the lifeless body of Lucy. A quick check confirms what they already suspected.

'Charlie Two Three to Force Control Room Inspector.'

'Force Control Room Inspector go ahead.'

'Can confirm one deceased female. Request CSI.'

'Roger,' replied the Inspector who then put the wheels in motion. He rang the duty CSI and appraised him of the situation and location. The control room operator put the duty undertaker on standby and all other protocols were set in motion.

While our lads were being taken to a police station in Leeds, PC666 had been listening to this conversation and informed them that it was true, Tom's wife was dead and that Tom was now wanted on suspicion of murder.

'So I would suggest he wasn't in that wood to be friendly!' said the officer. 'My guess is that he meant you two serious harm, maybe worse, so you were lucky to get away from him!'

A nationwide bulletin was passed so Leicestershire Constabulary would now be aware of the possibility of him heading to the De Montford Hall for the Elvis Convention on Sunday.

'If there are any police in attendance on Sunday I suggest you make yourselves known to them and inform them that you are probably the reason they are there,' continued PC666. 'They may also be able to tell you if Bowler has been apprehended prior to that, in which case you could stop worrying.'

Our two heroes, although worried about Tom, were itching to get to the railway station so that they could complete their journey to Leicester. Ian spoke first.

'What's happening to us then? Can we go to the station now to catch a train, like, or what?'

'Not just yet,' said PC666. 'We need a full statement from each of you then I will see what the Inspector says. We've got a couple of things to do before the statements so I'll take you to the canteen. You can have something to eat there. I guess you will be hungry.'

It was now mid morning. He purchased a sandwich for each of them and a mug of tea and sat them down at a table. They were exhausted after all that had happened so when they had finished eating they fell asleep, leaning on the table. It was a restless sleep but a couple of hours went by. It got busy as officers came in for something to eat then left when they finished, some of them giving our hungry, sleepy heroes a quizzical look. When they woke up, the day was getting on and the lads were keen to carry on with their journey. PC666 reappeared, with his partner, PC601.

'You come with me in this room Ian, and Barry, you go with John (PC601) in that one. The sooner we get your statements taken, the sooner you can get away.'

An hour later they had finished and were taken to the police canteen for something more to eat as they both said they were starving. The sandwich they had in the morning was all they had had to eat since yesterday and it was now late afternoon.

'How does Fish and Chips sound lads?'

'Great but I don't think we can afford that. We are on a budget.' said Barry

'Don't worry about it. It's on us,' said PC601.

'Wow thanks!' said Barry

'Yeh, thanks very much you two!' said Ian.

'You sit down over there and we will bring them over. Mug of tea?'

'Yes please,' said Ian and Barry, both now smiling brightly.

Their food appeared and the officers left them alone while they tucked in.

'Phew! I can't believe that he killed her!' said Barry, taking a mouthful of food and still a little shocked at the news.

'Neither can I. Or that he managed to find our campsite and tried to kill us!' said Ian, taking a swig of tea, 'aye, murder at least one of us.'

'That brother of his must have told him where he dropped us off and that's why he suggested we camp in the park. He was obviously gonna tell Tom where we could be found. He must have hated Lucy and thought his tittle tattle tale would get her into trouble, along with us. He could have got us killed as well as her, telling him that! He will know how powerful Tom is. What a bastard!'

Just then, PC666 came over to them.

'Hey officer, Tom only knew where we were because his brother told him. He was bound to know how Tom would take it. Doesn't that make him an accessory or something to Tom assaulting us?' said Barry

'And murdering his wife! said Ian.

'Don't worry. It's all in your statements. If anything needs to be done it will be but I can't see anything happening as regards to that. Who's to say he didn't say it in all innocence? Anyway, I've spoken to the Inspector and he agrees we have no real reason to keep you any longer but he asked me to inform you to be extra careful, keep your eyes open and your wit's about you. I know you won't take any notice but he strongly advises that you go home now and forget about the concert. Oh and I suggest you keep phoning in daily to check if we have apprehended Bowler. Its incident 162 of today. Here's the number you need to ring (he gave them a piece of paper with the contact phone number and the incident number on). The control room staff are aware you may call to check just in case you miss any media announcements.'

'Cheers.'

PC666 sat down beside them. 'If you do go to Leicester, just remember what I said earlier about making any officers there, know exactly who you are so they can keep an eye on you. Even if you take the Inspector's advice and go home, remember he knows which town you come from! His description has been passed out in case he changes his car or decides to travel by public transport. Obviously, if you go home, we will let you know as soon as we have Bowler in custody. From what you have said, I imagine he is going to plead guilty to his wife's murder. You never know, he might decide to give up looking for you and hand himself in. Fingers crossed lads. Finish your food and when you are ready you can be on your way and good luck.'

'Thanks a lot,' said Barry and Ian.

'And just to let you know, we will be going to Leicester. We don't want to miss the convention but we will remember what you told us and we have a radio so we will listen when we can and to see if it mentions him being arrested.' added Barry.

'Yes, we will and thanks for everything, especially the grub!' said Ian.

'Your welcome and behave yourselves,' said PC666 with a wink and a friendly smile as he left the table and walked out of the room.

'Time is getting on Ian, if you're ready, let's see if we can find the railway station. I think he said it was turn left out of here then next left and it's about a hundred yards further on so it won't take us long.'

'Yeh, that sounds right. Those Fish and Chips have done the trick Barry eh!' said Ian, 'aye, lovely Fish and Chips.'

'I was ready for them. Best meal since we left home.... after the Spag Bol!' They both chuckled and set off with renewed energy and a bounce in their steps.

It didn't take them long to reach the station. They checked the overhead timetables and eventually found the times for Leicester. It was now 6 in the evening and the next train to Leicester was at 1845hours from platform 3. They hurried to the kiosk to purchase a one-way ticket each, before making their way to the platform. By the time they got their tickets and reached platform, they didn't have long to wait form the train to arrive and when it did they climbed on board. The first carriage was fairly full and didn't have 2 seats together so they made their way down the aisle to the next carriage where they found some suitable seats. All the time they were on the train they kept their eyes pealed in case they bumped into Bowler but if he was still following them, they didn't see him.

They had to make one change on their journey, this train stopping in Peterborough at around 2008hours. They would then have to make their way to another platform to catch the Birmingham train which was due to leave at 2052hrs. 44 minutes was more than enough time for them to find the right train. When they got off at Peterborough, they needed platform 2 for the Leicester train. They asked a nearby porter where it was and he pointed them in the right direction. They set off, all the time looking about them. Tom could be anywhere, thought Barry. He would have been told by his brother that we were going to get a train to Leicester. Maybe he had been waiting in the station for us to arrive so he could follow us, they thought. Then again, no, that would be one coincidence too many.

They kept looking over their shoulders in any case. He was still haunting them, but he was nowhere to bee seen. They couldn't, however, be certain that he wasn't somewhere in front of them.

As they approached the platform they noticed a member of the British Transport Police near the train running a beady eye over everyone getting on board. That made them feel a little better. As they approached he spoke to them, having recognised them from a description he had been given. They had been seen by a Leeds policeman getting on the train and deducing correctly that they would change in Peterborough, they made contact, asking for an officer to see that they got on the train to Leicester safely, that task having been allocated to this officer.

'I haven't seen anyone matching Bowler's description so you should be OK for the journey down. Just be aware though, that there are plenty of other trains to Leicester and he could have taken one of them. Keep your wit's about you at the station when you arrive. He knows you are going to arrive there at some stage. As I say, just keep your wit's about you. Have you got a radio?'

'Yes we have,' said Ian, 'and we've been told to ring Leeds police station each day to check to see if he has been caught, like, just in case we miss hearing about it.'

'OK then. On you get lads and I will check everyone else that gets on. It's a big train but as you can see, they have to go passed me to get to it so I shouldn't miss him if he is planning to travel on this one.'

'Thanks a lot,' said Ian as they climbed on board. They found a suitable seat with a table in the first carriage they entered and managed to store their rucksacks underneath. Sitting down, they could still see the officer having a good look at the last passengers approaching. After a couple of minutes the doors were slammed shut, a whistle sounded and the train lurched forward as its wheels began to turn, slowly at first with a 'shunt, shunt' as if straining to pull the carriages. It didn't take long for the wheels to gain traction though and with a loud groan, the 2052 to Birmingham (stopping at Leicester of course!) lurched forward, gathering speed as it left Peterborough station on time. The journey time to Leicester was just under an hour. Our heroes checked the other passengers as they passed them by, looking for seats. Once the train started to move, they felt certain that Tom was not on board. They both now realised how tired they were despite their midday nap in the police station canteen but although they were of the opinion they were safe, the events of the last 24 hours stopped them from falling asleep - the steady swaying of the train under other circumstances would have allowed for instant slumber.

Ian had a rummage in his rucksack and broke open a packet of biscuit's and produced a bottle of water which they shared. They didn't feel like talking, instead they watched with interest the nearby passengers who were busy reading papers, having something to eat and paying visit's to the toilet. One couple were arguing about what they were going to do when they reached Birmingham which was their destination. Precisely on time - 2142hours - the train came to a lumbering halt in Leicester.

The station tannoy blared into action. 'Leicester! this is Leicester! The train now standing on platform 3 is the 2205 to Birmingham ....'

Our heroes decided to wait on the train until all the other passengers had alighted. This gave them the chance to make sure Tom Bowler wasn't one of them as they poured their eyes over as many as they could. They also checked the groups of people already on the platform waiting to welcome family or friends home. The crowd made it difficult to check but as far as they could see there was no sign of the one they feared.

When they were sure all those wanting to leave the train had done so, they decided to follow suit, but were prevented from doing so by an old lady who was struggling to get her case out of the train and onto the platform. She was wearing a black pleated skirt and black top and had grey hair on an extremely wrinkled face. Despite that, she seemed to pride herself in her make-up. Her case was almost as big was, being less than 5 feet tall. She was feeling a bit embarrassed at all the commotion she was causing. Passengers were trying to get on the train and she was preventing them. None of them thought to assist her and the nearest conductor was helping someone else at the far end of the train.

'Oh dear, oh dear !" is all she could say while moving from one side of her case to the other.

Barry saw the problem and said to her, 'Here you are, don't worry, I'll get this off for you,' grabbing hold of her case. 'If you folks would stand back please so we can get off, then you will be able to get on,' he shouted, at those on the platform waiting impatiently to board. There were a few grumbles among them but they soon realised that it was in their best interest to do as he requested. Barry soon managed to get the case onto the platform while Ian did his good deed by helping the old lady off. Eventually the grumbles of those wanting to get on the train abated as they realised their way was clear.

Barry turned to the old lady and said, 'How did you manage to travel with such a large case?'

'Oh I've had help all the way. My son-in-law got me onto the train and I was supposed to have been met by a porter when we arrived but he was nowhere to be seen, otherwise I would have been alright. If it hadn't been for you two kind young gentlemen I would have probably ended up in Birmingham tonight! Thank you! Thank you so much!'

'Your welcome,' said Barry, 'but how are you going to manage from here?'

'It's OK. I just have to ring my family and tell them I have arrived and they will come for me. They would have been here to meet me but you know what trains can be like, never on time, so I said I would phone them when I arrived to save them waiting too long. I will have time for a cup of tea in the café here while I'm waiting for them. I would be delighted if you would join me. You have been so kind.'

'Well, if you insist,' said Ian 'but let me take your case for you while you use the telephone kiosk, eh!'

The old dear gladly assented, despite not knowing anything about our two heroes, and entered the kiosk. Five minutes later they were sat at a table in the café - their new companion told them to sit there - while she got them all a cup of tea. She returned with her purchases on a tray and said,'Milk and sugar? I'll be mother. Let's face it, I'm old enough to be granny!' All three of them laughed.

She introduced herself as Edna Smith and explained that she had spent the last three weeks with her daughter and her husband, along with their two children, in Leeds. They would have driven her back home but the two children were not well and the journey would have been too much for them, so she insisted on going home by train. She went on to say that when she phoned her family in Leicester, she told them she would be waiting in the café so she didn't have to wait outside in the cold night air. Our heroes introduced themselves as they chatted away. During the conversation they mentioned what they were doing in Leicester. They also told her of the tragic events in Bramham which involved them.

'Oh my goodness! It was all over the TV, but they didn't mention two young men being involved!'

'No, I didn't think they would, eh! It will be for our safety really, aye, our safety,' said Ian.

'Yes, they haven't found her husband and they think he may still be after us,' said Barry who went on to explain their confrontation with Tom Bowler in Roundhay Park. He also mentioned that Bowler knew why they would be going to Leicester, but they were hoping he would be arrested soon because they were permanently on edge, in case he really was intending to follow them.

Edna was aghast. She couldn't understand how anyone could do such a thing. It was unthinkable to her. She said "Now then, you two, you've been so kind to an old lady. I live on Meadow Way in Wigston which is the south end of Leicester and if you want anything, if you get into trouble with this wicked man, then give me a ring or call round and maybe I can get you some help. I live with my son and his family and he is a Detective with Leicestershire police. His wife, Miranda, will be picking me up because he is at work but as soon as I see him I will tell him about you. I'm sure he will do what he can.' She then proceeded to pass them her telephone number and the house number on Meadow Way on a piece of paper.

Our heroes were grateful but insisted they would be fine and they didn't want to get her involved. She had time to wave their worries away before the café door opened and in walked her daughter in law. Edna introduced the lads and explained how helpful they had been but didn't mention their troubles. She did mention they were here for the Elvis Convention at the De Montford Hall. Miranda said she hoped they would enjoy it. Some more small talk passed between them before Edna and the lads said goodbye and she left Miranda.

'She was nice,' said Barry.

'Yes she was,' said Ian. 'I wonder if we will meet her son?'

'Probably not but then again, the way this trip has gone, I wouldn't rule anything out!'

'True!' said Ian as they made their way out of the café towards the station entrance. 'True'

Chapter Eleven

Victoria Park

As our heroes neared the main station exit, Barry sat down on a nearby seat and looked through his rucksack for the street map of Leicester but it was nowhere to be found.

'Shit! I can't find the map!'

'Damn. Do you remember packing it Barry? You must have, it's not like you not to, you're so organised!' said Ian,'Aye, so organised, eh!'

'I'm sure I did but it's definitely not here. I thought I put it in this side pocket but the zip on it is broken so maybe it fell out.'

While they were lamenting the loss of the map a man in his twenties heard them.

'Hey up lads, you got a problem?' he said in a local accent.

They looked up and saw a male with a full head of curly hair, heavy set, about 5 foot 9 inches tall wearing a black leather jacket and black jeans with equally black boots. He was standing there with his hands in his pockets as he spoke and a cigarette was hanging out of his mouth. He seemed an amiable sort.

'Yeh,' said Barry. 'I seem to have lost our street map of Leicester. We need to find somewhere suitable to camp for the night. Somewhere that is close to De Montford Hall,' he continued.

'Oh, what's going on at the De Montford Hall?'

'It's the Elvis Presley Convention there tomorrow. We've come down from Cumbria to see it.'

'Elvis coming to Leicester? I thought I would have heard if he was.'

'No. It's just his fans getting together, that's all,' said Barry.

'Oh, right! It just happens I live in Leicester so I know a couple of places not too far from there. You can either go to Spinney Park .... but that's about half an hour's walk from it ... or better still, you could go to Victoria Park. You should be able to camp in there. It's virtually next to it."

'Oh thanks. Can you point us in the right direction? Is it far from here?'

'Tell you what, I will take you there. I could do with a walk and it's not far from where I live. My names Albert by the way, Albert Hall.'

'Pleased to meet you Albert and thanks for that,' said Barry.

'Aye, thanks,' echoed Ian.

'I'm Barry and this is my mate Ian,' said Barry.

'Hi, you two. Ok, follow me.' Off he strode, turning right as they exited the station concourse.

'We shouldn't be too long,' said Albert, keeping the conversation going. 'Where are you from in Cumbria?'

'We are from a small town called Penrith,' said Ian 'aye, Penrith.'

'Oh I think I've heard of it but I've never been to Cumbria. Carlisle is in Cumbria isn't it?'

Aye, that's right. It's just a few miles up the road from us, like,' said Ian.

They were walking on a wide path next to a main road as they made their way from the station. Ian hoped it wouldn't be long before they were able to put their tent up. It had been a long enough day already.

'I had a bit of a fallout with my girlfriend tonight so I'm going home,' continued Albert. 'Let her stew, is what I say. She thinks she is the boss of me, well I'll show her! She will come crawling back to me tomorrow saying, 'I'm sorry Albert, I didn't mean to upset you. Come back with me now and I'll make you your favourite, leg of lamb with mint sauce', whine, whine, whine and then I will do what I always do - go back! I can't resist her roast lamb!' he said, laughing.

They were now going under a railway bridge on the A47 and Ian was becoming increasingly concerned that they were merely going for a walk because this bloke wanted someone to chat to before going home. He couldn't tell, but he guessed that Albert had been drinking. As they reached the other side of the railway bridge, Albert stopped to light a cigarette - he didn't offer one to the lads - and was looking back down the way they had come.

'Do you know, I could swear we are being followed but I can't see anybody now.' He shrugged and continued,'I must be imagining it. There doesn't appear to be anyone there .... strange though.'

While he was speaking, his back was to Barry and Ian. This revelation startled them but Barry signalled to Ian not to say anything. The less he knew, the better, Barry was thinking. Ian nodded quickly in silent agreement. Barry thought he would question Albert further, to try to find out what Albert thought he had seen.

'Following us? Was it one person or a number? What do you think you saw?' he asked.

'I dunno really. Just one figure, I think. It didn't seem to be somebody out walking 'cos they seemed to stop whenever we stopped and when I looked back earlier, whoever it was seemed to dodge behind a tree as if they didn't want to be seen. But don't take any notice of me. My eyes are playing up a bit tonight. I had a few drinks earlier.'

'Well I haven't seen anything so you might be right. It could be your eyes playing up,' replied Barry with another wink at Ian. He decided that he would keep his eyes peeled and Ian was thinking the same. Heaven forbid if Tom Bowler was behind them! Barry took this opportunity to light a cigarette for himself while having a sly look behind but the area under the bridge was pitch black. Easy for somebody to stand still and not be seen.

They started walking again, picking up the pace a little. The thought of Bowler caused them to move faster. After a while they reached the junction of Forest Road and Spinney Hill Road. Albert made to continue on the A74.

'Doesn't this road lead to Spinney Hill Park?' asked Barry, pointing in that direction.

'Yes, but if we carry on this way we will get to Victoria Park which is virtually next door to the hall. Trust me, I'll get you there. It's not too far now,' he said and strode off.

The night was now getting on and rather than make their own way in a strange city without a map they felt it was more prudent to stick with this local, even if he seemed to be taking them on a long walk. Also, they thought that if Tom Bowler was indeed following them then one more extra person might make him think twice before doing anything.

On they walked. They were still beside the A47. At least there were wide open spaces and the street lights ensured that nobody could come up to them without being seen from some distance. Barry and Ian kept looking back and on more than one occasion both lads felt they saw an ominous figure in the distance. Was this the person Albert referred to earlier? It seemed whoever this was, he was making sure they kept our group of three in sight. Our heroes were becoming increasingly concerned. Both lads were now getting tired. They wanted to get to the park as quickly as possible. The thought of putting their tent up was now becoming a chore they were not looking forward to, especially with the possibility of Bowler knowing where they were. Eventually Albert turned off the A47 onto Barnabas Road which consisted of a mixture of residential properties and businesses.

'We're not too far from where my parents live now but I'll walk on with you two to make sure you get to the park all right,' he said. The lads noted that he kept looking back which must mean he was also of the belief they were still being followed.

'Albert, have you seen any sign of whoever was following us, since the bridge?' asked Barry.

'I'm not sure mate. I said earlier I thought it might be the drink I'd had, messing with me but I still think somebody is following us. I'm sobering up now but I still think I can see someone every now and then. If there is someone there, whoever it is, they are making sure they keep well away, as if they want to see where we go and don't want to be recognised. Strange, really. I can't understand why,' he said.

Ian had an idea. 'You see that church on the left, let's run over there and hide in the shadows before he reaches the junction, then we'll know once and for all if we are being followed!'

'Yes, come on!' whispered Barry, who was already running towards it. Albert soon passed him and Ian followed until all three were behind a tree next to the church, and in a shadow.

'Keep as quiet as you can and try not to move!' whispered Barry, putting his rucksack down beside Ian's.

They crouched down and held their breath.

'If there is anyone following us they will have seen us turn down this road and I would guess they will make their way to the junction pretty sharpish just in case we turn off again,' continued Barry.

A tense couple of minutes went by with no sign of anyone. They were just about to believe they had imagined the whole thing when Albert ducked down and hurriedly whispered, 'Look out!'

They ducked back down hoping they hadn't been seen. They were still in the shadows so they thought they were OK. A figure had appeared at the road junction and was peering down the road. Whoever it was looked upset. He obviously couldn't see them. He made some careful steps down the road and started to move faster until he was almost at a run by the time he went passed our friends. It was a man, possibly in his late 20's with a shaven head, wearing jeans and a jacket. It wasn't Tom Bowler so who could it be? wondered Barry.

The mysterious person continued down the road until he reached the junction with French Road which was off to the left, all the time checking any alleyways leading off the main road. It was obvious he was searching for someone. He peered one final time, down Barnabas Road but when he didn't see anyone, he turned onto French Road and ran off.

As he disappeared out of view, Ian said, 'Let's get going. He may realise that we haven't gone that way and return, so the sooner we get down this road and out of sight the better chance we have of losing him completely.'

They gathered their things and ran to the turnoff for French Road. They looked earnestly down it as far as they could see. There was nobody in sight so they ran off down Barnabas Road. They decided that the further they got down this road, the better their chance of evading this male, so off they jogged as quickly as their heavy rucksacks would allow. It was impossible to go fast because of the weight but they hoped they had evaded whoever was following them. They couldn't even jog for long and slowed to a fast walk, reaching the junction with Leicester Street before any further words were passed between them. By now our heroes were out of breath.

'Who the bloody hell was that then?' asked Albert, looking suspiciously at our heroes.

'I dunno,' said Ian truthfully. He had never seen this man before today. 'No, I dunno.'

'No, neither do I,' said Barry.

'I'll tell you now, that wasn't just anyone, a mugger or thief. He was keeping an eye on us. Why? Is there something you're not telling me?'

They continued walking fast while this conversation took place, just in case their stalker had realised his mistake and came down Barnabas Road.

Barry looked at Ian and got a nod from him so he decided it was time to spill the beans. 'Albert, there is somebody out there who is looking for us ..... but it wasn't him.'

He proceeded to tell Albert what had happened and why they were being followed. He explained to him everything that had happened to them and their fears of what would occur if Tom Bowler caught them again. Albert was not aware of the murder in Bramham and was shocked to realise that the lads he had been walking with had been the cause of a murder and that's not all! They were earmarked as the next victims!

They walked on and all three became more alert in case Bowler should appear. Barry had described what Bowler had been wearing when they last saw him, although he did stress that he could easily be dressed differently now.

Soon after this revelation to Albert, they reached one end of Spinney Hill Park which consisted of 34 acres of sloping parkland with walks, avenues and areas for various sports.

Barry said,'I thought we were going to Victoria Park? We passed a turn-off for this park a long time ago. Have we been going in circles?'

'Err, no, we haven't ' stuttered Albert, 'but this was a safer way to go and Victoria Park is just further along this road.' We've sort of gone in a loop,' he said.

The first part of what he said was a lie, the reality being, he just wanted some company for a bit longer. However, now that he knew who they were he wished he had brought them the other way and got rid of them sooner! Barry and Ian were both sure that Albert was lying but realised they would just have to put up with it.

They continued on up the road with Spinney Hill Park on their right, our heroes becoming more weary and dreaming of being in their bed. Whether they could sleep knowing Bowler could be looking for them combined with the incident with the stranger, they didn't know.

Walking as fast as their aching legs could go, they reached the far end of Spinney Hill Park when they were startled by a figure who appeared out of some shade and approached them. Thankfully it wasn't Tom Bowler or the male that ran off earlier. This male was over 6 feet tall, was wearing blue jeans and a 3/4 length black coat. He had short cropped hair, a pock-marked face with a roman nose beneath which he had a pencil moustache. He spoke to our group while reaching for something inside his jacket.

'It's OK, I'm a policeman,'he said, pulling his warrant card out. He was speaking quietly as if to ensure nobody else could hear him. 'I believe you are Barry and Ian?' He pointed to our heroes as he said this, in answer to which they both nodded with their mouths open in wonder. Albert was equally in awe.

'We are aware of what happened in Yorkshire and have been following you since you arrived at the railway station,' he continued. 'It was for your safety but you obviously knew you were being followed, judging by the way you gave my colleague the slip back down the road. He must have spooked you, so I thought it would be better if I made myself known to you.'

Barry said, 'Does this mean that you believe he is here in Leicester, Tom Bowler that is?'

'Not really. To be honest, we don't know where he is. We haven't located his car yet either which is worrying but because of what happened and the threats he has made to you, we decided to keep you under surveillance. Am I right in saying, he knows you are coming to Leicester and the reason you are here?'

'Aye, that's right, he does,' said Ian.

'OK and where are you planning to stay the night?'

'I was taking them to Victoria Park. It's the closest to De Montford Hall.'

'And who are you?' asked the policeman.

'I'm Albert Hall. I live on Evington Drive,' said Albert, still unable to take in what had been going on.

'Ok Albert. In that case you're local so how come you've come such a long way round?'

Albert didn't know where to put himself. 'I just wanted some company on my way home. I'd had a few drinks...' his voice tailed off with embarrassment.

'Bloody hell! So we've walked further than we needed to!' said Barry.

'Yes,' replied the officer. 'The train station is only a short walk away.'

'I'm sorry lads. I just wanted someone to talk to after falling out with my girlfriend, said Albert, his head bowed.'

'OK, don't worry about it, Albert. We understand. No harm done,' said Ian, but inside he was fuming.

'I will take them from here,' said the officer to Albert in a firm voice and started to move off with our heroes in tow towards Victoria Park. Albert continued to apologise as they walked away. He headed off down Bradbourne Road with his tail between his legs and was soon out of site.

Our heroes were now in the company of a plain clothed Leicester police officer as they continued down the road with the straps of their rucksacks now chafing their shoulders and their enthusiasm for going any further and even for the convention, which was the reason for their trip, waning. The only consolation was they felt a lot safer. They didn't feel like talking, however, and the officer realised that his charges were tired and exhausted.

Eventually he said,'Not long now lads. Are you hungry?'

'Starving and I'm not in the mood to make anything never mind put up the tent,' groaned Barry.

'Aye, we are both knackered,' muttered Ian. For once, he didn't repeat himself, his mood being at a low ebb.

'There's a late night burger bar just up the road if you want something. I think it will still be open.'

'Sounds like a good idea to me,' said Barry.

'And me,' said Ian.

'Come on then'

They followed the officer across the road and thankfully the fast food premises was still open. A burger and chips was just what they needed. They enjoyed eating their food as they waked on. They weren't sure it was the taste or the hunger making them enjoy it but it did the trick. Their hunger was sorted and their mood improved as a result and they also had the chance to stock up on water.

By the time they had finished eating, they approached a junction with London Road and, at last, their first sighting of Victoria Park.

This was the city's racecourse until 1883. It has thoughtfully laid out pathways shaded by avenues of trees dividing its 69 acres of open parkland. It is a venue for large community and cultural events and has football and rugby pitches and other sports facilities. The northern edge has a wooded area with oak and ash trees, among others. There would be plenty of places here for the lads to be able to pitch a tent and they identified one area which would keep them from prying eyes and therefore have the potential of keeping them safe from Bowler, at least for the night, they hoped. The police officer agreed with their choice for a campsite and made a note of where it was.

'Now I know where you are going to pitch your tent, I'll be off. Don't worry, I will pass your location to other officers who are aware of the situation and between me and them we will pay passing attention. It won't be every minute, more like someone being nearby every half hour or so. We don't know if Bowler is even in the county so this is really more police time than we should be giving. Once again, don't worry. We won't be too far away. Have a good night's sleep and enjoy your concert or whatever it is tomorrow and if there is a uniformed officer there, make yourselves known to him or her. We have some female officers as well. They will be there because of you so it would be helpful if they know you by sight, OK?'

'Yes, we will and thanks for your help,' said Barry.

'Oh, one more thing, if you need to contact the police, tell them it is our incident number 523 of the 20th. Here, I've written it down for you.' He handed the piece of paper to Barry then quietly left the park.

They had been lucky with the weather. Some light cloud had gathered but it was a warm, windless night, perfect for putting the tent up and allow for a good night's sleep.

'I'll help you with the tent, Ian, and then make us a nice cuppa before we go to bed. How does that sound?'

'That sounds like a plan Barry, aye, sounds like a plan,' said Ian with a smile back on his face.

Barry was expecting a grumpy Ian after the day they had been through so he was quite impressed at this cheerier than expected version of his mate. He let Ian take the lead as he had assumed charge of the tent erection during their trip and Brian carried out any task he gave him. With two pairs of hands, the tent was quickly up and Ian took on the chore of sorting out the inside while Barry took out the gas stove and set about making them a brew.

Ian finished just as the tea was ready and he sat down beside his friend and relaxed for what must have been the first time that day. It was now gone midnight. No wonder they were feeling exhausted. They had had little sleep since they were disturbed by Tom Bowler in the early hours of Saturday morning. Ian gave out a big sigh as he placed both hands on his brew and Barry lit his first cigarette for a while.

'At least we know the police are looking out for us, Ian. That's something we weren't expecting. I might be able to sleep tonight, after all,' said Barry.

Ian took another good draft of his brew while Barry continued to enjoy his cigarette. 'Ahh, that hit the spot Barry. I must admit you make a damn good brew and I don't think anything will stop me from sleeping tonight. I'm bloody knackered!' he said, 'aye, bloody knackered,' he repeated, still with that smile on his face!

'Why do you look so happy?' asked Barry.

'Dunno. I guess it's because we've finally got our tent up after a knackering day or maybe it's because we are almost at the De Montford Hall. Or maybe I am becoming a bit less of a pain in the arse, eh?' said Ian, breaking into a laugh. 'Yeh, pain in the arse.'

'Well, Ian, we've been mates for a long time. I can take your 'pain in the arse' moments as you must know by now, just as you can take mine. Anyway, that's my ciggy finished. Time for some shut-eye, I think.'

'There's just one more thing I want to do before we go to bed, Barry. I think I will make us some weapons while nobody can see us. I'm going to cut some good strong branches so I can make them into spears for us. If Bowler does make an appearance, we might be able to fight him off, eh! Some to jab at him with and some longer ones as well. We can strap the smaller ones to our rucksacks so they are always with us.'

'You always come up with some good ideas, Ian. I'll help you. You know the saying, many hands make light work. I'm under your instructions of course because you know what you are doing. You're the practical one.'

They took a torch with them and selected a couple of long branches and some shorter ones. Ian had remembered the small axe they had been given by Mr and Mrs Nichol and they soon had the wood they needed. Ian quickly sharpened one end of each of the pieces of wood after first getting rid of any foliage. Although they were tired, they found this job satisfying. It made them feel a little safer.

'OK Barry, let's take one each of the longer ones into the tent with us just in case we need them tonight.'

'OK Ian. Oh and I've a little idea of my own. If we keep all our empty cans we can string them along some approaches to our camp the next time we pitch our tent. It might give us some warning of anyone approaching us. You never know, just a thought!'

'I agree. That's a cracking idea Barry.'

They were soon in bed with their weapons by their sides and it didn't take long for our heroes to reach the land of slumber. Despite their fears regarding the whereabouts of Tom Bowler, the day they had just experienced had taken it out of them more than they thought.

Barry, however, didn't sleep deeply for long. A sudden noise outside woke him with a start. He sat up and listened to the noise of an engine of some sort. It sounded like a motorbike. Ian must have been in a really deep sleep because he was still snoring. Barry decided not to wake him yet until he figured out what was going on. What the hell was a motorbike doing in the park at this time of night and what was it doing just outside their tent with the rider revving the engine so loud?

He heard a strange throaty laugh and he could see a shadow of the bike reflected on the tent as it started to move slowly down one side. Barry couldn't be sure at first but was that the guy ropes being lifted? The vehicle moved further round and he heard a grunt. Yes! The light from the bike was casting a shadow of the rider who appeared to be leaning over and removing the tent pegs! He was attempting to collapse the tent on our heroes! In fact, the tent was starting to bow in on one side already!

He shouted for Ian to wake up then moved to unzip the tent and get out as quickly as he could. He looked at the rider of the bike and to his he saw Bowler! He had found them! Barry ran towards the side of the wood, having forgotten the spear. He was intending to reach the main road at the edge of the park but the motorbike cut him off. He tripped over a tree root and fell. He screamed out in agony, holding his left ankle. He was sure he had sprained it. Tom had now got off his bike and was walking joyously over to him with the look of a madman on his face!

No police officers appeared, so there was no hope of any assistance and there was no sign of Ian! The only thing he could think of doing was to shout at the top of his voice, 'Help! Help! I'm being attacked! Help! Help!'

All of a sudden, Ian appeared, but, strangely, he started to shake him. He rubbed his eyes and after a while he realised he was still in bed. The tent was still standing and all was calm. There was no motorbike and no Tom Bowler and his ankle didn't hurt. Once again he had been having a nightmare!

'Barry, Barry, are you all right? I think you've been having a nightmare!' said Ian with real concern in his voice, 'aye, a nightmare.'

'Bloody hell, you're right, Ian, a bloody horrible one. I thought he was here wrecking our tent and I fell and twisted my ankle. I thought he was gonna get me then you woke me up.'

'We've had previous for nightmares on this trip! They are a pain in the arse, eh! I hope we don't have any more,' said Ian, 'aye, no more.'

'I know. I've never had a nightmare in my life until this trip. I almost wish I was back home,' said Barry. 'I need a cigarette ..... desperately!'

He finished speaking and went outside the tent with a cigarette in hand. He had a cursory look around and when he was satisfied that Bowler had not re-appeared, he lit his cigarette and took a long drag in an attempt to relax and calm his nerves. Ian came out and stood beside his mate. He too, had a good look around. What happened to Barry had spooked him a little as well. He would have been happier if he knew Bowler was locked up, then they might have been able to get the sleep their bodies and minds were craving.

'What time is it Barry?'

'It's 2 in the morning.' He looked up and said, 'At least there is no rain. There's a clear sky above. Look at all those stars.'

Ian was about to look up when a movement on the edge of the wood caught his eye. He tapped Barry on the shoulder and he looked in the same direction. Yes, a figure was moving towards them. It looked like one male.

'Oh, shit!' cried Ian. 'Shit, shit, shit! It can't be!'

Our heroes were ready to run when a voice said, 'Hey up, lads. Relax. I am PC Porter. Just checking your'e OK. I was over there when I saw some movement.' At this point he had reached the lads. 'I was just wondering what's disturbed you or is it you just can't sleep?'

He shook hands with the pair and they introduced themselves to him. He offered them a cigarette which Barry, although he had just finished his last one, accepted and lit gratefully, taking yet another good drag. His nerves needed some extra help to recover.

'I don't suppose you've got any more news about Tom Bowler, have you?' asked Barry.

'Not really,' said PC Porter. 'The only thing that might be news to you is that his vehicle has been located in Leeds and it wasn't far from the railway station,' he finished slowly, knowing the conclusion the lads would come to.

'So that means there is a good chance he is in Leicester now then,' said Ian.

'I won't beat about the bush. That's the possibility we are working on and that's why we are paying more attention to you two. The thinking is, if he is coming here it can only be to get to you and to be honest, you are our best hopes of our apprehending a murder suspect, so you should feel safer with the attention we will be giving you. You should be able to get to sleep no problem now and I would suggest, once you have finished your cigarette, Barry, that you do just that.'

'Yeh, well, now that we know we are getting special attention we will, eh!' said Ian.

'Don't worry. I, or one of my colleagues, won't be too far away. You've got plenty of time until the do at the hall so you can have a good long sleep. You look as though you need it to settle your nerves.'

'Yes, you're right. We are out here now because I've just had a nightmare. Ian had one the other night. This trip is beginning to get to us a bit!'

PC Porter moved away, with our heroes watching him until he eventually disappeared through the trees. They didn't tell him about their weapons in case it got them into trouble and they didn't want them confiscated, citing them as dangerous objects. Instead, the friends went back to their tent and, at last, fell asleep.

Chapter Twelve

Concert Day!

They woke at 7a.m, having slept like logs with no more nightmares. It wasn't a long sleep. Because of the time of year the sun was already shining brightly through the tree canopy, directly onto their tent. Despite this, their mood had improved enormously. It was the big day! The one they had been waiting for all these months! It was almost like Christmas, the excitement building in their heads. Barry gave out a big yawn and noted his mate was awake.

'Time for a brew, Ian?'

'Yeh, I would love one, said Ian with a stretch and yawn.'

Barry got the gas stove on and used some of their diminishing supply of water to make the anticipated brew. Water to them was more important for drinking, cooking and washing the pots than for personal cleanliness! While it was boiling he had a walk around their campsite and lit his first cigarette of the day. There were a number of people he could see in the distance on the paths in and around the park but none of them gave him any cause for concern. There was no sign of anyone acting in a remotely suspicious manner. Ian joined him and had a look around before the pair returned to their campsite and sat down to enjoy their brew. They were both feeling good and were looking forward to the convention.

'Ah, what a great day for the concert! Unbroken sunshine! said Barry.

'Perfect!' replied Ian. 'Perfect!'

They were finishing their cup of tea when once again they were approached by a single male. They assumed it was a police officer and they were right.. He was in plain clothes and his task was to check that they were OK. He got them to confirm their plans were for the day. They told him that after having breakfast, they were going to pack their gear and go to find somewhere to replenish their food stocks, before heading for the convention - did he know of anywhere nearby that would be open on a Sunday? He said there was a spot down Evington Road where they would find Patel's Convenience Store. He pointed out where it was and said they would be able to acquire everything they needed there. After telling him that they would probably return to this spot to camp for the night, after the convention, he told them there was no further update on Bowler. He hoped they would enjoy the concert and wished them good luck before departing.

'Right, a big day today, Ian, so let's have a good breakfast, eh?'

'Aye, I'm starving. Must be all this fresh air Barry! A good nosh up will go down well. While you're doing that, I will do myself usual and strike camp.'

They got on with their respective chores and once again, Ian finished just as breakfast was ready. Barry handed him another brew, having used the last remnants of their water and put food onto their plates. They ate in silence, each tending to his own thoughts which were mainly about the convention.

When they had finished, Ian threw the extra large 'spears' under some bushes to hide them from any children or dog-walkers. They wouldn't be able to take them to De Montford Hall so he made a mental note of where they were because they would feel better with them close by on their return from the concert. They would be able to sleep easier with them back in their tent.

It was a lovely sunny day again so they decided to wear jeans and T Shirts. Nothing like a bit of sun on your skin, they thought. They didn't have any water to wash their dishes so they wiped them as best they could before packing them away. Barry would clean them before they were used again. When everything was packed they picked up their rucksacks and headed in the direction of the shop the police officer had mentioned. He said it was down Evington Road which was just across from where they had been camping.

The shop was only a short walk down from the road junction. It was run by a local family of Indian origin and it was a veritable Aladdin's cave and, as the officer had told them, contained everything the lads would need. They helped themselves to eggs, bacon and bread rolls along with water and stocked up on other items they were short of.

As they were waiting to pay for their goods at the counter, the shopkeeper asked if they were going to the Elvis thing at the De Montford Hall. When they told him they were, he asked if they were by any chance, Barry and Ian! Our heroes were surprised and concerned at this. How did he guess? Who had he been speaking to? Had the police already been in and for some reason, mentioned them? Our heroes looked at each other with incredulity.

Without acknowledging anything, Barry said, 'Why do you ask?'

'Oh, there was a man in yesterday evening, and he said he was looking for a couple of lads with northern accents like yours. What's the matter? You both look like you've seen a ghost!' said the shop assistant.

What he said, made the hairs on the back of their necks stand out, and if they were truthful, they would have admitted that they were quaking in their boots!

'He said to let him know if I saw you,' he continued.

Barry's brain was now turning over fast and he had the presence of mind to ask if this person was planning to come back to the shop or had he left any kind of contact details.

'He said he was intending to call back in this afternoon but he didn't leave any other details, not even his name, sorry. Is he a relation of yours? You're not on the run from home or anything are you?'

'Don't be daft!' said Barry, 'Do we look like we are on the run? If you give us a description of this fella, I'll have a better idea of who it is you're talking about,' he continued. 'And you're right. We are just here for the Elvis Convention at De Montford Hall.'

They continued paying for their purchases while the Indian described a male that could only be Tom Bowler! He was right here in Leicester! He had obviously changed his clothes. He was now wearing some brown canvas trousers tucked into a pair of Doc Martin's and a blue, full sleeved shirt despite the warm weather. He was also wearing a black baseball cap.

'Right,' said Barry, 'this guy is wanted by the police for murder. His name is Tom Bowler and he murdered his wife on Friday in their home in Bramham which, if you don't know, is a small town in Yorkshire not far from Leeds. If you don't believe me, call the police. They will tell you what I am saying is true. He is after us because he is blaming us for it.'

'Aye,' chirped up Ian, 'and I think you should call the police anyway, if you think he is coming back this afternoon, eh! The police are expecting him to be in Leicester, because he knows we are going to the Elvis do and they think he could still be after us. And we know he is! Call them and tell them what you told us. Aye, tell them what you said.'

'A murder? You're pulling me leg!' said the shopkeeper with a disbelieving air.'

'No, we are deadly serious! No pun intended! We've been told to let the police at the hall know when we arrive there. Your description makes us believe it is him so we will pass this on to the first policeman we see, whether at the hall or on this street when we leave here,' said Barry.

'Aye, and we will tell them that we said you should phone them as well, eh! So you better had!' added Ian, staring forcefully into the man's face.

'We don't mean to sound bullying but this could be a matter of life and death .... ours! ....Oh, tell them it's incident number 523 of the 20th, they'll know what you are talking about if you tell them that.' Barry got a piece of paper from the counter and took the shopkeeper's pen and used it to write the incident details down before passing the paper and pen back to him.

It was now time for the shopkeeper to look shocked. When they left, his was still in wonder at what he had heard but Barry still wasn't convinced that he would contact the police.

Outside, they kept their eyes peeled for anyone matching the new description they had of Bowler and were impatient to find a police officer to pass this on to but there were none to be seen in the immediate vicinity. To make matters worse, the ones they had been in contact with were in plain clothes which would make them harder to find, even if they were still on duty. Also, it might be that most uniformed officers currently on duty might not be aware of the danger they were in at all, thought Barry, this being the first indication that Bowler was, indeed, in Leicester!

They walked back towards Victoria Park and made their way onto Granville Road which would take them towards De Montford Hall itself. Their plan, seeing as it was such a lovely warm sunny day, was to find a place in the park which was close to the hall where they could do some sunbathing in full view of the locals. When the time came to make their way to the hall, they would only be a short walk away. They thought that with so many people in the park taking advantage of this weather, Bowler wouldn't risk doing anything. They gambled that he would wait until he got them in some secluded place. Half way along Granville Road, they saw a phone box. Ian ran towards it and said "I'm gonna phone the police and tell them what that shop fella said."

'OK, I'll keep my eyes peeled. You've got the incident number, Ian?'

'Yeh, I've got it,' came the reply as Ian entered the phone box.

Barry kept checking around to make sure there was no sign of Bowler. Surely he would leave them alone and not try anything here ..... or would he? Ian seemed to take an age on the phone and Barry was starting to get a little nervous but thankfully he reappeared and told Barry what had been said.

'I've told them that we'd been into Patel's on Evington Road and all about what was said, eh. I told them what Bowler is now wearing and I said that we'd told the guy to phone the police, aye, to phone them. But he hasn't yet.'

'Any more info on Bowler?'

'No,' said Ian, 'but they said that now it looks like he is here, they will update all officers and pass on the new description, aye, let officers know what he may now be wearing.'

'Did you tell them what we are doing?'

'I nearly forgot but luckily the woman on the other end asked me so I told her. She is gonna make sure everyone knows, eh.'

'That's good. Well done Ian. I wouldn't have thought of calling them.'

'No probs Barry. Oh, they said they were going to get someone to visit Patel's so I said tell them to go in plain clothes otherwise you might alert Bowler, aye, alert him, and she said 'you should be a police officer' so I just laughed.'

'She's right though. You would probably make a good one, Ian,' said Barry with an appreciative smile.

At the end of Granville Road, still checking everyone in sight, they took a path into the park. Barry noticed an unoccupied bench just ahead and said, 'Let's park our bums here and enjoy the sun. There's an ice cream van over there if you fancy one.'

'Yeh, Barry. I do. Can't remember the last time I had one, eh. I'll have a 99 if they have them, said Ian, 'aye, a 99.'

They reached the bench, which looked like it had seen better days. It was made of wooden slats which had once been painted red but a lot of it had been worn off by years of bodies sitting on it. Someone had carved their initials on both arms and there was a plaque in the middle which could only just be read. It was placed there in memory of a friend of the park who died before our heroes had even been born and judging by the state of the bench they had been dead and forgotten a long time before that! Ian put their rucksacks on one side while he sat on the other, having first checked that the local bird population hadn't christened it recently.

Barry did indeed manage to purchase two 99's and handed one to Ian who took it with an appreciative look, after making space for Barry on the bench. He immediately bit off the piece of flake protruding from the ice cream. They both sat back and looked around. The park was criss-crossed with wide paths with trees planted on either side, forming lovely avenues. It was the middle of summer so the trees were in full leaf and included Ash, Beech, Sycamore and some Oak. In the distance they could see some football pitches, one of which was showing some activity, probably preparation for a match due to take place later that day. The sun was still beating down so the players were going to get hot, thought Ian. Behind them, they just had to cross the road and they were within yards of De Montford Hall.

'Ah, this is the life,' said Barry, 'at least it would be if it wasn't for that fella after us, eh?'

'Aye, you're right there Barry, if it wasn't for him!' repeated Ian.

'I'm gonna try to not let it bother me too much right now. There are a lot of people around so we should be safe. Need to keep our eyes peeled, though, just to make sure. We still have our sticks on our rucksacks as well, remember.'

'Aye, you're right again,' said Ian, stretching out on the grass next to the bench with his arms behind his head, having finished his ice cream, his rucksack close by.

A couple of minutes later they were approached by a male they recognised as the officer who had taken them to Victoria Park the day before.

'Hi again! Any news for us?' asked Barry.

'Nothing really. We've been to see Mr Patel. He did phone in the end. He wasn't sure if what you had told him was true, but thankfully he decided it would be better to contact us just in case. Giving him the incident number is what motivated him to call. He was demanding police protection when we confirmed your story but we told him what to do with that. I don't know why he thought he was in any danger. We've passed the latest description of Bowler to all officers in the city, now that we are just about certain he is in the area. We've beefed up numbers looking for him as well, however, it is Sunday so we don't have as many officers available as we would have liked to have. We've got someone posted near Patel's just in case he does return there but Mr Patel couldn't help us with any timings. He is aware to let us know should he turn up.'

'That's all comforting to know. Thanks for that,' said Barry.

'Aye, thanks for that,' echoed Ian.

'At least we now know where you are and where you are intending to go so we can organise our people,' said the officer, whose eyes were continuously checking the area for anything unusual.

'Oh and by the way, we will be back where we were last night in Victoria Park for one last night after the show,' said Barry.

'Aye, for one last time,' echoed Ian again.

'I'll make a mental note of that and make sure the night shift are aware. By the way, you helped my mother at the railway station. She can't stop talking about how helpful you were. I'll let her know your'e well and good luck and enjoy the show,' said the officer as they parted company.

'Give her our best,' shouted Barry to which the officer gave a thumbs up.

Our heroes felt a little better after that so they settled down to enjoy the sun. Their suntans were coming along fine. A little while later, the sound of a whistle woke them up. Both our heroes had nodded off. They hadn't intended to but it happened despite their fears of being attacked by Bowler. The whistle, they found out, signalled the start of the football match on the pitch in the distance.

'Hey Ian. Its later than I thought! We better have something quick to eat! The show starts at 2. I'm starting to get a little excited. It's nearly time Ian, after all the planning and waiting!'

'Yeh, I can't wait, but something to eat will go down well now, eh. I'm ready for it, Barry, are you?'

'Yep. I'll get cracking with it now. I hope there is no rule to stop us lighting a camping stove on this land.'

'I shouldn't think so, Barry. No, I shouldn't think so. We will soon find out anyway.'

Barry got cracking with the stove. He found a tin of stew and peeled a couple of potatoes, cutting them into small pieces so they would cook quickly along with some onion and the best ingredient, curry powder, which Patel had suggested would be good. He said it would make a boring stew more tasty and he told them how much to add. Never having made a curry before, they followed his instructions. He did suggest rice but they had plenty of potatoes so he said potatoes would do for a filling meal. Barry wasn't sure if it would work but, in for a penny, as they say! It smelled delicious while it was cooking and he kept tasting it to see how it was going. He was pleasantly really pleased with it. When it was ready, he served it up and passed Ian his plate.

Ian took a tentative mouthful. 'Wow!' he said, 'that's bloody good! I wish we'd tried this earlier! Curry powder goes brilliant with it, yeh, brilliant Barry. Well done!'

'Your right Ian, it's bloody lovely and because I used two tins of stew there is plenty for a second helping!'

The second helping was soon demolished and the lads sat back with a cup of tea to finish off.

'I think you added the right amount of curry powder, Barry, eh!'

'Yes, I think you're right. I followed Patel's instructions. We'll definitely have that again before this trip is over!'

'Aye, I'll give that a big thumbs up, said Ian, 'yep, a big thumbs up!'

When their tea was finished, it was time to make their way to the convention so they packed everything up and prepared to move off.

Picking up their rucksacks, they crossed the road, heading for the hall.

As they were not far away, they joined an already growing throng of people of all ages heading in the same direction and judging by their chatter they were going to the same event. Our heroes were soaking up the atmosphere. The day was here! It was really happening after all this time and they were mingling with like minded fans! Despite this, they kept their eyes peeled, just in case Bowler made an appearance and they also kept a lookout for a uniformed police officer.

They caught their first glimpse of the hall shortly after. It was a purpose built building, erected by the Corporation of Leicester and had not been a stately home, as Barry had originally thought. It was finally completed in 1913 in a new classical style, the front of the building being supported by a number of white columns. The indoor auditorium can seat up to 2,000 people and this evening they would be among a crowd that would fill it to capacity.

They stopped near the entrance while Barry opened up his rucksack. He rummaged inside one of the compartments and when he removed his hand, he was grasping their tickets.

'Don't worry Ian. I didn't lose them. Here they are,' he said, with a big smile.

'I didn't for one minute think you would, Barry, eh. You're too organised for that ... although you did lose the street map of Leicester, aye the street map, if I remember,' said Ian, teasing his friend.

'True,' said Barry, still smiling, 'True.'

One final look about them and at last they spied a policeman standing not too far away, keeping a wary eye over the gathering crowds. Our heroes walked over to him and, probably as a result of the rucksacks they were carrying, he recognised them almost immediately.

'Hey up, you two. I would hazard a guess that you are Barry and Ian, is that correct?'

He was very tall, even for a policeman. He must have been 6'6" at least. He was fairly slim and probably around 30 years old. He had an air of authority about him and an obvious intelligence and looked as though he wouldn't take fools lightly. He also had a friendly smile, at least towards Barry and Ian.

'You are Barry and Ian,' he had said.

'Yes, that's us,' replied Barry, 'Is it that obvious?'

'It wasn't difficult! The rucksacks gave you away and you fit the description I was given. How has your day been so far?'

'We've had a bit of a sunbathe just over there in the park, eh, and just had a good feast, so we are ready for the show now. Ready and excited, like!' said Ian. 'Do you know if there will be any plain clothes officers inside the building?' This last he said in a whisper.

'Don't worry. The organisers are aware. Only fans with tickets will be allowed in ..... you do have tickets don't you?'

'Yes, of course we do,' said Barry, producing them.

'Thank god for that! In that case, just go ahead and enjoy yourselves and leave the rest to us. Nice to meet you, now off you go lads,' said the officer, ushering them along .'

'Aye, cheers!' and off they went.

In front of the entrance was a large lawn laid out with neat flower beds, dissected by a wide path. Our heroes made their way down this path, following the ever growing throng of fans and settled at the back of the queue. The noise from the chatter was growing and the lads noted accents from the four corners of the country. Fans had travelled from far and wide, some even from Europe.

Immediately in front of them was one female fan, possibly in her mid 20's, with long black hair, wearing tight black jeans. Down her right leg the word 'ELVIS' was sewn in large white letters and down her left leg she had sewn the word 'PRESLEY'. Our lads realised she must be a huge Elvis fan and were in awe of her.

The queue slowly made its way forward and eventually they reached the ticket office where they presented theirs. They were accepted and seat numbers issued. Following the crowd towards the auditorium, Ian noticed a cloakroom.

'Look Barry, I think we can leave our rucksacks over there, eh!' said Ian, 'aye, over there in that cloakroom. What do you think? It would be better than carting them into the auditorium. They would be a nuisance in there.'

'Good spot Ian, let's do that. I don't think we need anything out of them.'

They handed their rucksacks over at the cloakroom and the female attendant gave our heroes the impression that she was expecting them. Barry and Ian wondered if maybe the police had passed on their description so they could look out for them. They were given a ticket so they could retrieve their rucksacks at the end of the show and they headed into the auditorium. as expected it was absolutely packed! The atmosphere was electric! They were pleased to find they weren't too far from the front and had an aisle seat and the one next to it. The female with the black 'Elvis Presley' jeans was another few rows further forward and she also had an aisle seat.

Elvis songs were playing in the background as the place filled up and this female kept dancing in the aisle whenever she heard what must have been some of her favourite ones.

Barry looked at his watch and said, 'It's almost time for the Convention to start!'

He had only finished speaking when the curtains opened to reveal Todd Slaughter who was the host of the show. He was head of 'The Official Elvis Fan Club of Great Britain.'

'Ladies and gentleman! Welcome to the De Montford Hall in Leicester!'

The lights went out and a hush came over the expectant crowd. Todd Slaughter continued, 'Ladies and gentlemen, without further ado, let's start the proceedings with one of Elvis favourite films..... King Creole!'

Loud applause, whistles and cheers accompanied the film credit's but gradually subsided until there was complete silence. This didn't last long as Elvis made his first appearance in the film, singing 'Crawfish'. The building erupted with deafening cheers and applause which drowned out his first words. Silence gradually ensued again but some of the songs, especially 'Hard Headed Woman' and the title song 'King Creole', had fans dancing in the aisles. The film was in black and white but that didn't dampen the spirit's of the audience. Most fans believe this to be one of the best films Elvis ever made.

The film finished with rapturous applause. When it died down onto the stage walked the well known DJ, Emperor Rosko. He had flown from Paris especially for the convention. More loud applause. He was recognised by everyone in the audience, his love of Elvis being well known. He introduced the audience to Ian Kaye and the Dykons, whom Ian and Barry had never heard of. They performed a number of Elvis songs, including 'Guitar Man'. The crowd showed their appreciation. The female wearing wearing the Elvis' jeans was back dancing in the aisle. It took no time for others to join her and soon the whole aisle was rocking. Fans who couldn't get to the aisle, started dancing in their seats. The atmosphere was incredible. Our heroes were also in the aisle, clapping and singing but not really dancing - they weren't any good at it so clapping and singing was all they could do.

At the end of their piece, another DJ and confessed Elvis fan, Peter Aldersley, came on stage. He was clapping wildly and said, 'Ladies and gentlemen, Ian Kaye and the Dykons!' More rapturous applause from the audience who enjoyed being able to dance to songs by the king of rock and roll. Ian Kaye, now covered in sweat, gave an exaggerated bow before exiting the stage with the other members of his band.

Peter Aldersley, then introduced several guests including Albert Hand, the editor of Barry's favourite magazine, 'Elvis Monthly'. Between them, they attempted to answer questions from the audience, including the one asked by Elvis fans all over the country, 'When will Elvis come to England?'. Those who's questions were chosen, received a copy of the 'Speedway' LP, personally autographed by Elvis. Lucky buggers, thought Barry. When the questions were over, Todd Slaughter presented a check for £875, the proceeds of the convention, to representatives of the Guide Dogs for the Blind.

Following a short break, when Elvis records and memorabilia could be purchased, the audience was treated to Elvis' latest film 'Speedway', just as Barry had predicted. Before the film started, a letter appeared on the screen signed by Elvis himself, thanking them for attending. He apologised for not being able to attend in person but hoped they had enjoyed themselves.

The film was enjoyed by everyone present. They were Elvis fans, after all, but in reality, Nancy Sinatra stole the show!

— — — — —

Back in the foyer, while the convention was in progress, a male approached the cloakroom. He pointed out the rucksacks and said, 'I've been sent to collect those rucksacks.'

The girl behind the counter said, 'Can I have your tickets please, sir.'

'Oh, er, I don't seem to have them.'

'Sorry sir, but we can't give anything out without a ticket,' she replied in a disinterested attitude and continued with whatever she was doing.

'They belong to my mates and they have already left. They didn't give me any ticket. They've just asked me to call in and collect them. One of my mates fell ill and they forgot to pick them up when they left.'

'I'm sorry to hear that, sir, but it's more than my jobs worth to hand anything over without a ticket. We've had people sneak in off the street and claim things which didn't belong to them and I don't want to get into trouble.'

A voice from behind another door was heard. 'Is there a problem, Linda?'

Linda turned round and walked into the cloakroom.'Yes, Jack, there's a gent out here says he's come to collect those rucksacks but he hasn't got a ticket.'

'Hold on, Linda, don't let him take them. I'm coming through,' said Jack as he made his way to the counter.

Linda turned round to speak to the male but he was nowhere to be seen! She had no idea why, or which way he had gone.

'Bloody hell, he's gone, Jack!'

'Did he get the rucksacks?' asked a worried Jack as he arrived at the counter.

'No, they are over there.'

'Those rucksacks you booked in, belong to two teenage lads who are watching the show. The police told me that someone may attend to cause them trouble and to let them know if anything happened. What did this man look like? What was he wearing?'

'He had a beige duffel coat with black toggles. It looked well worn, quite dirty, and blue jeans. I didn't notice anything else, oh, apart from a black woollen hat. Come to think of it, it's a bit warm for that sort of gear, Jack!'

'Look after the counter, Linda, I'm going to see if that policeman is outside,' said Jack, leaving quickly 'and don't let anything go without a ticket!,' he added.'

'I won't,' shouted Linda, feeling badly thought of.

— — — —

Back in the concert hall, the compere returned to the stage and talked through a slide show of recent Elvis photos and all too soon the convention came to an end. There was a lot of applause, whistles and shouts as the audience slowly made its way to the exit. Our heroes joined the queue for the cloakroom. It seemed to take an age but they were eventually reunited with their precious rucksacks with the pointed sticks still in place.

It was Jack who handed them over and he took them to one side, out of earshot of everyone else.

'I think you better speak to the policeman outside. I think you are already acquainted with him. There's been a fella in here trying to get your rucksacks. He made some excuse as to why he didn't have the cloakroom ticket. Thankfully my staff are told not to hand anything over without one. He left as I was coming from out back to find out what was going on. I went outside to tell that copper all about it. Seems it's something he's aware of. They haven't told me much. What's been going on?'

'It's a long story.' said Ian, 'aye, a long story which we'd rather not go into right now, eh! But thanks for telling us. We'll have a word with the policeman. Cheers for that.'

They walked off towards the exit, leaving the man looking perplexed.

They left the hall and sure enough, the officer was still outside, like a sentinel, checking all around him for anything untoward.

Barry and Ian walked up to him. 'Hiya again. We believe you are aware of someone trying to get our rucksacks,' said Barry.

'Yes I am but whoever it was has eluded us. Although we don't know for certain, we have to presume it was Bowler.' He then went on to pass an updated description. "He seems to have a range of gear with him so he may be going to change again which makes be believe he is aware we are out in force looking for him. This is going to make the search that little bit more difficult. If he has any sense he will be well away from here...... for now. You better keep your wit's about you, though.'

'Thanks for that. We are going back to where we were camped last night in Victoria Park if any of your people don't already know,' said Barry.

'They are all well aware of it. Anyway, did you enjoy the show?' he asked, changing the subject.

'Yeh, it was great, eh! Really good,' said Ian, 'aye, better than we expected.'

'Yes, we really enjoyed it,' said Barry.

'I'm glad to hear it. You obviously didn't let all this spoil the highlight of your trip. Well done, but I can't stress this enough, without trying to worry you, he is still out there somewhere!'

'No problem and thanks for that. Oh, do you know of anywhere we can get a burger that will still be open on a Sunday night?' asked Barry.

The policeman told them of somewhere nearby that should still be open and they said their farewells.

Chapter Thirteen

Discovered!

Our heroes walked off towards Victoria Park with mixed emotions. They were still buzzing after the show of a lifetime but this was tempered with the knowledge that Bowler had only been wiped from their minds for a few hours and it looked like he had tried to get his hands on their rucksacks. He was in Leicester and that was too close for comfort!

They kept their eyes peeled as they set off to buy some food. In an attempt to lighten the atmosphere, Barry said, 'What did you think of the show, then?'

'It was great Barry, aye, great. Pity it had to end. What time is it anyway?'

Barry looked at his watch. 'It's 9pm. That burger spot is down here, Ian. I would rather get one of them than cook at this time of night if thats OK with you? What do you say?'

'Aye, that's all right Barry. By the time we get back to our campsite and get the tent up it will be far too late, eh.'

Sure enough, the officer was right - the burger spot was open. It was burger and chips each and a short walk to Victoria Park. There was a bench by a street light on the edge of the park so they sat down to eat their food. There were now only a few people about. The concert goers had dispersed and there were only a few dog walkers in the area. The heat of the day had now given way to a slightly nippy evening air. Once they had finished their meal, they put the rubbish in a bin beside the bench and walked back to their old spot in amongst the trees.

'That filled a hole, Barry. I love what they put in burgers here, eh! Yeh, I love them.'

'Yes, they are quite tasty and I was ready for it as well.'

It was still light enough for them to make sure there was nobody in their camping area to worry them. Once satisfied, Ian retrieved the spears he had hidden earlier, before putting the tent up with Barry's help. Ian sorted the inside and made sure they each had a spear next to where they would sleep - just in case!

Happy that everything was in order, Barry got the stove out and started to make a brew before lighting a cigarette and sitting on a tree stump. Ian sat on the grass, opposite his mate. 'I'm pissed off, Ian,' groaned Barry. 'If it wasn't for Tom Bowler we would be having a great time. Instead, we have to watch our backs and worry about him turning up to try and kill us, night after night.'

'I know, Barry. I feel the same. I wish he was caught or better still, dead, eh! Aye, DEAD!' said Ian with some feeling.

'Bloody right! You know what, Ian, why don't we prepare a nice welcome for him? I have some old tin cans I've been keeping. I've been looking around and there are a couple of tracks in these woods which he would more than probably use. We could string some cans up and hide them as best we can and hope they will give us a bit of a warning if he stumbles on them. We could also dig a few holes big enough for him to break his ankle if the steps on them. Or maybe even his bloody neck! I can't see anyone else walking in the woods at this time of night. All we need to do is remember where all these places are so we don't come a cropper ourselves!'

'Bloody hell! That's a lot to take in but yeh, I get the gist of what you are saying, eh, and I have another idea. I will make some more spears and place them on the edge of this wood, in case we have to make a run for it, eh! If we need to run, he will see us running away probably with our hands empty and won't believe we would be crafty enough to have some weapons hidden. We could then give him a big surprise, aye, a BIG surprise! Especially when we pick them up and face him. Hahahaha, I can just see the surprise on HIS face for a change,' said Ian, now in full flow, the frenzy of emotion and hatred for all things Bowler, evident in his voice. 'And you never know what might happen to him, aye, what might happen in the dark!' he finished.

'Brilliant! I like it,' said Barry, 'Between us I think we have a good plan. Time's getting on so let's get on with it ...... but remember, we must do it quietly and keep our eyes peeled!'

Our heroes set about preparing this welcome for Bowler, should he care to make an appearance. It took them a good hour or more but when done, they were pleased with their endeavours. They made one final check and a mental note of where all the traps were and where they had hidden the spears.

'That's a job well done,' said Barry. 'Just one more thing, Ian. If nothing happens tonight I think we should try to give Bowler the slip by going south tomorrow. He won't be expecting it. We've still got the rest of our holiday to have yet, anyway. What do you think?'

'Aye, Barry. Sod him. Let's do that,' said a now determined Ian.

'I will take the first stag tonight, Ian, if that's all right with you' said Barry, lighting a cigarette. 'Agreed?'

'That's fine by me, Barry. I'm really tired now anyway, eh,'

Barry said he would wake Ian after about 4 hours. He had cigarettes to keep him awake although he realised he would have to hide the light from them as much as he could because Bowler may well have been able to follow them from the concert. He didn't really think that was the case but better safe than sorry. Bowler could well have made an educated guess.

Because the street lights weren't too far away it didn't get pitch black in the wood, but they had positioned themselves in an area which was just dark enough to force Bowler into a search if he hadn't followed them. It was getting cooler so Barry draped himself in a blanket while Ian took himself to bed.

Barry walked around while he was finishing his cigarette, his blanket still draped over his shoulders and mentally reminded himself of where they had placed the various obstacles and the route to the edge of the wood where they had hidden the spears in the event that they needed to run for it. He noticed it was all quiet outside now. No footsteps could be heard. It seemed like the whole city was asleep. No birds singing, no cats meowing, no dogs barking. An eerie silence, thought Barry. Quite spooky. Barry was no friend of the dark, in fact, like Ian, he hated it.

He looked at their campsite and the sports fields and tree-lined avenues further out. His eyes then looked skywards where he noted the bright moon and a few slivers of light cloud. The moon was in a dominant mood, casting its light everywhere, the clouds being too weak to stop it. There were one or two oasis of thicker cloud which defied the moon but these were few and far between. The moonlight shone through the trees and danced on the ground in the more open areas, somehow reminding Barry of the concert.

He began to realise that if Bowler did turn up there was a good chance he would see their tent well before he got anywhere near. All the more reason to keep a good look-out. Better if they saw him first!

Returning to the safety of the tent, he sat down again for a moment on the tree stump when he heard a noise. It was Ian snoring again. Barry chuckled to himself, his cigarette now finished.

He looked at his watch. 12:30 am. He planned to wake Ian at about 4:30 am, but how was he to stay awake until then? He walked carefully to the edge of the wood and looked out onto the fields again. He hadn't really noticed it during the night. The moody silent, seemingly endless stretch in front of him was broken by trees here and there, like sentinels standing to attention waiting for the order to march off, the moonlight giving them a preternatural glow. Some straddled either side of one of the paths forming an avenue and was the furthest point Barry could make out.

Once again, he made his way back to his favourite tree stump and carefully lit another cigarette, making sure as little light as possible in case Bowler was out there searching for them. There was a sudden breeze which murmured as it made its way through the leaves of the trees but otherwise the wood was deadly silent. He had another drag of his cigarette while looking about. The night air had a chill to it after such a hot day so he began to appreciate the warmth of the blanket.

Wait! What was that! A rustling roundabout 30 yards in front of him! It wasn't the breeze! He had a rough idea where the noise was coming from. He dropped his cigarette and stood on it, making sure it was out and picked up his spear, standing up slowly, his heart starting to beat faster. He peered through the darkness. There it goes again! Just a light rustle. What could it be? Tom Bowler? or hopefully the police checking to see if they were OK? He could see nothing despite the moonlight. He didn't want to wake Ian just yet but he didn't relish checking out the noise by himself. He wasn't that brave! He also felt too embarrassed to wake Ian.

Rather than risk Ian laughing at him, he took a deep breath and found himself moving very slowly forward. He had his spear pointing to his front. A break of a twig directly in front of him! Barry gasp and stagger back! Still no sign of anyone approaching! Strange! What could it be? All of a sudden there was a rushing noise in the grass! Barry nearly fell backwards. He thought he was going to have a heart attack as an equally frightened rabbit approached, saw him, turned and ran away. 'Bloody hell!!! You bastard! You scared the living daylights out of me!' This he muttered to himself quietly as he watched the rabbit disappear into the undergrowth. Putting his hand on his chest, he realised his heart was racing fast. Fancy being scared of a bloody rabbit!

He looked around and seeing nothing else to alarm him he made his way back to his tree stump. He had a little chuckle to himself while he was recovering. Fancy being frightened of a rabbit! For god's sake, what a wimp I am! He sat down to give his nerves some time to recover. It had sharpened his senses though. He realised that if Bowler was around, he could have heard the commotion and be aware of where they were, so he kept alert, just in case. Another cigarette. That will help his nerves return to normal. The last one was put out prematurely. This time he couldn't be bothered to shield it from any prying eyes. He took a deep drag and held the smoke down before exhaling. Another long drag seemed to help him get a proper hold of himself. He stood up and had another good look around but saw nothing to worry him. He took yet another drag from his cigarette. It was in quick succession to the others and it made him feel a little dizzy. He decided it would be best if he put his cigarette out before it made him fall over.

It took a while but eventually he summoned up the courage to make another patrol of the site. He was growing tired as time ticked by so he kept walking around to keep from falling asleep. With the help of the moonlight, he got to know the wood very well, especially where the strings of cans were and the holes they had concealed in the hope that Bowler would be tripped up and break an ankle or maybe something worse!

Satisfied that everything was OK and all was peace and quiet with no more rabbit's lurking around to give him a heart attack, he set his spear to one side and made a brew. When it was ready, he entered the tent. 'Sorry Ian but it's now your turn to keep a lookout,' he said, while giving Ian a shake. Ian woke up and rubbed his eyes. 'OK Barry, no problem. What's it like out there?'

'Not bad. A bit chilly but it's dry and it's just starting to get light. Would you believe it, I got spooked by a fucking rabbit! I thought I was being attacked! I can laugh about it now but at the time I nearly shit myself!' said Barry, chuckling at the memory.

'Hahaha! laughed Ian. 'Was it armed and dangerous?'

"Fuck off! laughed Barry. 'You'll have to find out yourself.'

Barry watched Ian putting his boots on. There was no hurry, he thought.

'By the way, I've made a brew for us. While we are having it I will remind you of where the traps are. I've kept myself awake by walking round and making myself familiar with them. I feel I could walk it blindfold now,' said Barry.

"Sounds like a good idea. I think I will do the same,' said Ian.

Barry now made his way out of the tent to get his brew with Ian almost ready to follow. He stood up and decided he would have one last cigarette as well. He reached for his packet but before he could get them out he was struck an almighty blow which knocked him to the ground! Ian was just exiting the tent and saw it happen. Tom Bowler was looking down at Barry. He wasn't expecting Ian at that moment and wasn't prepared for what happened next. Ian had left his spear inside. It was still by his bed so he charged out and pushed Tom as hard as he could. Once again, Bowler tripped and fell. This gave Ian time to grab Barry who, in his slightly dazed state, was trying to get back to his feet.

'Run!' shouted Ian. 'You know where!' He pushed Barry ahead of him while he looked back. Bowler was getting to his feet. Barry's constant walking about the wood aided him in his flight. He knew exactly the route needed to get to the spears they had hidden so he set off as fast as he could. He was still staggering a little because of the effects of the blow he had received but he kept going. Ian was right behind him, shouting encouragement.

'That's right, Barry. Keep going. I'm right behind you!'

'Why is it always me he hit's first?' shouted Barry.

They heard a yell back in the wood. Bowler had found one of the traps they had set. It sent him head first to the ground. This gave them an added few seconds, allowing them to reach the edge of the wood and the hidden spears. Barry, now fully compos mentis, passed one to Ian and picked one up himself. They waited for Bowler to approach. They squatted down so he wouldn't see them, allowing them to spring their surprise.

'Right, Barry, when he is close enough, I will count to 3 then we hurl these spears at him. If we throw at the same time, it will be difficult for him to avoid them both. We'll then pick the next ones up and charge him! I'm fucking sick of him!' whispered Ian quickly.

'Gotcha Ian. I'm ready for the bastard!' said Barry, determined to get his own back.

He had only finished speaking when Tom appeared, limping towards them. He had changed again. He was wearing a black leather jacket and black leather biker style jeans and his favourite Doc Martin's. He saw our heroes and gave out a great yell. He seemed really angry and was about to charge them!

Ian said, 'One, two, three, FIRE!'

Both spears were released at exactly the same time in Bowler's direction. He let out a yell of surprise and pain which meant at least one of the spears had found the target. They were not sharp enough to cause deep wounds but enough to cause him pain. He never expected the lads to be ingenious enough to turn his ambush on its head and was even less prepared for what happened next.

Our heroes had already picked up their second spears and were bearing down on him as fast as they could, yelling at the top of their voices! Closing with him they both jabbed at him, striking his torso again and again. Although Bowler had a leather jacket on, the spears had the desired effect. Bowler kept yelling out in pain as the points of the spears struck their target, sometimes piercing his skin. No matter how much he lashed out, he couldn't disarm them, they were too fleet of foot. It didn't take long for him to concede that he had been bested yet again and although not badly hurt, he growled in frustration and turned tail, running back through the woods towards the main road. He was also worried that all this unexpected noise would alert the police.

They knew he was nearing the edge of the woods when the noise from some tin cans were heard, followed by another loud curse. The cans didn't make a lot of noise but would have done the trick if he had stumbled on them earlier. Barry and Ian gave a loud cheer. It must have been pure luck that Bowler had got to their tent without stumbling on one of their surprises.

'Quick, let's get to the phone box and tell the police,' said Barry.

They reached the phone box which was illuminated by a nearby street lamp. This gave them a bit of safety, thought Barry but also highlighted their location if Tom Bowler was crazy enough to have another go at them, so he stood guard outside with his spear still in his hands while Ian called the police.

He got through to them quite quickly and quoted the incident number. He explained to the control room officer the events that had just occurred and was asked to wait there while they got a police response vehicle to them. Exiting the box he explained to Barry what was said so they did what they were told while keeping a good lookout for Bowler.

The police vehicle arrived at the same time as a plain clothed officer. It just happened to be time for him to check on them. When he saw the police car arriving, he realised something had occurred. The police car came round the corner and stopped beside the phone box where Barry and Ian were waiting, the relief on their faces, evident. The plain clothes officer also joined them. If Bowler was around, he was keeping well out of sight. Barry explained to the officers what had occurred and, when asked, pointed in the direction of their campsite. The officers asked to be taken there and on their way, they told them about their traps and how they seem to have saved them from serious injury or even worse.

'You had better pack your gear and come with us to the police station. It's obviously not safe for you to stay out here. He knows where your site is now and who knows, the mental state he is in, he could easily make another attempt to get at you. He now knows you are intelligent enough to arm yourselves, so he may decide to do the same,' said the first officer.

'OK Ian, let's get cracking,' said Barry and they proceeded to pack everything away. Barry made sure he retrieved the cans. He was thinking that they could use them at their next campsite if Bowler was still at large.

Once they had completed packing, they followed the officers back to their vehicle and were taken to the nearest police station. On arrival, they were asked if there was anything further they could add to his description. They told them about the leather gear he was now wearing and Ian said he thought it may mean he had a motorbike. The officers thanked him for that. They were given a cup of tea before being taken to a room where they could sleep for the night without being disturbed by Bowler. Barry asked if they could be woken if they managed to apprehend him during the night.

Before going to bed, Barry nipped outside for a cigarette. While there, he met the plain clothes officer who had taken them to Victoria Park on Saturday night. They had a chat and Barry told him that they were going to head south in the morning in the hope of throwing Bowler off their scent, believing he would be expecting them to be heading back up north.

'Does he know where you live?' asked the officer.

'I can't remember if we told him we were from Penrith but he picked us up just outside the town so he might do,' said Barry.' Whether he would try to find us, there I don't know. If he looked in the phone book he would see lots of Davidson's listed which would make it difficult for him to find out exactly where we live. I'm also not sure if he knows our surnames anyway.'

'OK. It won't do any harm if I make Penrith officers aware, just in case.'

The officer wished them luck and left Barry to finish his cigarette, after which he rejoined Ian who was already asleep and found his own space in the room. He seemed to take longer to fall asleep, his last waking thoughts being a hope that he didn't have another embarrassing nightmare!

Chapter Fourteen

Leicester

It's now Monday morning. A police officer enters the room and wakes our heroes. There had been no nightmares for either of them. A result!

'Morning lads! Time to get up' said the officer.

'Morning' said Barry and Ian. Barry looked at his watch. It was 8am.

'So what are your plans for today?' asked the officer.

'We've decided to carry on south. Bowler won't be expecting it. He will be thinking that now the convention is over, we will be going home. I take it there is no news of his arrest yet then?'

'No, not yet. I don't know how but he is managing to evade us. We will keep trying, don't you worry about that! Believe me, there are a lot of officers involved in this now.'

'Hopefully it won't be much longer. He's a slippery eel, eh. I thought we had him last night but we didn't dare chase him when he turned and ran,' said Ian, 'aye, turned and ran from us, he continued, smiling at the thought.'

'No, you did the right thing contacting us. At least you had the sense to prepare yourselves last night. I'm sure it will have saved you at least from a good beating, if not worse! Quite inventive if you ask me, lads.'

'Thanks. We wanted to make sure we could defend ourselves if he turned up, eh! And I'm glad we did. I just wish we had been able to capture him, aye capture him, but we know how powerful he is so we didn't dare chase him,' said Ian.

'Well done anyway. What time are you thinking of setting off?'

Barry said, 'I think we would like to find somewhere we can go for a bath first. We haven't had one for a while. Is there anywhere you can recommend?'

'How about the Crossington Street Sports Centre in the city? It's got a swimming pool, or you could just use the showers in their changing rooms, said the officer.'

'That's a good idea. Is it far away?'

'Not too far. Tell you what, I'm going off duty now. My car is in the yard out back. I could drop you off there if you like.'

'Oh, yes please' said Ian.

'Ok. I will see you outside. Is ten minutes OK?'

'No probs,' said Barry.

They quickly packed and found the yard. The officer was waiting for them and soon had their rucksacks in the boot and the lads in the back seats. He drove them to the Sports Centre and dropped them off.

'By the way, there is a cafe in there. They do a mean bacon butty if you're hungry,' said the officer before driving away with a wave.

Our heroes walked into the building and paid for the use of the pool.

'Where's the café?' asked Barry. The cashier was a small, grossly overweight woman, unlike what they expected to see in a place supposed to be for fit people! She pointed out the café to them. They were hungry after the events of the night so they made their way in anticipation of one of the highly recommended bacon butties.

They opened the café door and found no other customers, so they could sit where they wanted. They chose the table nearest the café window so they could look towards the entrance - just in case! A female waitress came over to serve them. She was exactly the opposite to the receptionist, being a real beauty who must have worked out a lot to look so good. She had blonde hair in a pony tail and a smile to make any young man drool, with a figure to match. Both lads ordered the recommended bacon butty and a cup of tea and away she went.

'Bloody hell, Ian! She is well fit!'

'Aye, Barry. She's bloody gorgeous, eh! bloody gorgeous!'

Taking his mind off the waitress, Barry said, 'It's a pity we didn't bring any swimming trunks. I could have done with a good swim. Never mind. The showers in the changing rooms will have to do.'

'Aye, Barry, that will be fine, eh! I'm looking forward to a good shower. At least you had one in Bramham!'

'Yes, but the least said about that one the better! I wish it had never happened. We wouldn't be in the pickle we are in now, Ian.'

'Aye well. It can't be helped now, Barry.'

The gorgeous female returned with their order. 'That's a bacon butty and a pot of tea for two. Will there be anything else?' she asked, while she leant provocatively over the table, presenting them with a lovely smile. She seemed to detect what the lads were thinking and thought she would have some fun at their expense.

'No, that's all thanks,' stuttered Barry, feeling embarrassed and aware of what she was doing.

She gave them another cheeky smile and left with a pronounced wiggle. Our flustered heroes got on with their butties, both applying lashings of brown sauce.

Half way through their food the female shouted over, 'Where are you from, lads?'

'We are from Cumbria, Penrith to be exact,' said Barry.

'Oh, that's a long way. What are you doing in Leicester?'

'We were here for the Elvis Convention in the De Montford Hall yesterday,' said Barry

'I don't believe it! I was there!' she said.

'Were you?' said a disbelieving Ian.

'Yes, I was on the aisle opposite that girl with the black jeans on with Elvis Presley stitched into them. Did you see her?'

'Aye, we did. We were about half a dozen rows back from her, aye, about half a dozen rows back,' said Ian.

'Oh, we weren't far from each other then. I really enjoyed it and to have it in my home town, well that was just lucky for me. I see you have rucksacks with you. Did you camp out then?'

'Aye, we did. We hitched down here, like, and intend to hitch home, don't we Barry, but first we are in need of a good shower, eh, in real need!'chuckled Ian.

Just then, another customer came in so the conversation came to an end. The lads finished their meal and made their way to the café door, saying goodbye on their way out. They found the changing rooms and went inside. There were slatted benches along walls with drab grey lockers above. Once they had removed their towels they locked their rucksacks away and went to the showers. They both allowed the hot water to play on their bodies and sighed with pleasure. They spent a good 20 minutes enjoying getting all the dirt off. They hadn't paid much attention to their personal cleanliness since they set off on their journey. Apart from Barry's momentous shower in Bramham on Friday, water had been reserved on the whole, for drinking and cooking with! When they were finished and had dried themselves they retrieved their rucksacks and got dressed into some cleaner clothes. The time in the shower and the cleaner clothes made them feel a lot better.

With everything packed away, they left the changing rooms and started to walk towards the sport centre exit but were stopped by the gorgeous female who came out of the café, gesturing to them.

'I think there has been a fella in the café asking after you. It was a muscly fella, wearing black biker leathers.'

'Oh shit, what did he say?' asked Barry.

'He said he saw two lads come in here earlier and described you. He asked where you went. He sounded a bit fishy to me so I said I didn't know.'

'You did right,' said Ian. 'Aye, you did right. That guy is after us, eh! You won't believe me but he's wanted by the police for a murder and he's after getting us next. Can you do us a favour and phone them? It's all to do with log number 523 of the 19th. If you tell them that, they will know what you are on about. We are gonna make our way back towards the city centre and then try to go south on the A6 towards Bedford, if they ask. Remember, it's log 523 of the 19th.'

'Your joking!' she said but the look on their faces told her otherwise so she wrote the details down. 'OK, I'll do that. You two take care of yourselves. He went out about quarter of an hour ago but I didn't see which way he went, unfortunately.'

'OK, don't worry and thanks for that,' said Barry as they continued to approach the entrance door, but a bit more apprehensively.

'Jesus wept! This is getting passed a joke! Why can't he just do one? Why can't the police arrest the git? How does he keep finding out where we are? I wonder if there is an informer in the police?' said Barry, with despair in his voice.

'I know exactly what you are saying, Barry, eh, but I think he has had some good luck and we've had some bad luck. I tell you what, though, if I had a gun, I would willingly use it on the bastard, aye, empty the fucking magazine!' said an annoyed Ian. 'do for him!'

Ian was first to the door. He opened it and had a good look around but couldn't see anyone matching Bowler's description. It was fairly quiet outside. They went down the steps to the street and turned left and made their way back towards the city centre, both with raised heart rates and sharp eyes.

A hundred yards or so along the road and no sign of Bowler. They started to relax a little ..... but not too much. He was around somewhere! They got as far as St Matthews Way which formed part of the ring road round the city centre and all was OK, even getting as far as the junction with Queen Street. Their aim was to continue on the ring road until they got to the A6 heading south where they would start hitching, if it seemed feasible. There was a sign earlier for the A6 to Market Harborough so they knew they were heading in the right direction. They had to rely on these signs because Ian had lost the Leicester street map.

After a while, Ian turned to look behind him and couldn't believe his eyes. There, about 30 yards behind them, was none other than the dreaded Tom Bowler! He was still wearing the black leathers! He was was making ground on them. Surely he wasn't going to start anything in broad daylight and in the middle of a busy city!

'Shit! he's behind us!', said Ian to Barry in shocked surprise.

'Oh shit! I tell you what we should do, Ian, let's split up. He can only follow one of us. The other can get to a policeman, or get to a telephone box and call them. You go towards the city centre and

I'll carry on round the ring road. Whatever happens, let's plan to meet near the railway station, where the ring road and the A6 meet.'

'Got ya Barry.'

'That's the way to the city centre.' Said Barry, pointing down a street. 'Don't forget we still have our sticks if he tries anything. Yell like hell if he does, to attract attention! See you later,' said Barry and they went their separate ways as quickly as their rucksacks would allow.

Neither looked back for a good 30 yards or so but when Barry glanced over his shoulder he saw Tom Bowler who had chosen to follow him. He was on his tail! Bowler had let Ian head for the city centre.

Barry had a nauseous feeling in the pit of his stomach and his heart started to pound. Tom Bowler was a strong man and he knew he would have no chance if a fight should ensue, even though he still had his spear to aid him. He started to look around as discreetly as he could, in the hope of spotting a policeman but there were none to be seen. Why can you never find one when you need one? Barry was getting more and more anxious! He presumed that Bowler had realised there would be more chance of catching Barry away from the city centre than Ian in the busier streets where there would be more chance of a policeman or good spirited member of the public to come to his aid.

Barry summoned up some courage and decided to stop and turn to face Bowler who, for reasons known only to himself, was keeping his distance. Barry placed his rucksack on the ground and un- tied his short spear, making sure Bowler knew what he was doing. He slung his rucksack onto his back again and held the spear in one hand. He took another look at Bowler who had also stopped. Barry then turned away from him and continued his way on the ring road, hoping a miracle would cause a policeman to suddenly appear as if by magic but that didn't happen, at least not yet.

He now realised where he was. They had been along this street with Albert Hall who had taken them on that unnecessary long walk to Victoria Park. If he continued in this direction the railway station was just around the next bend! There are always policemen in big railway stations like this. Barry hoped there would be one in there now. As a last resort there would be railway staff who would be sure to help and commuters who may also come to his rescue.

It seemed that Bowler was biding his time until there was nobody else around. He was obviously going to try to take Barry out at some stage, otherwise why keep following him?

Barry was hoping Ian had managed to make contact with the police and hoped they would rescue him sooner rather than later!

He continued walking, occasionally looking over his shoulder. Bowler had closed the gap to about 15 yards but didn't seem in any hurry. He was also looking around, obviously keeping a wary eye out for the police. He was wanted for murder, after all. Barry's hands started to feel clammy as his fear was rising. Would he make it to the station in time? He wasn't sure. If Bowler was going to make a move before he did, it would have to be soon so Barry suddenly picked up his pace.

His hopes of reaching the station rose as he rounded the bend. He had about 50 yards to go! He now realised that Bowler appeared to be waiting until they had passed the busy railway station, not expecting Barry to go inside, but Barry began to calm down a little as he realised he was going to spoil his enemy's plans.

When he reached the station entrance, he made his way inside almost bursting into a run, in an attempt to put some more distance between himself and Bowler. He had a quick look for a police officer but couldn't find one. He did, however, see a porter dealing with a commuter, a few yards away. As he approached him, he had a nervous look over his shoulder and was relieved to see no sign of his would-be murderer. He also spotted a telephone kiosk close by so, instead of interrupting the porter for now, he decided to call the police. He reasoned he might struggle to get the porter to believe him anyway.

There was a woman using the phone, which made Barry anxious again. He kept looking around but there was still no sign of Bowler and, thankfully, the woman soon completed her call. One final look around, then Barry picked up the phone and made his call. He gave the incident number and explained what had just occurred. The operator told him to wait there and make himself known to railway staff who would keep an eye on him. She told him that they had received a call from Ian who was now speaking to an officer in the city centre. They would let him know where Barry was. She told him there was no officer in the station at this time but based on the information Ian had given them, some were already on their way to the planned RV and she would direct them to the station itself. Barry reiterated that he hadn't seen Bowler enter the concourse which could mean he was waiting outside. The operator said she would pass that information on.

Feeling a little easier, Barry went to a porter and told him his story. As Barry thought, the porter found it a bit difficult to believe at first but he noticed the urgency in Barry's voice and the anxious look on his face and decided to take him to the staff rest room to let him wait there. He took him passed the ticket office to a room where there were three other porters having their break. He explained to them a little of what Barry had said and left him with them.

One porter was 6' tall and skinny. He had a pencil moustache below a hooked nose and close-set bloodshot eyes. 'Hi there, I'm Jack. Did he say that you are being chased by someone who has committed a murder?'

'Hi, yes, that's right and now he wants to kill me and my mate,' said Barry.

'Why?'

'To cut a long story short, he is blaming us for his wife's death. He killed her but it was because she had been playing around and she told him that one of us had been with her and that was the last straw. After he killed her he came after us and nearly killed us as well. We managed to get away that time but he hasn't given up on us. He seems to appear wherever we are and keeps evading the police. I don't know how he manages it! He seems to have decided that he may as well go to prison for two or even three murders as go down for one. We've been running from him ever since,' said Barry, finishing his tale.

'How long has this been going on?'

'Since Friday night, or Saturday morning to be more exact,' said Barry who kept looking at the door, expecting Bowler to come in any moment.

'He's a big muscly fella,' continued Barry. 'He works out and knows how to handle himself! We are sure he has flipped, gone completely nuts, 'cos when he first confronted us, he didn't seem to care if he got caught, as long as he did us in. He had wide staring eyes just like a madman. He was pissed as well and thankfully that's what allowed us to make our escape. He said something about killing us then handing himself in.'

'Hell! Not a nice predicament to be in, pal,' said another of the porters, lighting a cigarette.

'I wish he would just hand himself in!' said Barry, lighting a cigarette for himself while checking the door again.

He managed to sit down on a bench just as the door swung open. A startled Barry stood up quickly, but to his relief, a police officer entered.

'Hi, I take it your Barry?' he said.

'Yes, that's me.'

'OK mate, come with me please,' said the officer. Barry noted his caller number - PC698.

He got up and said goodbye to the porters and left the room with the officer.

'Good luck!' shouted the railway staff.

'We've got people checking but there is no sign of Bowler. He must have heard our sirens and made himself scarce but we are still looking. I'm going to take you back to the police station to reunite you with your pal. I believe it's the same station you slept in last night', said PC698.

'Oh, OK,' said Barry.

On arrival at the police station, Barry was taken to the same room they slept in and there was Ian waiting for him.

'Barry! Barry! Are you all right?' asked Ian, going over to his mate.

'Yes, I'm fine. I went to the railway station. After we split, he followed me but when I went into the railway station for help, he didn't come in. He must have thought I was gonna walk passed so I think I have spoiled his plans by going inside. I phoned the police and, well, you know the rest,' said Barry.

'What happens now officer?' said Barry to the policeman.

'It would be advisable if you stayed here just for now while we finish checking for Bowler, then we will see what's best to do. I'll be back soon,' said the policeman before leaving the room.

Ian and Barry looked at each other, both wondering how much more was going to happen to them.

'By the way, Ian, what happened to you when we split?'

'Oh, aye, not a lot really. When I got to the city centre, Bowler wasn't following me, eh, so I knew he was going for you. I saw a policeman fairly quickly and explained what had happened, like, and where you would be. He took me back to the police station while others were sent out looking for you and I've been waiting here ever since, aye, ever since.'

'Anyway, it seemed to do the trick. That road I was on, took me passed the railway station so I decided to go in, gambling that he wouldn't follow and I was right. I phoned the police and the railway staff let me wait with them in their bate room,' said Barry.

'Bloody hell! The sooner we get out of Leicester the better, aye, the sooner the better! Hey, here's a thought, I wonder if the police would give us a lift to somewhere down the A6, just to get away from Bowler once and for all, eh? Who knows, he may be watching the police station somehow.'

'That's a thought, Ian, but I don't think they will do that. We could always ask though.'

They sat there in the room for about an hour before anyone came in to update them. It was the same officer who had left them there, PC698. He told them that they had conducted an extensive search for Bowler but he had evaded them once again. They were at a loss as to how he could be keeping one step ahead of them and they were beefing up the search. As for our two heroes, they couldn't stay there. His advice was to get the next train home. They explained to him that their original plan was to do that but they still wanted to continue with their holiday. They didn't want to go home just yet and definitely not by train. They told him that they had a plan which, if it worked, would lead them to escaping Bowler's clutches, hopefully once and for all. He would be expecting them to go home now so they thought they would do the opposite and head south instead for a day or two. The A6 towards Bedford would suit them but how to get out of Leicester without the possibility of him seeing them was the problem.

PC698 said, 'Leave it with me. I will see if the Sargent will allow us to take you to the outskirts of the city on the Bedford road.' He turned and left the room, leaving them to their own thoughts again.

It didn't take long before he returned and was sporting a big smile.

'Your in luck lads,' he said. 'The Sargent has agreed to let me take you down the road now, so if you get your things together, we will get you on your way. Follow me.'

Our heroes thanked him and followed him out into the yard to the police vehicle. They dumped their rucksacks in the boot before settling in the rear seats and were taken out of the city for the next leg of their adventure.

Chapter Fifteen

The Journey South

The police officer took them as far as Oadby before dropping them off at a road junction and gave them directions to a shop so that they could replenish their food and water stocks. As they were getting out of the vehicle, the officer said, 'Just a word of advice for you. I wouldn't go telling everyone you meet what has been going on. These wagon drivers have CB radios and chat to each other all the time. Tom Bowler is a wagon driver and may have access to one. That might explain how he keeps one step ahead of us. Also, despite what he has done, he will still have some friends about who probably don't believe he has done it and they might be keen to help him. Just bear that in mind.' He then gave them a wave goodbye.

Our heroes picked up their rucksacks and headed in the direction the officer gave, with a spring in their steps. Surely they had given Bowler the slip now? They were just about certain but there was enough of a healthy doubt to keep them a little on their toes, especially when they thought of what the officer had said.

While looking at the map, Barry said, 'if we head south on the A6, we might get to Bedford or at least somewhere near it, by nightfall. That should be far enough away from Bowler.

'That's sounds good, Barry, aye, that's fine,' said Ian.

It was mid-afternoon when they reached the shop and bought the necessary provisions. The shopkeeper suggested they go down London Road and they would reach the A6 so they set off in the direction he pointed out but it took longer than they thought to get there.

'Thank god for that! I thought we were never gonna get here. I'm sure it would have been quicker if we had walked back to where the policeman dropped us off!' said Barry.

'Yeh, I was beginning to wonder the same thing, eh, but we're here now,' said Ian.

'Let's cross the road so we can start hitching as soon as possible. It would be a change to get to our next campsite in daylight,' said Barry.

'Aye, it sure would,' replied Ian.

Their luck was in. A wagon, bearing the company name of Perrins Haulage, pulled over within two minutes of them starting to thumb.

'And where might yer be going today, lads?' said the driver.

'Hiya, um, we were hoping to get somewhere along the road to Bedford,' replied Barry.

'Aye, Bedford,' echoed Ian.

'I can get yer to Irthlingborough if that will suit you lads,' said the driver.

'Where's that? asked Barry.'

'I take it yer not from round these parts then. Yer from up north aren't yer?' he asked.

'Aye, we're from Penrith in Cumbria,' said Ian. 'Yeh, Penrith.'

'Aye, northerners as I guessed. Well, Irthlingborough is a place I can get yer to which is nearer to Bedford than here. Yer could go on from there or maybe yer could camp near one of the lakes that you'll see.'

'Thanks for that,' said Barry, climbing into the cab with Ian following.

'Aye, thanks for that,' repeated Ian.

'No problem, I'm Liam, by the way. And what might you two be called then?'

'I'm Barry and this is my mate Ian. We are on a camping holiday. We have been to Leicester for a music convention. It was a gathering of Elvis Presley fans. We still have a week to go before we need to get back home so we thought we would head a bit further south. We've never been this far before so we thought we would like to see a bit more of the country,' said Barry.

'I've been all over in me time,' said Liam, 'that's because I'm a lorry driver, see. Gets yer everywhere really, although of late I've been doing jobs local, like, since I settled in the area. Yep, I've got a contract that looks like it will see me through to retirement, I hope,' he laughed.

He lit a cigarette but didn't offer our heroes one. Barry got his packet out and politely asked if he could light up as well. Liam said he didn't mind at all.

Liam liked to talk a lot, particularly on his CB, so all the lads had to do was listen. When he wasn't talking on his CB, he told them he goes up to Oadby for his pickups. Sometimes he is able to return home the same day but there are occasions when he has to stay overnight. He has relatives in Oadby for those occasions. He went on to say that on those days he at least gets a lay in. He rambled on about all sorts of subjects and even mentioned that he used to like Elvis but didn't like his films. He said Elvis couldn't act. He was also a big football fan and a supporter of Sheffield United. The lads gathered that he was originally from up north. In one break in the conversation, Barry offered Liam another cigarette which he accepted and they carried on down the A6, Liam now back to chatting on his CB.

At last, Liam said, 'We are coming into Irthlingborough so I'll find somewhere to drop yer off. I'm going off the A6 onto the A45 and up passed Stanwick Lakes. It's a nice area open to the public and if yer want, yer could camp in there, lads. You'd enjoy it I think.'

'What do you think, Ian? Time is getting on now and we said it would be better to camp in daylight for a change.'

'Aye, I agree, Barry,' and turning to Liam, he said, 'the lakes will do fine, Liam, thanks.'

At the junction with the A45, Liam turned left and headed up by the lakes until he got to a point opposite the Stanwick Lakes Hotel opposite which was a road to the lake area. He stopped and pointed to the entrance. After dropping them off they thanked him for the lift and wished him a safe journey home. He said 'cheers lads' as he drove off.

Our heroes picked up their rucksacks and walked down to the entrance and into the lake area.

'Liam Perrin couldn't half chatter, couldn't he, Barry', said Ian with a chuckle.   'Your telling me! He was certainly full of himself!' laughed Barry.

'His name rang a bell with me but I can't put a finger on it,' said Ian.

'Do you think we should have told him not to mention us on his CB? I was just thinking what that copper had told us, aye, not to tell anyone who we are?'

'You're probably right, Ian, but at least he didn't mention us while we were with him so it should be OK,' said Barry.

'I hope so,' replied Ian.

Barry shrugged and they walked on, into the park where they noticed there were plenty of wooded areas. They were certain there would be somewhere not too far down the road where they could camp for the night which was far enough away from any disturbance from the night time traffic on the A45. Their mood lifted again as they walked on. Sure enough, to their right was a possible area with some tall, mature trees in full leaf where they felt they would find a camping place.

They found a track heading into the wood. They followed it and sure enough, there was ample room for their tent on a dry, grassy piece of ground, far enough from the road to keep them safe from prying eyes.

Barry gave Ian a hand with the tent this time. Although they were sure they were free from Tom Bowler, Ian said they should make another large spear each, just in case and suggested they should resume guard duties later. Barry agreed.

'You're good at making those spears Ian. Do you want to make some while I sort tea? I can't stop thinking of food. It seems an age since we had anything!' said Barry.

Ian said. 'Aye, that suits me, Barry. We seem to have settled into a rhythm with our camp chores. Besides, you make a mean brew, hint hint!... oh, and you're grub's not bad either,' said Ian with a cheeky smile.

'Get lost,' laughed Barry.

They believed they were safer, now that they were away from Leicester, and felt they could at least enjoy this evening, Bowler free, they hoped. Barry started to sort the cooking gear and set about making something nice to eat while Ian sorted the tent. They decided it was OK to light a fire and

Barry set about gathering fuel from nearby. Once it was well lit he placed some potatoes inside, thinking they would cook to a treat.

It wasn't long before Ian had the tent up and sorted. He forayed into the wood and returned with what he needed to make the spears with and sat down near Barry to began his whittling.

'I'm gonna make these sharper than the last ones, aye, a lot sharper! He won't like these ones if he comes near us, Barry, no, he won't like them at all by the time I'm finished!' said Ian with grim determination on his face.

Barry had a brew ready for him and handed Ian his mug. 'Here's a mean brew for you Ian,' he said with a cheeky smile.

'Ta,' said Ian, happier then he had been for some time.

Barry told him about the potatoes. Ian didn't care. As long as they were edible!. The cheery and somewhat relieved atmosphere continued in the campsite as they kept themselves busy with their respective jobs. Once Barry had finished making the meal, he called Ian over and handed him his plate, complete with the cooked potatoes.

'Thanks Barry, I'm ravenous, eh! This is gonna go down well!'

'Yeh, me too. I could devour a bakery!' said Barry, tucking in.

The potatoes were a big hit with both of our heroes but although they were enjoying their feast, Ian couldn't help thinking of their nemesis, wondering what he was up to and where he was.

'Do you think we've got away from Bowler at last?' asked Ian, his mood turning somber.

'I don't see why not, although the only thing that bothers me, is his knack of finding us no matter what we do, which is a good reason to do our stags tonight as you said ... just in case,' said Barry, 'but I think, or should I say I damn well hope, that we are now free of him, at least for tonight.'

'I dream of him getting tired of chasing us and handing himself in, aye, handing himself in to the police, but I doubt that is gonna happen, eh?' said Ian.

'No, I doubt it.'

It was a calm, balmy night as they ate their meal. There was no wind and apart from the tap tap tap of a woodpecker somewhere nearby, not a sound could be heard. Their hopes of picking a site which was far enough away from the road to sufficiently limit the noise from any passing traffic had been successful which meant they would be able to get an undisturbed sleep.

'Hey, Ian. Just a thought. I'm gonna put the radio on. You never know. It might give us some good news about that bastard. It will be nice to listen to some music anyway.'

'Bloody hell, I forgot all about the radio, eh!, said Ian. Aye, forgot all about it!' said Ian.

Barry got it out of his rucksack and switched it on, tuning into whatever station they could find that was playing their sort of music - Young Girl by The Union Gap was heard along with Rainbow Valley by the Love Affair, among others. When they finished their meal Barry set about washing the pots. The fire was lovely and warm and although it was only early evening, Ian laid back with his hands behind is head and before he knew it, he was sound asleep. Barry soon noticed and kept the noise down to a minimum as he busied himself. He turned the radio down as well in case it woke his friend.

Barry was humming quietly to himself as the music was playing. His chores completed, he decided to leave Ian sleeping while he checked out the wood. He walked back along the path they had used to enter it and was pleased to note that when he turned around to look back, he couldn't see their tent or even the fire. He had concealed it well, at least from that direction. The only indication that anyone was in the wood was their radio which he could just hear, even though he had turned it down. He would have to sort that on his return to the camp once night fell. Sound seems to travel well in the dark night air. He continued to skirt round the rest of the wood which he noted was big enough to conceal them from any prying eyes. Just that radio to sort.

He hadn't had a cigarette for a while but he now felt the need of one so, while deep in thought, he removed one from the packet and lit up. On his tour of the wood, he noted two other tracks which, if needed, they could use to escape in the unlikely event that Bowler should somehow know where they were and turn up like the ogre he was.

Back at the campsite, he turned the radio off and put some more fuel on the fire which had burnt down and settled close enough to it to feel it's soothing warmth and enjoy the tranquility of the beautiful area they were in. He realised how much he loved camping. It felt good to be out in the fresh air under the canopy and quiet of the woods with the trees in full leaf. It made him feel content.

Ian was still asleep where he left him, lying on his back, snoring merrily away. Barry chuckled to himself. He heard some birds twittering about in the trees, the woodpecker having ceased its labours for the day. Late in the year for a woodpecker to be active, he thought. The fire crackled a little and the warmth and otherwise quietness of this idyllic little place was like a lullaby and it worked it's magic on Barry. His eyes slowly closed and he joined Ian in slumber, despite their decision to keep a wakeful watch!

A couple of hours passed and night fell before Barry woke up, needing to go to the loo for a leak. He realised what had happened and was annoyed with himself. He walked to the edge of the wood away from the road and completed his toilet before quickly returning to the camp. He shook Ian until he woke up.

'Wakey, wakey, Ian. I think you would be a bit more comfortable in the tent. I know it's been a warm day but temperatures are gonna drop soon. I'll take the first stag. You look beat.'

'Bloody hell, Barry. I was enjoying that,' said Ian, feeling grumpy at being woken up. He soon came round and said, 'But you're right, I'll be better off in the tent, eh. Wake me when it's my turn to stag. Bowler may be miles away but we shouldn't both go to sleep at the same time, just in case, eh.'

'Yeh, sorry I woke you. Get yourself off and I'll wake you when I can't stay awake any more.'

He didn't dare tell Ian that he had fallen asleep earlier. What he doesn't know won't hurt him, he thought.

Once he knew Ian was safely ensconced in the tent with his spear by his side, Barry lit another cigarette and decided to check the periphery of the wood again, just to make sure he could remember where the tracks were that he spotted earlier. He didn't feel there was any need to put out the tin cans or to dig any holes to act as traps this time. He felt sure Bowler was nowhere near. What they were doing was more of an insurance policy. Everything appeared fine so he returned to the camp fire and enjoyed the warm glow of its dying embers. He didn't add any more fuel, his intention being to let it burn itself out. They could light it again in the morning if they needed to. He dug his map out of his rucksack and had a look at it. He wasn't sure which way they should go tomorrow so he wanted to have a look before making any suggestions to Ian.

It was now Monday night. Tomorrow was Tuesday. Although they had only just turned south today, he thought that maybe they should be thinking of making their way slowly back in the direction of home after all. If they could get passed Leicester tomorrow and up to somewhere around Derby, following the A6, or maybe even further, they could then relax. The need to get passed Leicester felt strong as that was the last place they saw Bowler. He was sure that if they got passed there and near Derby, they could easily make it home by the weekend if not before. It seemed the more sensible move as far as he was concerned. It would save panicking later because their money wouldn't last much longer. He just hoped Ian would agree.

He lit another cigarette. Blimey, I'm almost chain smoking, he thought. While enjoying it, he was contemplating possible scenarios and what Ian might think of his plans and how he would handle any negative reaction from him. He sat back with all these ideas going through his head. The embers of the fire died about the same time as his cigarette. He lay back, feeling nice and comfortable and in no time he fell asleep again!

He woke with a start. It was daylight! There was a loud rustling nearby! Bowler? Barry jumped up and grabbed his spear and looked all about. No sign of him. The noise came again, directly in front of him. All of a sudden a Cocker Spaniel appeared from behind a tree, sniffing about, its tail wagging furiously. A whistle sounded. It came from the road, thought Barry. The Spaniel's ears pricked up and it ran off in the direction of the sound and disappeared from view. When Barry was sure they were not about to be attacked, he breathed a sigh of relief and looked at his watch. 7.30am! It must have been somebody taking his dog for an early morning walk.

Both he and Ian had slept solid for about 10 hours! Barry wondered how Ian would react when he told him he had fallen asleep. Ian wouldn't trust him again. Never mind. He would have to face it. Time to give him a shake.

'Morning, Ian,' said Barry, as he gently woke his mate.

'Morning, Barry. Morning? What happened to the night, aye, to my stag?'

'You looked knackered, Ian, so I thought I would leave you a bit longer. I must admit though, that it meant I got tired and, don't get mad, but I did eventually fall asleep. I don't think it was for long though.'

'I must admit I needed that sleep. like, but you should have woken me, Barry, aye, you should have woken me up! I know that there wasn't much chance of Bowler turning up, eh! but we couldn't be certain, could we?' said Ian, but he wasn't too upset, he had enjoyed a good sleep.

'Yeh, you're right Ian. Lesson learnt,' said Barry, feeling suitably scolded. As he switched the radio on, he said, 'You would never guess but a bloody dog woke me up! Somebody was out walking it but when he whistled, it ran off. I don't think whoever it was would have seen our camp. I checked it out earlier and we are well hidden. I'll put the kettle on and make you one of my epic brews before we decide what we are gonna do today.'

'Ah, now your'e talking, Barry! Now your'e talking!'

While the kettle boiled, Barry had another cigarette and was glad Ian had taken it so well. A good long sleep had done both of them good.

'Brew's ready Ian!'

'Great, I'm here,' said Ian, appearing from the tent.

'Ah, that's good' he said as he started on his tea. He sat down before adding, 'so, what's on the menu today Barry, and I don't mean to eat,' he said, good-humouredly.

Barry told him what he he had been thinking during the night and asked Ian what he thought. He was pleased to find that Ian agreed with him. Barry needn't have worried.

While Ian was having his cuppa, he got up and had a good walk around the wood and when he was satisfied that all was well he returned and started looking at the tent.

'I'll make breakfast then Ian, if you want to do your thing.'

'Yeh, I like to sort the tent. I'm not much of a cook anyway and you seem to have got it off to a tea, aye, a tea, hehe, no pun intended,' laughed Ian.

He made short work of the tent and sat down while Barry continued to prepare the breakfast. Barry had buttered some bread and sliced a tin of luncheon meat and dry-fried it in a pan while some beans were cooking. He finished off with two fried eggs each and shared this offering between two plates. They would need to find somewhere to restock before their next meal but he was sure that wouldn't be a problem. They had always managed to find somewhere to replenish their supplies. He handed a plate to Ian and they began to eat.

'A good feast, Barry, as usual, aye, lovely,' said Ian, tucking in.

'Yeh, I thought we'd better fill up. I don't think we will have any problem getting more stuff so a good feast now will be OK even if we don't know when we will be able to sit down like this again. There's bound to be somewhere near where we end up.' said Barry.

While they were eating, they discussed their hopes for the day, settling on reaching Derby as Barry had hoped, all being well. It was still relatively early so Barry lit a cigarette before washing up. He was walking around, deep in thought and decided that as soon as they saw a phone box, he would contact Leicester police and see if there was any update on Tom Bowler, having heard nothing on the radio which he switched off and packed away along with everything else.

'OK Ian, ready when you are, mate.'

'Yep, let's go and see what the world is going to throw at us today,' said Ian, in an upbeat mood.

As usual, they checked they hadn't left any rubbish before moving down to the road which led to the park exit and the A45.

Chapter Sixteen

To Chapel-en-le-Frith

It didn't take them long to reach the main road which they quickly crossed so that they could head back towards Irthlingborough and the A6 north. There wasn't a lot of traffic but what there was, didn't want to know. It was 9am and another lovely Summer's day so they decided to walk towards Irthlingborough and the junction with the A6 which would take them back north, all the time attempting to hitch a lift from what vehicles that did pass. They were unsuccessful but they didn't mind. It took them about 40 minutes to reach the road junction. They crossed over to the other side and recommenced hitching. Due to the amount of gear they were carrying, there wasn't much hope of any cars stopping but they tried all modes of transport anyway.

They now had plenty of experience in hitching and adopted the best strategy which was to wait at the junction, rather than walking down the road. At one point, however, Barry was looking up the A6 with his thoughts on other things when he heard the sound of an engine and without looking back, he once again raised his arm and attempted to hitchhike. He nearly curled up in laughter and embarrassment when a motorbike passed by, the rider tooting his horn. Ian hadn't noticed Barry thumbing but when he realised what had happened, he couldn't help laughing as well. Barry should know what a motorbike sounds like! Lesson learnt.

It was just after 10am when a wagon approached. They immediately recognised it as belonging to Liam Perrin! He must be on his way back to Oadby! Liam stopped and with a wry smile on his face, beckoned them on board.

'I thought you two were heading further south today! That's in the other direction, yer do realise that, don't yer lads?' he said, guessing they had changed their minds.

'Yeh, we know but we decided to start making our way back home, like. We thought that if we take our time we will still be able to see some of the country, eh, and not have to panic about getting there in time for work next week,' replied an embarrassed Ian, 'aye, it will save us rushing back.'

'No worries lads. I sought of guessed so. I tell yer what I'll do, I'll drop you off in Oadby, where I picked you up yesterday if that's all right?'

'Yes please, Liam. That would be perfect for us. We will be well on our way then,' said Barry.

During the journey they couldn't help but tell him about Tom Bowler and all that had transpired over the last few eventful days. Knowing how prolific he was on his CB, they pleaded with him not to mention it because they thought it was possible Bowler had access to one. He looked at them with disbelieving eyes but told them that their secret was safe with him. He would say nothing about it. The journey would take around an hour, their story a lot less, so as soon as they had finished, Liam was once again busy on his beloved CB, chatting to all that would listen. he did keep his word - nothing of their secret was mentioned. The time passed quickly and on arrival in Oadby, he dropped them off at the junction with London Road, roughly opposite where he had picked them up. They gave him their thanks and wished him a safe journey home.

Unfortunately for them, Liam was a bigger chatterbox than they thought and he couldn't resist broadcasting what the lads had told him in confidence! For some reason, he hadn't believed a word of what they said and continued to ridicule them until he reached his destination. Thankfully, the journey to his depot only took a few minutes.

There was a phone box only a short walk away from our heroes. It was vacant so Barry entered it and phoned Leicestershire police. Quoting the incident number, he asked if there was any update on Tom Bowler. Did they know where he was? Had he been arrested? The answers came back in the negative. He was told Bowler's last description had been passed on TV stations and in the newspapers, the manhunt now having gone nationwide, so they remained hopeful. They also said that judging by the many calls they had received, of possible sightings, there was a good possibility that he was still in the Leicester area. The operator asked where they were and what their intentions were so he told them there intentions before thanking the operator and replacing the phone. He told Ian what he had learnt and they sat down on their rucksacks for a moment, both feeling a little disconcerted about the news. When, oh when, were they going to catch him?

Barry lit a cigarette and said, 'I can see a shop up ahead. It will save us going to that one at the far end of London Road so when I've had this, we'll call in and stock up with some more food before we try to get a lift through Leicester.'

'Yeh, we need to make sure it will get us all the way through the city, eh, and as far away as possible. I don't want to see Leicester again for a long time!' replied Ian. 'Aye, a long time.'

They enjoyed this spell of sunshine while Barry had his cigarette before going to the shop. It was turning out to be another glorious day. They had been blessed with good weather for most of their trip. Entering the shop, they were able to replenish their food stocks and Barry's cigarette supplies, which they carefully packed away once they were outside.

It was now time to begin hitchhiking. Once again, they were lucky. They only had to wait a minute before another wagon pulled up. It was even better when the driver told them his destination was Derby which was their target for the day.

'So what have you been up to then?' he asked.

'We've been to the Elvis Presley Convention in Leicester. It was on Sunday. Since then we've just been looking round the area. We are from Penrith in Cumbria,' said Barry.

'Oh yeh?' said the driver, lighting a cigarette. 'I used to like Elvis but mainly his early stuff. Don't like him much now,' he said, taking another drag from his cigarette. He opened his window and flicked his ash outside. 'Did you hitchhike all the way down then?' he continued.

'Aye, we did. We cut across the A66 to Scotch Corner and came down that way, aye, down from Scotch Corner,' said Ian.

'Has it been fun, then?' said the driver.

'Yeh. More of an adventure than we expected!' said Barry who, forgetting the advice the police had given him, then proceeded to tell him of the tragedy that had unfolded and their worry that Bowler was still after them.

'Well, well, well. I saw something on the TV about that. They didn't mention you two though. You're not pulling my leg are you?'

'No, of course not!' said an indignant Barry. 'It's as true as we are sitting here. We've nothing to gain by telling a tale, have we? And he's still out there, after us!'

'No, I suppose not. Come to think of it, I heard someone on the CB a few minutes before I picked you up, going on about two lads he had just dropped off here. He didn't believe a word you said. So it's true is it?'

'Oh no! He promised not to say anything! The police believe that Bowler may have access to a CB. He hasn't believed a word we have said, Ian!' said Barry, turning to his friend.

'I don't believe it! The only good point is he was only a few minutes from his depot when he dropped us off, so he can't have had time to talk about it for long, aye, not for too long,' said Ian.

'Maybe not but I heard it so maybe others did,' said the driver.

Between them, Barry and Ian explained everything and with the little the driver had already heard about the incident, he believed they were telling the truth. They spoke for a little longer. Barry wanted a cigarette so he offered the driver one, which he took. Barry was hoping he would, because he was in desperate need of one and didn't want to light up without at least offering him one first. They talked of other things which engaged them all the way to Derby. The driver said he was going to Duffield which was a place north of the city. It was on the A6, which was were they wanted to be, so he said he would drop them off there. Our heroes were happy with that.

It was early afternoon when they arrived. The driver dropped them off and wished them luck. They thanked him for the lift as they left his vehicle and waved him off.

'That was good, Ian. We've already reached our target for today. If things carry online this we will be home in no time. Tell you what, I'm getting hungry. I can make us a quick sandwich here and then we can see if we can get any further today. How about that? said Barry.

'Perfect, Barry. I'm hungry as well, eh. A sandwich will go down well right now', replied Ian.

They chose a grassed area just off the road where Barry took what he needed out of his rucksack. A sandwich was quickly made and gratefully devoured by our hungry pair. When he had finished eating, Barry had another cigarette and sat back while he enjoyed it.

'I wonder if we should have kept quiet about our problem and not mentioned it to that driver? The problem is I can't help myself,' said Barry, with a feeling they had once more made a big mistake in doing so.

'Don't worry, Barry. I didn't see a CB so we should be OK'

'Good point Ian ....ah, but he did say he heard about it on his CB so he must have one!' said Barry.

'Oh yeh, he did, didn't he!'

'There's nothing we can do about it now except hope.'

Barry finished his cigarette then said, 'OK, let's make a move and see how far we can get before we need to make camp. Are you ready?'

'Aye, Barry. I'm ready to go. A little bit further today would be good, like, so let's see what fate throughs at us.'

They enjoyed the walk. Their legs were a little stiff after the cramped conditions in the last vehicle and the exercise would do them good. They could easily see if there were any vehicles coming and stopped to raise their thumbs when anything with potential went by. Once again, their luck was in. They had only been walking for a couple of minutes when a wagon stopped and offered them a lift.

'Hiya, fellas. I'm going to Buxton if that's any good to you. It's just over an hour away.'

'Hiya, yes, that will be perfect,' said a thankful Ian.

'Hop in then, I need to get going.'

Our heroes hurried on board and as soon as they closed the door the driver set off. His physique reminded them of Tom Bowler because his arms were full of muscles. Barry and Ian introduced themselves.

'And I'm Alexander, Alexander Palace, said the driver, 'but you can call me Alex, he quickly added.'

Ian couldn't help but snigger.

'I know, I know,' laughed the driver. 'My farther must have been having a joke when he named me but it's set me in good stead. I didn't have any problems until I reached my teens when kids were old enough to know what the Alexander Palace really was. I had to toughen up quickly so I took up boxing. When I became good at it, people suddenly became friendly and left me alone. Hahaha.'

'Amazing! You still look fighting fit. Do you still box now?' asked Barry.

'I don't box any more but I still like to work out at the gym. I enjoy keeping fit. Driving lorries isn't exactly good for you, you know, hahaha.'

'I don't think boxing would suit me,' said Barry with a giggle.

'No, you're too weedy,' laughed Alexander again. 'Anyway, where exactly are you heading, lads?'

Our heroes, between them, explained the reason for their trip and that they were now making their way home.

'Have you enjoyed your time away then, lads?' asked the muscly but cheerful Alex.

Once again, Barry couldn't help but tell the story of what had occurred in Bramham and that they were not sure if they had given Tom Bowler the slip. Alex looked incredulous.

'I know I laugh a lot, but *you're* having a laugh now, aren't you? You must have watched that bit on the telly last night about this and now you're having me on!'

'No, what Barry said is all true, like! Aye, all true, eh! We haven't seen a TV or picked up a paper since we left home!' said Ian with a serious look on his face. This guy isn't going to believe us, he thought. And I wouldn't if I was him, either.

'You must admit that's a bit hard to believe. Still, you're safely on your way home now. He won't be able to hurt you while you are with me, anyway, hahaha!' laughed Alex.

'Yeh, we're glad about that,' laughed Barry, 'at least until you drop us off!'

The jocularity continued for the rest of the journey which took them passed Buxton and into the tiny village of Dove Holes which is where Alex lived. He dropped them off but before he could drive away, Barry said, 'Oh, by the way, please don't mention anything on your CB. We've been told that Tom Bowler may have access to one and he has some wagon driver friends who don't believe he killed his wife. It's possible they will let him know where we are if you say anything!' said Barry in his most serious voice.

'OK, lads. Enjoy your journey home. Cheerio!' and that was the last they saw of Alex.

'Time to stretch our legs again, Ian, so let's have a little walk up the road here. We are well ahead of where we expected to get to. I was checking the map earlier and I think we are now in the Peak District. Look at the view! It's almost as good as the Lakes,' said Barry with a smile.

'Aye, it is nice Barry, especially on a nice warm day like today, eh!'

'Yeh. The map shows another village no too far away. Let's see if we can walk to it. We've made good progress today and the exercise is welcome.'

— — — — — —

Meanwhile, Alex was driving the short distance home when he heard a conversation on his CB. He soon joined in and was asked where he was. He told them he was now back home in Dove Holes and explained that he had just dropped off two teenagers who told him a wild tale about them being chased by some guy who murdered his wife in Bramham. He said he watched something about it on the TV last night and there was no mention of the lads. He said thats where the lads must have got the information and that they must have been having him on! One of the other drivers said he had heard a rumour that 2 northern lads were somehow involved. It was then that Alex realised that the lads had been telling the truth. He made his way home without speaking any more on his CB and prayed neither Bowler nor any of his mates had heard the conversation.

— — — —-

Back on the A6, Barry and Ian had walked for over half an hour, enjoying the view and the warmth of the sun. There was a sign ahead of them which told them they were approaching a place called 'Chapel-en-le-Frith'. Barry lit a cigarette as they left the A6 onto a minor road which led into this small town.

The Main Street took them passed grey bricked buildings which seemed to be a feature of the place. There were a number of shops either side of the road but thankfully they didn't need anything for the time being. They carried on making their way through this quaint town, looking for clues for somewhere to pitch their tent for the night when they saw two teenage girls and a young boy, eating something out of paper.

"I think they've got fish and chips, Ian. Should we ask them where they got them from? I know we've stocked up but I really fancy some. How about you?'

'You know what they say, Barry, great minds think alike, eh. I fancy some as well.'

'OK, here we go.'

They waved at the group to attract their attention. 'Hiya you lot, is that fish and chips you've got there?' asked Barry.

The girls giggled at their Cumbrian accent.

'Yes they are, see,' said one showing them the contents of her paper. She had black hair in a pony-tail and was about 5ft 4ins tall with a neat figure. Quite pretty.

'Where did you get them from? We really fancy some,' said Barry.

The second girl was not as good looking as the first. She wore spectacles and was a little shorter. She had a reasonable figure, with large breasts for a girl of her age. She was wearing a short pleated skirt. She was the next to speak.

'The chippy is over there,' she said, and pointed up a side street. 'Go up there and turn right. You'll see it. It's not far away.'

'Oh thanks. Let's go Ian.'

As they were about to go, the black haired girl said they would show them where it was so they walked together, our heroes allowing their new acquaintances to take them there. The one in the black hair introduced herself as Paige Turner. The other girl was Lorna Reid and the young boy, who was about ten years old, was Bobby Baker. Our heroes told them who they were. By the time they had completed the introductions they had reached the chippy. Our lads went inside and bought some fish and chips. When they made their way out, the two girls and boy were waiting for them.

While tucking into his food, Barry took the opportunity of asking them a question. 'We are looking for somewhere we can put our tent up for the night. Do you know of anywhere nearby?'

'Yes. You could go to the Memorial Park. It's not far away. We'll take you there!' said Paige excitedly.

All five set off, while continuing to eat their fish and chips.

'Where are you from?' asked Bobby, while fiddling with a catapult he produced from the back pocket of his jeans.

'We are from a town called Penrith, eh! It's in Cumbria in the Lake District,' said Ian.

'I've heard of the Lake District at school,' said Bobby.

The girls continued to ask questions while they walked along. What were they doing in Chapel, where were they going next, why were they hitchhiking etc. By the time our heroes answered, they found themselves on Rowton Grange Road, not far off an arched opening into the park area they had mentioned. Bobby took out his catapult again and fired a small stone at a sign about 15 yards away and hit it almost in the centre!

'That was a cracking shot!' said Barry. He was truly amazed at the accuracy.

'Yes, he's brilliant! He's had practice. He never puts it away!' said Paige.

Bobby looked a bit bashful at all this attention but fired another shot which was equally as accurate and the power of it caused a big dent in the sign. Barry and Ian couldn't believe what they had seen.

'Look at the dent that has caused! I wouldn't like to be hit with that!' said Barry, examining the sign.

'If that was an Olympic sport, you would win a gold medal, Bobby! said Ian with real appreciation in his voice.

Bobby looked very embarrassed and once again put his catapult away.

'This is Memorial Park. We'll show you a good spot to put your tent up,' said Paige.

She seemed to have attached herself to Ian while Lorna seemed to have taken a shine to Barry. Into the park they walked, the lads quite happy to be led to wherever it was the girls were taking them, trusting they would know a good spot. They walked over some well tended football pitches, continuing their chatter until they approached a small wooded area containing some large Oak trees, along with some Ash and a lovely Copper Beech. There were several bushes in the area, along with a copse of small firs. A few yards short of this wood was a wooden building which was about 40 feet long and 12 feet wide which had been partitioned into two rooms, each with its own entrance. It had seen better days. There was a bench outside, along the entire front wall, facing the playing fields and on looking inside, a similar bench on 3 sides. Barry assumed that these were or had been used as changing rooms for teams using the football pitches with the ones outside for spectators.

'That wood over there should be a good place for our tent,' said Barry, pointing in its direction.

'Why don't you sleep in there, said Paige, pointing to the wooden building. 'It would save you having to put your tent up!'

'No, we need to be out of site in the woods, eh! Anyone looking for us would automatically check in there. Aye, they would check inside. The woods will do for us, thanks,' said Ian.

While they were looking around the building, Paige thought about what had just been said.

'Who's after you? Is it the police?' she said, excitedly, coming to the conclusion that our heroes were on the run.

'No, no. Nobody's after us. We like camping in woods, that's all,' replied Barry.

'Then why mention it, if there's nothing in it?' continued Paige, pushing for a better answer.

'Barry, let's tell them. There can be no harm in telling this lot, eh?' suggested Ian.

Barry hesitated for a moment or two before agreeing. It took them a while to relate all that had occurred because the girls found it difficult to believe, so they kept interrupting and asking questions. Eventually they got their story across and hoped the girls understood their reason for caution. Barry gave them the last description they had of Tom Bowler just in case he should turn up, although he never for a moment expected him to do so. He believed they had given him the slip at last but they were not going to relax their guard until they were back home.

The afternoon sunshine could be felt on their skin so, instead of putting the tent up, they decided they would a sunbathe while having a chat with their new companions. It wasn't long before Bobby said he was going home but he said he wanted to come back in the morning to see them before they left. They agreed they wouldn't leave without saying goodbye. This seemed to satisfy him and off he went.

After spending some time chatting with the girls, Ian decided it was finally time to put the tent up so he picked up his rucksack and, looking towards the wood, he said, 'I think I'll put the tent up now Barry, eh! Do you fancy helping me, Paige?'

'Yeh! I'd love to! she said, and linked Ian's right arm.

'You needn't bother, Barry. Paige and I will manage, eh,' and off they went.

Lorna and Barry chatted away about nothing in particular for a while before she wandered back into the wooden building.

'Have you seen this, Barry?' she shouted.

He made his way inside and saw Lorna looking at the wall.

'What is it?' asked Barry as he joined her.

'That's where my last boyfriend carved our names. Just there,' she said, pointing at the carving in the wooden wall.

'Your last boyfriend? Does that mean you don't have one now?' asked Barry.

'No.'

'Why is that?'

'He wanted me to take my knickers off but I'm not that sort of girl. I know what he was after, so he chucked me.'

Barry was a little startled at this revelation. He said, 'Oh dear! Did you like him?'

'Not enough to do that with,' she replied.

Barry was hoping she would be willing with him but soon realise he wasn't going to be that lucky.

'I don't want to be called a slut so it will be a long time yet before I do that,'she said.

Barry, although disappointed, had a look at the walls and saw a few other carvings by lovers as well as some graffiti which left nothing to the imagination.

Realising he was going to get nowhere, he suggested they go and see how the tent was progressing. They walked over to the wood to discover it was already up and the inside was sorted. Ian and Paige were nowhere to be seen but they soon appeared from the other side of the wood, loaded with some tree branches. Ian explained that he was going to make some more long spears for their protection tonight - just in case. Paige had helped him collect them. They both appeared to be happy and were chatting away merrily as they joined Barry and Lorna.

'Paige gave me a hand with the tent and helped me get these,' said Ian.

'I really enjoyed it! I didn't have to do much with the tent. Ian is brilliant at putting it up,' said Paige.

Lorna gave her a cheeky look.

'I'm talking about the tent, you cheeky bugger!' laughed Paige.

All four laughed while Ian made a start with the spears. Seeing him working, Barry gave him a hand. The girls didn't have a knife so they just watched.

Lorna said, 'What are they for, Barry?'

'They're our secret weapon against Bowler if he comes. Well, not so secret because the last time he tried to tackle us we had some, so he knows we will probably have some more,' said Barry.

'That's a good idea,' said Lorna, impressed by their ingenuity.

'Aye, it saved our lives last time, eh!' said Ian, while whittling away. 'If we hadn't made them he would have crucified us, aye, crucified us!'

'Yeh, but we gave him a taste of his own medicine. He had to run or we would have really hurt him. Trouble is, he got away ... again!' Said Barry. 'I don't know how he does it but every time the police get close, he manages to evade them. That's why we've decided that every time we camp up, we will make sure we are prepared for him.'

'Does he know where you are then?' asked Paige.

'We don't think he has a clue where we are now, but we aren't taking any chances. These are our insurance policy,' said Barry.

'I wouldn't like to be caught by him without these to fight with, eh! He's a right nutter. He seems to think that because he has murdered his wife, it won't make any difference to him if he murders us as well! Aye, murder us as well! said Ian.

'He sounds really dangerous! Is he a big man?' asked Paige.

'Not so big but he has muscles. He works out a lot in the gym, he told us. As we told you before, he gave us a lift from our home town to Scotch Corner. That's where he dropped us off,' said Barry.

Paige looked at her watch. 'Well, I hope you're both safe tonight. I think it's time for us to be going now though. Lorna, are you ready?' she added, turning to her friend.

'Yes, I'm coming,' answered Lorna. 'But we'll be back in the morning. Don't leave without seeing us first.'

They said a friendly cheerio and the lads watched them walk away.

Chapter Seventeen

Campsite Prepared

When the spears were finished, Barry lit a cigarette. 'I'll just have a walk round this wood to check it out, as I usually do, Ian.'

'I've already done that Barry, so I'll come with you and point some things out. I don't think we can put the cans out here, eh. It's too well used. And we shouldn't dig any traps either. I honestly don't think Bowler will have a clue where we are anyway.

'I will feel better with these spears, Ian. You make a good job of them as well!'

'Cheers, Barry.'

Ian spoke about the layout of the wood and what was on the other side. Barry was happy with their information and they returned to their tent.

'If anything does happen, we should make for that entrance off Rowton Grange Road or whatever they call it, where we came in down passed those football pitches. Let's make it our rendezvous point. What do you think, Ian?' said Barry.

'Yeh, I agree with that. At least we know where it is and it's near some houses so we can call for help if he follows us there, eh!' said Ian.

'True,' was Barry's reply.

Barry looked around and wondered where the time had gone. The light was starting to fade.

'Time's getting on now Ian. Do you fancy something to eat before we organise stags for tonight, because I think we should still do them .... and I promise not to fall asleep,' he said, with a sheepish smile.

'Aye, all right, Barry. Come to think of it, I'm starting to get a bit peckish. Aye, it's a bit now since we had those fish and chips. Some grub would go down well, I think. Do you want a hand?'

'No, I'm fine, Ian. I quite enjoy doing it. Tell you what, I'll put the kettle on first and make us a brew before setting to with something. It won't be anything special tonight. I was thinking, we still have a tin of that stew your auntie gave us. I can add a couple of taties to it. How does that sound, with some bread?'

'Yes Barry. Oh, and don't forget to add some of that curry powder as well! We both enjoyed it last time!' asked Ian.

'Good thinking, Ian. I forgot about that.'

'I'll have another walk round the wood,' continued Ian, 'then I'll stand over there where those wooden changing rooms are. At least, that's what I reckon they are, changing rooms. I can see almost all the way to the park entrance from there so I will see if anything, or anyone is coming, eh!' said Ian.

'Good idea. I'll give you a shout when grub's up but wait for your cuppa before you go. It won't be a sec.'

While the kettle boiled, Barry switched the radio on and began peeling the potatoes and cutting them into small chunks. The DJ was playing 'Lazy Sunday' by the Small Faces. Barry produced a pan from his rucksack and put the potatoes in. When the kettle boiled, he poured out the tea and handed a cup to a grateful Ian who took it with him on his tour of the wood, the remainder of the water being used to boil the potatoes.

Ian completed his tour and was relaxing in the vicinity of the wooden building when he heard Barry shout 'Grub up!' Licking his lips, he made his way eagerly to the waiting plate of stew and potatoes. He noticed some buttered bread for them to share.

'Cor! This looks good! I know we had those fish and chips earlier but this fresh air ....'

'Yeh, I know what you mean, Ian. Here you are, tuck in, mate!'

'Did you remember the curry powder?'

'I sure did. Have a taste. It's really good!'

Ian sat down beside his mate and started to eat. He said, 'Wow! That's even better than last time, Brian, yeh, definitely better!'

'Isn't it!'

They listened to the radio and cheered when he started to play 'US Male' by their beloved Elvis.

Whilst enjoying the music and the food, Ian said, 'It's all quiet out there, Barry. Just a couple of dog walkers, that's all.'

'Jolly good. Let's hope it stays like that'

The rest of the meal was eaten in relative silence, both of our heroes enjoying the last of the tins of stew Ian's auntie had given them. The addition of the curry powder was a master stroke. They loved it! When they had finished, Barry lit a cigarette and sat back while he enjoyed it, taking in the calmness of the evening. The washing up could wait until he had finished, he thought.

'I wonder if we can make it all the way home tomorrow, Ian?'

'All we can do is try, Barry, aye, all we can do is try. I hope the police have got Bowler before we get home, eh!'

'Yeh, he's become a pain in the arse! I still can't understand how he keeps finding us!'

'It must be something with those CB's as that copper said, eh. Let's just hope we never see him again though,' said Ian.

When Barry finished his cigarette, Ian volunteered to do the first stag and suggested Barry get his head down while he washed up for a change. He would stay up as long as he could before waking Barry and promised not to fall asleep. Barry eventually agreed. He was tired anyway. He picked up his spear and made his way into the tent. It didn't take long before Ian knew Barry was in the land of nod. He wasn't the only one who could snore!

With the washing up completed and all cooking implements packed away, Ian stood up and looked around, wondering how he would spend the time. He picked up his spear and decided to make his way to the edge of the wood and do a walk of the perimeter to start with. He thought this was a good practice they had adopted. He noticed a few spots of rain but hoped the good spell of weather hadn't broken. He decided if it got any worse he would have to go and get his jacket, but for now he would do without. He continued to check the perimeter of the wood just as the rain became heavy. He made his way back to their campsite and put his jacket on before continuing his patrol of the area.

He looked across the playing fields to the main park entrance. Again, he could make out a couple of dog walkers quietly exercising their animals but the rain seemed to curtail their activity as they scurried quickly away. It was beginning to cool down, the night air and rain having its effect. He had a bright idea. He would gather some wood before it got too wet and make a fire. He would find somewhere to screen it, somewhere away from the tent and prying eyes and somewhere under the canopy of the trees in the hope of keeping the rain off it. He wished he had grabbed his blanket before Barry got in the tent but it wouldn't be right to go in and disturb him while he was enjoying his sleep. It didn't take him long to gather enough wood and soon he had the fire going. He found an ideal spot in amongst the group of small fir trees which were about 20 yards from the tent. The branches of two large Oak trees towered above the firs, shielding them with their leaves. No rain would get through for a while at least. When the fire was lit, he had a quick walk around the area to make sure it was well enough concealed and was pleased to find that it was better hidden than he was expecting. He stayed round the fire while it built up and was pleased with its warming effect. Satisfied that the fire was safe and established, he kept walking round the edge of the wood and on the completion of each circuit he returned to the fire for a quick warm-up and at the same time, added some more fuel to keep it going. This seemed to be a successful strategy and the walking would keep him awake until it was time for Barry to take over.

As the night crept in, thankfully the rain abated. Tiredness started to take hold. He began to imagine all sorts of things lurking in the wood. Was that something moving slowly over there? What's that, flickering in the shadow? Was that someone's foot landing on a broken twig behind him? He felt brave enough to check out each possibility, telling himself to buck up, it was just his imagination playing with him...... which it was.

Due to the late hour and the effect of the earlier rain, he saw no more dog walkers. He even made one trip to the wooden building and checked it out. He put his head through both doorways but decided not to step inside. The building appeared empty anyway. He made his way back to the wood and decided that his bravery, or lack of it, was such that he wouldn't go back to that building again. He would leave it to Barry to check it out during his stag.

Finally, at 3a.m. he decided it was time to wake Barry otherwise he would be doing his mate's trick and falling asleep. Before waking him, he stoked up the fire, adding more fuel and made sure it was nice and warm when Barry got up. Satisfied that all was well, he unzipped the tent and entered. Barry was still snoring and woke with a start when Ian gently shook him. He soon recovered and realised it was time for him to do his bit outside.

'Hello, Ian. I take it all's well then?' queried Barry, slowly removing himself from his lovely warm bed space.

'Morning Barry. Aye, all's well. Not even any dog walkers now, eh, not that I would expect any at 3 in the morning, like. I suppose they will all be in bed now. I've got a fire going for when the night air gets to you. It's over in those firs so it can't be seen from outside the wood, eh! Ive just topped it up so it will be nice and warm when you go out, aye, just right! There's also a big pile of fuel near it, so you can keep it going. I must admit I'm looking forward to getting into bed. I'm so tired I'm beginning to imagine all sorts of things, aye, all sorts of spooky things out there!' finished Ian with a chuckle.

'Charming! Just the sort of thing I want to hear, NOT!' chuckled Barry.

While Ian had was talking, Barry got dressed. He picked his spear up as he made his way outside. 'I think I will have a quick walk around and then make myself a brew. Do you fancy one before you go to bed, Ian? he asked.

'Thanks Barry but I'm knackered. A good thought but I'll just go to bed if you don't mind, eh?'

'No, that's fine. I didn't want you to think I was selfish if I only made one for myself, that's all.'

'Ah, it's OK, Barry. I'll just grab my spear and be off. That's where the fire is, by the way.' said Ian, pointing out the group of firs. 'Have a good stag and hopefully you will wake me up and nothing will have happened, eh, yeh, all will have been fine, like last night. Oh and don't fall asleep now!' he joked.

'No, I won't. Goodnight, Ian. I'll be as quiet as I can,' said Barry, getting the kettle out and filling it with water while Ian disappeared into the tent.

Barry lit the stove, looking forward to his brew. Once it was ready, he stood up and took his mug and trusty spear with him to check on the fire. He warmed himself up while he finished drinking. Making his way back to the tent, he quietly set his mug down and began his first tour of the wood. He noticed it had been raining while he had been asleep. Ian hadn't mentioned it but on looking up, the stars were now out so he was happy there wouldn't be any more tonight at least.

He had the camp torch in his pocket but was aware that if he used it, he could give away their position, should Bowler be in the area looking for them. Instead, he relied on his eyes which gradually became accustomed to the night, knowing it would improve as time moved on and morning approached. At the end of his first tour he walked over to the wooden building and checked inside. Here, he used the torch to penetrate the dark areas. There was nothing to be seen, but the silence and the spooky atmosphere inside, caused Barry to retreat rather quickly with a slight rise in his heart rate. He, too, wasn't the bravest of people, especially when on his own in the dark. He blamed Bowler for this, although, in reality, it had been something he had suffered from for as far back as he could remember. He was glad to return to the warmth of the fire and grateful to Ian for having the good sense to light one and leave plenty of fuel for him so he could feed it from time to time.

He mirrored Ian's idea of touring the wood and returning to the fire at the end of each trip to warm up and stoke it up, adding fuel when necessary. This would be the best way to stay awake. The new day began to make its appearance and Barry was, by degrees, able to see further and further. A lot of the worrying dark shadows in the wood were gradually bathed in the increasing morning light, much to Barry's relief. He was beginning to believe that they had escaped Bowler's clutches and, feeling thirsty, he decided it was time for another brew so the kettle was brought into action once again.

While it was boiling, the increasing light emboldened Barry into checking the wooden building again. This time he left the torch behind. He didn't feel the need to take it with him. As he expected, the building was empty. He looked over the football fields towards the park entrance and noticed some movement. All was fine though. It was just the early morning dog walkers. He didn't believe Bowler had a dog anyway. There hadn't been one in his house when they were there and he couldn't remember seeing any dog bed or dog food or any other indication that they owned one. So far as he was concerned, anyone with a dog was not a threat.

Barry returned to the campsite and by this time the kettle had boiled, so he made himself only his second brew of the night. He was beginning to feel happier and pleased with himself for not falling asleep. He took his brew over to the fire to make sure it was still burning, adding some more wood to it, while warming his hands and enjoying a cigarette. Once his brew was finished, he replaced his cup by the stove and resolved to do another tour of the wood, his trusty spear in his hand. He was surprised how much lighter it had become. Thank god it's Summer, he thought. As he walked around, his mood lightened further. All was fine. There was nothing to worry him and he started to hum to himself the Elvis song, 'Good Luck Charm' while making what he hoped would be his final check.

He realised it was now Wednesday and they may only need to spend one more night under the stars. Maybe they would receive news that Bowler had at last been arrested! He resolved to make another phone call to the police to check and if he was still at large, he would make sure the police knew their movements in case they needed to adjust any of their plans.

Chapter Eighteen

Bowler!

Barry was returning to the tent, when some movement near its entrance caught his eye. He thought at first, maybe Ian had been to the loo, but this guy was a bigger built male! His heart dropped and his knees felt like jelly as he realised he was looking at Tom Bowler in his biker leathers!

He heard Bowler shout into the tent. 'This is what CB's can do for you and now you're gonna pay for what you've done to me!' were the words Barry heard.

Barry took a deep breath and ran up to the would-be murderer as quietly as he could. By the time he arrived, Bowler had completed unzipping the tent and was beginning to step inside. He had woken a now startled Ian with his shouting, but it took Barry's mate a while to understand what was going on.

Barry shouted 'Oy, Bowler!' as loud as he could, in the hope of startling the man.

This had the desired effect. Bowler was, as intended, visibly surprised by the shout. He must have been expecting both lads to be in the tent. He had checked the wood and hadn't seen anyone outside. This must have been when Barry was over at the wooden building.

'Oy, Bowler!' Barry had shouted. He started to turn. As he did so, Barry lunged as hard as he could with his spear. Bowler yelled out in pain but, being sober this time, he moved faster than Barry, managing to wrestle the spear out of his hand. He had the nerve to break it over his knee before throwing it away, in a show of contempt. Barry was petrified and dithered long enough to allow Bowler to launch his left fist at him aiming for the side of his head. Luckily, Barry saw it coming and managed to duck. He was unable to avoid the fist completely but it meant the blow was only a glancing one.

Barry hadn't fallen down this time. The sun was now in the sky and there was a glint of something in Bowler's right hand. It was a knife! In his anger, Bowler lashed out at Barry but he saw it coming. He raised his arm defensively. The knife shone in the morning sun's rays, striking Barry's upper arm. It caused a deep gash and blood began to flow immediately. Bowler swung his other fist which struck Barry for a second time. This blow sent him crashing to the ground. He landed with a thud, this second blow nearly knocking him out.

All this occurred in a few seconds. Bowler was intent on finishing Barry off but he had forgotten about Ian who had seen what had ensued. Before Bowler could move towards his mate, he had picked up his spear. Without needing to step out of the tent which was now fully unzipped, he gave an almighty thrust with his spear at Bowler's back. His spear was sharp enough to penetrate the leather jacket. It caused some damage to his back. The shock of the strike and the power Ian used, was enough to force Bowler to attempt to turn and face this new threat.

Ian cried out in pain as a large splinter lodged itself in his thumb. The pain was enough to make him drop his weapon.

Bowler, realised that at last he had the upper hand. His elation was short lived though. Before he could do anything, he heard a shout from about 10 yards away. He turned his head to see what the noise was and was greeted by a stone which hit him on his chin. He shouted in pained surprise and peered through the trees in an attempt to see where this unexpected attack had come from, forgetting all about Ian. A sudden movement revealed young Bobby with his catapult. He unleashed another stone from it which was just as accurate as the first one, this time striking Bowler a fraction above his left eye. A millimetre lower and he would have been blinded. Bowler was stunned by this strike and shouted out in agony. The stone had caused enough damage for blood to flow into his eyes, blurring his vision. His head was hurting and he felt dizzy. The stone had nearly knocked him out.

He cursed heavily and his fury at this unexpected attack reached boiling point. However, before he could do anything, Ian had removed the splinter ignoring any pain and had picked up his spear. He renewed his attack on Bowler's back and jabbed him again as hard as he could. He realised this was working when he noticed a trickle of blood visible from his first jab. Bowler once again winced in agony.

Bobby noticed some dog walkers nearby so he yelled, 'Help! Help! He's attacking my friends! He's a murderer! Help! Help!'

He reloaded his catapult and let loose another missile. Bowler was now more concerned about Ian so he didn't see this one coming. Once again it hit its target. Bowler was now side on to Bobby so it struck his left ear. The pain was unbearable!

A further jab from Ian! Bowler realised he was once again beaten. Caught between this two pronged attack and hearing a number of dogs barking and several voices, he realised that the two scrawny teenagers had thwarted his plans again! He was in excruciating pain. Feeling feint as well, he realised he was in danger of being caught before he had inflicted punishment on the 2 scrawny teenagers.

He staggered through the trees, away from the direction of the approaching people. Blood in his eye impaired his vision so much that he bounced from tree to tree. He let out a blood curdling roar of frustration and eventually exited the wood and negotiated a fence into somebody's back garden before once more disappearing from site. He had evaded capture yet again, but at least our heroes, with Bobby's timely help, had survived the madman's assault.

The youngster put his catapult in his back pocket and ran to the tent where Barry was just regaining his senses with Ian attending to him.

'Am I glad to see you!' said Ian to Bobby. 'What are you doing here at this time of morning, anyway?' Ian had noticed the cut on Barry's arm and before waiting for a reply, he went back into the tent to get the First Aid Kit.

'I wanted to make sure you hadn't left without saying goodbye, Ian. Barry, you're bleeding!' said Bobby, noticing the blood for the first time.

'So I am!... it's bloody painful as well!,' cried Barry, clasping his arm.

Ian returned with a bandage. At the same time a couple of dog walkers entered the wood.

'Oh my goodness! What's been going on?' said a female with a Labrador in tow.

'We've been attacked, aye, attacked by a man who is already wanted for murder! My mate has got a cut to his arm. The guy had a knife. Look!' said Ian.

'Give me that bandage. I'm a nurse. I better do that for you.'

Some other dog walkers had arrived. They checked the area for their assailant but when satisfied he had left, they returned to the campsite. Once they had learned what had occurred and realised there was nothing else to see, they left them in the good hands of the nurse.

The female continued to attend to Barry's wound. She said, 'You're going to need some stitches in that and it looks like you've had a blow to your head as well! We will need an ambulance to get you checked out.'

Ian turned to the young lad and said, 'Bobby, what you did was great, eh! You probably saved our lives but now we need you to do something else. Can you go to a house, any house, and phone for an ambulance. Barry will need some stitches, like, and they will need to check that bruise on his head. He may have been knocked out for a bit, you see, aye, knocked out when he was hit.'

'Ok Ian,' and without another word, he ran off as fast as he could.

Satisfied that Barry had Ian to look after him while they waited for the ambulance, the female nurse left, saying she would have to get to work. Barry and Ian thanked her as she exited the wood, her Labrador dog by her side. She hadn't given them her name.

'Bloody hell, Ian! My arm is sore and so is my head. I'm so glad Bobby turned up. If he hadn't, I think Bowler would have done for us!'

'Aye, I reckon it would've been curtains! How's your arm?' asked Ian, looking at the bandage.

'It's a bloody sore as I have just said but I think it will be fine, Ian. She did a good job. I'm glad she was a nurse. Let me just sit here a minute. I think I am in a bit of shock. I wasn't expecting him to turn up here. I'm bloody glad Bobby did though!'

'Yeh, he was brilliant with that catapult! I tell you what, Barry, I'll put the kettle on. I reckon you could do with a brew.'

'Ah, a good idea, Ian. I would love one….. and a cigarette,' he said, searching for his packet.

When they finished their brew, Ian went to the edge of the wood and looked over the playing fields just as a police car and an ambulance were negotiating the park entrance. There was a small figure talking to the driver of the panda and pointing in their direction. This could only have been Bobby. The vehicles formed a convoy and headed in their direction. Ian noticed two other figures with the catapult hero and all three were running behind the ambulance, chatting excitedly.

'There's a police car and an ambulance coming over the sports fields and guess what, I think Bobby has told Lorna and Paige. I think it's them running after the ambulance. Wait a minute, there are some other people heading this way as well. I wonder if it's their parents or maybe just nosey parkers because they've seen the ambulance?' shouted Ian, watching the cavalcade.

As the vehicles approached, Ian made himself visible, waving at the panda, pointing in the direction of their tent. The driver of the panda waved the ambulance on and when it reached the edge of the wood, it stopped, the medics emerging to follow Ian to their campsite and his injured friend. The police officers followed the medics and while Barry's injuries were being treated, they spoke to Ian who, in answer to their questions, explained what had happened and why. The history of all the events over the last few days was told. The officers gave no indication if they were aware of Bowler and continued with their questions.

Barry's arm was checked by the medics who confirmed the nurse had done a good job. They also stated that they would need to take him to hospital. They said he would need a tetanus jab and confirmed he would require stitches. They checked his head and after asking Barry what seemed to be a myriad of questions, were happy that he would fully recover from the blow.

When the police were satisfied they had all the information they needed, they returned to their vehicle and radio'd back to their base.

By this time, Bobby arrived with Paige and Lorna to see our heroes. Bobby had told them what had occurred.

Barry said, 'I have to go to hospital for a tetanus jab and some stitches.'

'We can look after your stuff while you are away if you want!' suggested Paige.

'Are you sure?' said Barry.

'Yes, we'll enjoy it!' It will save you having to pack it all up.' chirped in Bobby.

Barry gave a questioning look to Ian.

Ian nodded to Barry before saying to their new friends, 'OK, you've convinced us. The ambulance staff are wanting us to go now, eh, so we don't have time to pack it all away anyway. Hopefully we won't be long,' said Ian. 'Aye, we won't be long.'

Some adults were joining the throng in the wood. One couple introduced themselves as Bobby's parents, John and Margaret.

'Your son saved our skins today. His skill with that catapult was the difference,' said Barry.

'That doesn't surprise me. He has it with him all the time, but is it safe for them to be here? We heard you had been attacked by a murderer!' said John, not quite knowing what to believe.

One of the police officers heard this conversation and said, 'Don't worry folks. We've been told that one of us has to be in the vicinity, but we're sure that the attacker has cleared away from the area. My colleague has checked around and there is no sign of him. An occupant of a house over there said they saw a male matching his description, make off on a motorbike and they confirmed his head was bleeding, which ties in with what we have been told. I doubt if we will see him here again.'

'That's because I got him with my catapult!' beamed a delighted Bobby.

The medics helped Barry to the ambulance. Ian joined him after making sure everyone was happy with the arrangements and off they went to Buxton Hospital. Barry had stitches applied and was given a tetanus jab. He was told to change the bandage regularly. Ian was given instructions on how to put the bandage on and was given enough to last them until they got back home to Penrith. The hospital staff kept Barry for about another hour before satisfying themselves that he would be OK with Ian looking after him. Ian was told to get him to a hospital if he didn't show signs of recovering from the blow to the head. They told him what symptoms to look out for. After a while, an ambulance was able to return them to Chapel-en-le-Frith and their campsite.

They arrived to find their three friends in the wood along with all three sets of parents! They agreed that the lads should pack up and go as soon as possible. They didn't tell Barry and Ian that the reason was that they were worried their children were in danger, even though the assailant was probably well away from the area.

'It's lunchtime now so, if you don't mind, we will have something to eat before we pack up and leave,' said Barry.

'Where are you from?' asked Trevor, Paige's father.

'Penrith in Cumbria, so we need to get onto the A6, aye, the A6 takes us back home,' said Ian.

'I tell you what,' said Trevor, 'get Paige to take you to our house when you're ready to go and I will take you in my car, a little way up the A6. I doubt if that nutter will be on the lookout for a while and it might give you a head start at least.'

'Thanks very much! That would be great! said Barry in a weak voicer.

'I can do better than that, said Paige's mother, Barbara. 'Get your stuff packed up and come to our place. I will make you some lunch.' She looked at her husband and added, 'If that's all right with you, love?'

'Well ...... yes, that's fine Babs. Paige, bring them over once they are ready, will you! See you later, lads.'

All the parents seemed happy with this arrangement and didn't feel the need to stay any longer. They all left together, chattering away as they went. Ian told the police officers the details of their plans and they were more than happy with what they were told. It meant they could go for their own lunch break after making their report and updating the control room.

As his cooking skills weren't needed, Barry did what he could to help Ian with the tent. It was packed away in no time and with everything else sorted, it was time to leave the wood.

'This way, you two,' said Paige and our two heroes shouldered their rucksacks and were taken out of the park, their three new friends once again excitedly chattering away about the morning's events. Bobby's skills with the catapult left Paige and Lorna in awe and admiration for their younger friend.

'It looks like you saved their lives, Bobby!' said Paige.

'Yeh, I think I did!' beamed Bobby. 'I really enjoyed it, especially when my shots got him in the head! I wasn't frightened at all, either. I just concentrated on hitting that bastard!'

'Bobby! Language!' said Paige in admonishment.

Lorna laughed. Paige kept looking at him in awe. They arrived at Paige's parents house on Eccles Road and were ushered into the kitchen by Paige's mother.

'Sit down at the table lads and lunch won't be long. Do you want a cup of tea?' she asked.

'Yes please, I could murder one,' said Barry. Ian agreed.

'From what I hear, it was you two that were nearly murdered!' said Barbara. 'How do you like your tea, both?' she added, changing the subject.

Both replied that it was 'milk and two'. Barbara gave Paige the task of making it for them. Our heroes detected an aroma of bacon and other lovely smells coming from one end of the kitchen as Barbara busied herself.

149

'You two go and wait in the living room and give Ian and Barry some room. There's the Beano and Bunty to keep you occupied while your'e waiting,' said Barbara in a commanding voice to Bobby and Lorna. They both protested at first but were made to obey her instructions.

'Now, you two, is it right that with all that's happened today, you haven't eaten yet?'

'Aye, Mrs Turner. Barry would have made us breakfast this morning when *he* turned up, I mean Bowler, aye, when Bowler turned up,' said Ian.

'I thought that would be the case so I've cooked you a good breakfast. Here's some toast to be getting on with,' she said, placing it on the table, 'the rest will be just a sec. There's butter over there.'

'Here's your tea,' said Paige, placing two big mugs in front of them.

'Thanks,' came the grateful replies.

They had time for one sip each before their breakfast was placed in front of them. As they had guessed from the smells that greeted them, they were treated to Bacon, Fried Eggs, Sausage, Mushrooms, Beans and Tomatoes! It was a feast fit for a hungry pair and they got stuck right in.

'Wow, Mrs Turner! This is fantastic. Some bread and jam would have done us but this will go down a treat. Thank you! Pass the salt, Ian,'said Barry who, until he started eating, hadn't realised how hungry he was.

Barbara just gave them a broad smile.

'Right, Paige, you go in the living room and join your mates. Let Barry and Ian eat their meal in peace.'

'Oh, do I have to?' pleaded Paige.

'Yes you do, now off you go!' said Barbara, forcefully.

While the lads were eating, Barbara made herself a cup of tea and sat down at the table, delighting in watching them eat so heartily.

'How's your arm?' she said to Barry.

'A bit sore but it could have been worse. They gave Ian plenty of bandages and showed him how to put them on so I should be fine,' replied a quieter than usual Barry. He was still suffering a little from the shock of what had occurred.

'So when do you expect to get home?' she asked.

'Hopefully by Friday,' said Ian, between mouthfuls. 'Aye, Friday we think.'

'It's Wednesday today. Where are you planning on getting to tonight then?"

'That depends on what lifts we get,' said Barry. 'We would like to get as far as Lancaster, then one more lift would get us home.'

The conversation continued and Barbara asked Barry once more about his injuries. He showed her the bandage on his arm and she could already see the bruise on the side of his head. He said he felt OK and was ready to continue the journey home with Ian, once they had finished this delightful plate of food. There was so much on their plates that Barry wasn't sure he could finish it all, but somehow he managed.

As they were finishing, Barbara made them another brew and finally allowed Bobby, Paige and Lorna back into the kitchen for a chat. Her husband had realised he was low on petrol and had gone to the garage to fill up.

'OK you lot, you've got about five minutes until Paige's dad returns then these lads will have to be on their way. They've got a long way to go, you know!' said Barbara.

The five minutes went by quickly as this little group had their last chat with Bobby getting special praise for his part in repelling Bowler's attack. Bobby was floating on a cloud at this. Trevor returned and took their rucksacks which he placed in the boot of his vehicle, a black Ford Zodiac Mk 4. Our heroes said their final goodbyes while thanking Barbara again for the meal.

'See you later, Babs. I'll take them to Disley. I shouldn't be too long,' said Trevor and off they went.

Chapter Nineteen

To Garstang

'Well lads, I gather you enjoyed your meal,' said Trevor.

'We sure did,' said Ian. 'It was unbelievable, eh! We were only expecting a sandwich, like, or some toast. Aye some toast or something like that would have done, not the feast that Mrs Turner put in front of us!'

'She's a good cook and I knew she would do you proud. It will set you on until teatime I would think."

'Easily!' said Barry. 'That's the best meal we have had since we had Spag Bol on Friday, that *eventful* Friday!' said Barry.

'Aye, Friday,' echoed Ian.

Trevor continued to ask questions about what had occurred. He preferred to get it from the horse's mouth rather than second hand from his daughter. He realised that, although Paige had exaggerated slightly, the information she had passed was just about right. Having said that, he also realised the lads had kept some of the details from his daughter but he didn't dig any deeper.

It wasn't too long before they arrived in Disley. Trevor found a place to park on Market Street, near the junction with Fountain Square. The lads got out as Trevor opened the boot to retrieve their rucksacks which he passed to them before wishing them good luck with a shake of the hand. They thanked him and asked him to pass their thanks to Paige and Lorna for looking after their gear while they had been to the hospital and asked him to give some special thanks to Bobby whom they were adamant had saved their lives.

When he left, they got their bearings and began their wait for the first wagon to go by. Being a Wednesday, traffic was light, so Barry lit his first cigarette for what seemed an age. They were both silent, taking in, for the first time, what had happened since the day had dawned. Barry finished his cigarette before saying, 'This is as good a place as any to thumb a lift. We may as well stay here instead of walking on. What do you think Ian?'

'Aye, you're right, we've learnt our lesson with walking on, eh. We may as well save our feet and hitch from here,' said Ian.

It took about twenty minutes before a wagon pulled alongside them. Ian opened the passenger door to be greeted by a rotund, balding male who was giving him an almost toothless grin.

'So, me lads, where will you be going to on such a fine day?' said the driver in a broad Irish accent.

'We are heading for Cumbria, so anywhere in the right direction will do, won't it Ian.'

'Aye, that's right, we're from Cumbria,' said Ian.

'Well, bejesus! Would you believe it, I'm going that way! Not all the way to Cumbria mind, but I can get you to Garstang in Lancashire. That's most of the way, isn't it! I turn around and go back down south from there. So up you get then, lads, up you get now!'

'Thanks,' said our heroes as they climbed on board.

'I'm Seamus,' he said, 'but you can call me Paddy, OK?'

'OK Paddy. I'm Barry and this is my mate, Ian.'

'Welcome aboard, then.' said Paddy.

He set off up the road and immediately got on his CB and started a conversation with a couple of other truckers in the area. Before either Barry or Ian could speak, his first words were to inform them that he had picked up two hitchhikers and was taking them to Garstang. The conversation continued until eventually Barry managed to interrupt him.

It took Barry nearly half an hour to explain all that had occurred over the past few days and get him to understand that they didn't want it mentioned over the CB. Barry went on to suggest that he got back on his radio to tell anyone listening that they were going to get off at Stockport or some such place, just in case Bowler had heard his earlier transmission, or even one of Bowler's friends, who might be helping him find them.

'Well, would you believe it, I've got two passengers here who are on the run from a murderer. It seems to me, it does, that this is a bit hard to believe, you know. Where did you say the dastardly deed was done?'

'In Bramham in Yorkshire, eh! and it was over last weekend. Friday night we think,' said Ian, wondering why nobody seems to believe them?

Paddy, who seemed to have an obsession with his CB, was back talking to his trucker friends, asking if anyone knew about this murder! The lads winced as he asked the question. The first replies were in the negative but after a while, one trucker confirmed everything they had said, even confirming that the murderer was looking for the two lads. Paddy looked at them in a new light and at last was more careful about what he said, although Ian thought it was probably too late. They had just gone through Stockport and were heading in the direction of Manchester.

'Bejesus! You weren't telling me porkies, were you now! Would you believe it! Two lads on the run and a murderer on the loose looking for them and I blather me mouth off on the radio. Me wife tells me I talk too much, aye, a woman telling a man that *he* talks too much! That certainly *is* Irish, isn't it, me lads, eh, isn't it! Bejesus!' said Paddy, now in fits of laughter.

'Yeh, but hopefully no harm done. Tell them that you have dropped us off some place, though, just in case, will you?' said Barry.

'I certainly will, lads, I certainly will.' He thought for a moment before joining another conversation on the radio and after a while he subtly mentioned that he had dropped the lads off in Stockport because they wanted to see a relative before returning home. Barry thought that was good and thanked him for it.

They continued the journey through Manchester and on towards Preston without a break. That included without a break from Paddy's constant chatter on the CB. Our heroes wondered why he ever wanted their company. He just seemed to ignore them! At least he didn't mention the fact they were still in his vehicle. That's something, at least, thought Barry.

When they were approaching Preston, Paddy finally paid them some attention. He said, 'Would you believe it, lads, but didn't you see I haven't mentioned youse two on the radio, not once, and would you believe that I did it on purpose, you know?'

'On purpose?' replied Barry.

'Bejesus! Think about it! I told them I was dropping you off in Stockport. All my CB friends know that if I have no passengers when I talk and talk like a typical Paddy, you know. So that's what I've been doing, see? So they all believe I DID drop you off, like!'

'Oh, I get it, said Ian, 'I get it! Yes! Well done! Thanks!' said Ian.

Paddy now concentrated on splitting his chat between the lads and his CB, telling the lads about his life in Dublin before he left to settle in Derby. Once again he was in full flow, first chatting to the lads and then, before they could make any sort of reply, he proceeded to talk on his CB. He said this was to maintain his cover, that the lads had already been dropped off.

Looking ahead, Ian noticed a signpost for Garstang and was looking forward to getting out of motormouth Paddy's vehicle. He was sending them crazy! Reaching the outskirts of the town, Paddy had to concentrate on the road which meant a gap in his conversation which allowed Ian to speak.

'It's late afternoon now Paddy, eh, so we will be looking for somewhere to pitch our tent! Do you know of anywhere near the A6 we could use, like, aye, anywhere nearby?' asked Ian.

'I do. Would you believe it, there is Kepple Road Park just up the road here! Aye, you will be able to set your tent up there, no problem, lads. We are nearly there now. It's off this road here. I'll just turn down it and park outside.'

He turned down Kepple Road and parked directly outside the park entrance. The lads got their gear out of the vehicle and thanked Paddy for the lift.

'Good luck lads. I hope they get that fella soon so you can sleep easy. Take care now!' With that, he reversed his wagon up a side street before making his way back to the A6 and out of sight.

Barry lit his first cigarette since they met Paddy, picked up his rucksack and walked into Kepple Road Park, the entrance being through a car park. Ian was right behind him. The park was formed from an old tip and was now a lush park of open spaces, a children's play area and a small wooded section. As our heroes entered the park, the wooded area was immediately to their left. It wasn't an extensive wood but once inside, they happened to see a piece of ground big enough for their tent which was almost hidden by trees with just a small gap by way of access! It was perfect for them! Opposite the entrance to the park were a number of houses and bungalows so if they needed help, it could be obtained close by.

They set up camp according to their now well established routine - Ian putting up the tent as usual, with Barry preparing the food. The radio was switched on, partly in the hope that there may be some news about Bowler being arrested. The search for him had gone nationwide now. 'Yummy, Yummy, Yummy' by Ohio Express was playing so Barry hummed and sang along.

'This song has got me feeling even hungrier, Ian. I'm looking forward to have something in my 'tummy' soon. That feast Lorna's mother gave us was great but that was hours ago!'

'Snap!' was Ian's one word reply.

As usual, Ian finished the tent before the meal was ready and was about to check the wood for anything he could use for spears when Barry thrust a mug of tea in his hands.

'Ah, cheers Barry,' said Ian. He took a couple of swigs and said, 'That's almost as good as the one Mrs Turner gave us, aye, almost as good as hers.'

'Cheers Ian,' laughed Barry. He knew Ian was only joking but at the same time, he knew he was correct.

'Not a bad place here, Ian, and despite what Paddy said on the CB, I doubt we will be visited by Bowler, but if you want to make some spears then go ahead. Tea won't be too long though.'

'Aye, OK Barry. I'll finish this brew and see if there is anything I can make spears with, eh! As long as I don't wreck any of these trees, like! I don't think the locals would be too happy if I did,' said Ian.

'No probs. If you do get some branches, I will help you sort them out. It's early evening so we should have plenty of time.'

Barry continued making the tea while Ian finished his brew and started searching round the wooded area for anything he could use to make weapons with. He was hoping to make a few but he could only find a couple of specimens that would suit. They would have to do. He didn't want to damage the trees. He returned to the tent area just in time for Barry to say, 'Grubs up!'

'Perfect!' said Ian, 'I'm ready for it!'

They both sat down and tucked into the fare Barry had prepared. They listened to the radio while eating, hoping Bowler's arrest would be mentioned. No such luck. 'McArthur Park' by Richard Harris, was playing. They couldn't believe how an actor could sing such a good song! Once they finished eating, Ian got on with making the spears while Barry sorted the washing up, helping Ian once this domestic chore was completed. It was early evening by the time the spears were completed to Ian's satisfaction.

He looked at Barry and asked how he was feeling and how his arm was. He said he felt fine and didn't think the bandage needed changing until the morning. Ian was more concerned about Barry's head but his mate gave him no cause for concern.

They decided to have a walk around the area to familiarise themselves with it, a habit they were now used to. The wood was very thin and was bordered by a road on one side, some small industrial buildings on another and open playing fields on the other two. It was a small park compared to the ones they had become used to but it would suffice for tonight, especially as they had found a tight knot of trees within the wooded area itself which hid them from view. Barry was hoping this would be their last night under the stars. He was looking forward to a nice comfy bed and a whole night's sleep - no stags!

On return to their tent, they discussed the stag question and Ian, with a little difficulty, persuaded Barry that they should still continue with them. Better to err on the side of safety! It was vital that one of them was awake at any one time, said Ian during their discussions and Barry felt a bit embarrassed about it, having fallen asleep on more than one occasion.

In the meantime, they just lounged about on the grass, listening to the radio. Thankfully, they hadn't used it too much so the batteries were still OK. A good job because they didn't have any spares. Ian complained that they had hardly heard Elvis, not even his latest song 'Your Time Hasn't Come Yet, Baby', but as Barry explained, it only scraped into the charts for one week so they shouldn't expect it to be played.

Barry changed the subject. He asked Ian what he thought of Paige. He said she was OK but she couldn't hold a candle to his Rosemary back home. Good on you, thought Barry. He thought Rosemary was a really nice person and they appeared ideally suited. He wished he had someone to go home to as well. Lorna wasn't his type so he was glad she had been confined to history, to be remembered only as a passing acquaintance on this memorable trip. Yes, memorable beyond their wildest expectations!

The evening drew on and a fine mist began to form, making it dark before it's time. Not knowing the intricacies of meteorology, Barry presumed this was because of the heat of the day, the evening chill being a marked contrast.

Ian suggested Barry should have the first sleep because of the injuries he had suffered that morning at the hands of Bowler and Barry was only too ready to agree. He stretched and gave out a big yawn before bidding Ian a good stag. He made his way into the tent, not forgetting the spear Ian had fashioned for him. The day's activities had taken their toll and it wasn't long before he was asleep. Ian had been right when he suggested he should get his head down first.

Outside, Ian had made the decision that he would stay awake for as long as possible to allow Barry to have a good long rest. He would be better for it. Ever the one to do his duty properly, he picked up his spear and started his first patrol of the wood. As previously stated, it was small so he was never far from the tent. He could see the residential area across the road, with its mix of bungalows and houses. Some of them still had lights on but as the evening progressed, he gathered that the occupants were retiring to bed, as one by one the lights went out, leaving the street in darkness.

After a while, Ian noted that the mist was becoming unexpectedly worse, making it increasingly difficult to see more than a few yards in front of him. He hoped it wasn't going to be as bad as the mist at Catterick but as time went on, it thickened and he was starting to become a little disoriented. On one occasion, he nearly stumbled into the tent! He was sure it was a few yards further away. This made him feel creepy. One consolation - if anyone was looking for them, they would have great difficulty in finding them in the worsening visibility and that included Bowler. He decided he wouldn't wander too far from their camp. In fact, he lit the gas stove so he could make himself a brew. He felt he was getting a little tired and thought that making some tea would help to keep him awake and pass a little more time. He didn't want to wake Barry yet.

Whilst enjoying the drink, he thought his eyes were beginning to play tricks on him. He was sure that he could see, through the thickening mist, what appeared to be a group of people heading towards him. No, this can't be! They vanished again. He must have imagined it, so he relaxed. Wait a minute! Was it the mist or was that someone a few yards away to his left? It was difficult to tell if it was, or even how far away. The mist swirled and the figures he imagined, vanished again. He was getting tired. Surely it was just his imagination. They had been through a lot these last few days ... or was it? He kept alert, keeping his spear close by him as he tried to understand what was happening. Was there really someone out there? But why would there be? Wait! Was that a whisper? Yes, he was sure he heard voices but the mist seemed to prevent the words from reaching him properly. What's that to his left now? Someone is approaching!

His heart began to beat faster as he could make out two figures! He felt transfixed, unable to move, other than to pick up his spear! He couldn't shout to wake Barry even if he wanted to - his mouth was now too dry despite the tea. No sound came out, fear beginning to take over. Was this Bowler with someone to help him? Had he decided he needed help to do his dirty deed? If it was, this would be the end of them! They couldn't possibly fight off two! All he could think of doing was to adopt an aggressive pose. If he could only manage to yell out, he might wake someone in one of the houses but he couldn't utter one word!

The approaching figures finally noticed Ian and one of them, in a strong Lancashire accent, shouted out, 'Police ! Who's there?'

Police? Ian took in a great gulp of air. He realised he had been holding his breath. The fear of impending doom had badly affected him but he recovered sufficiently to yell back in a weak, breaking voice, 'Did you say police?'

His voice only just carried to the two, now stationary figures in front of him. Ian hadn't realised it but he was still posing an aggressive stance with the spear pointed in the direction of the officers.

A demanding voice shouted, 'Yes, police! Put that thing down!'

Ian immediately dropped his spear as if it was made of red hot coals, suddenly realising how it must have looked, and wiped his hands on his jeans while saying, 'Oh, sorry, I forgot I was still holding it!'

One at a time, the officers brushed the trees to one side to enable them to access the campsite and one of them asked again, 'What are you doing here?'

'We've been on a hitchhiking holiday and are on our away back home, aye, back home to Penrith. That's in Cumbria, stuttered Ian.'

'Yes, we know where Penrith is!'

'Are we doing something wrong in camping here?' asked Ian, still shaking.

'Some of the local residents have reported a couple of young men coming into the park and acting suspiciously. There have been a number of burglaries in the area over the last few months so they are naturally a bit nervous,' said the taller of the two officers.

'You won't believe how happy I am to see you. You may already have heard of us. Can I make you a brew? I will explain all while you are drinking it', uttered Ian, a little more relaxed.'

'I could do with a brew actually, and I'm interested in what you have to say,' said the tall one. His colleague allowed him to do all the talking while he looked about their campsite.

With the warming tea ready and in their hands - Ian having to do without because they only had two mugs - our hero began to explain all to the waiting officers.

'Most of the police in the country seem to know about us,' said Ian as the officers supped their tea. He continued to tell them all that had occurred over the last few days and it became obvious that the officers had heard something. It had been mentioned in their briefing that they could be in the area en route to Cumbria. They hadn't realised that these were indeed the teenagers they were told about. They now looked at Ian in a different light.

'Where's your mate then? Asleep, I take it?'

'Barry? Yes. Because Bowler seems to have a nasty habit of finding us, we decided to take turns on watch and Barry was the one who got hurt when we were in Chapel-en-le-Frith, so I took the first stag, eh. I don't mind admitting though, that if you had been Bowler with a mate, we would have been done for, because I froze and couldn't even speak, never mind yell out!'

The officers giggled.

The tall officer said, 'You've done the right thing. I must warn you that Bowler is still at large, so I suggest you keep alert. Now that we know who you are, we will give what passing attention we can to make sure you are safe. You've got yourselves in a bit of a situation with him. I don't want to worry you but it seems Bowler is hellbent on finding out where you are. I suggest you leave in the morning as soon as you can and get yourselves home. In the meantime, if we have any more news about Bowler we will pop in and let you know. Good luck then ..... oh, by the way, don't forget to let your mate know you have spoken to us. I don't fancy a spear in my chest if we return!'

'Cheers,' said Ian. 'Don't worry. I'll tell him.'

'Just one more thing. If we can find you, even in this heavy mist, then Bowler can. As I said, keep alert at all times!'

'Oh, we will. Don't worry about that!'

The officers left to continue their night's work.

Ian sat down to take stock. Although the officers had given him a scare, at least they now knew where they were and would give them some passing attention, they had said. It was now into the early hours of the morning and the scare had woken Ian up a bit, so he decided to leave Barry asleep for a while longer. The mist hadn't got any worse but he wasn't keen on walking away from the perceived safety of the tent so he washed the mugs which the officers had used and made himself another brew while wondering what drama might be waiting for them in the coming day. He hoped it would be peaceful and that they would be informed that Bowler had been arrested but he didn't hold out much chance of that.

When he nearly fell off his seat, he realised it was now time to wake Barry for his stag. He looked at his watch and thought he had done well to last until 4 a.m.

He woke Barry and asked him how he was feeling. He said he was fine and felt suitably refreshed - no nightmares! - so Ian told him all about the visit of the policemen and suggested he didn't wander far from the tent because of the disorienting affect of the mist. Barry thanked Ian for letting him sleep for so long and told him to get to bed.

It didn't take long at all before Ian's snores, reached Barry's ears. He just smiled and continued making himself a brew. While the kettle was boiling, he had a quick look around, taking care to keep the tent in site, adhering to Ian's warning. The mist was still swirling about and it was thick enough in places to disturb Barry's happy mood. He cheered up again when he recalled the ghostly mist they had encountered in the field at Catterick, almost breaking into laughter at the recollection. He yawned as he picked up his now steaming mug of tea and stood up, making sure he had his spear in his other hand.

He had another walk round the immediate area, humming to himself one Elvis song after another. He found it a good way of staying awake, although after the sleep he had just had, he didn't for one minute think he would fall asleep.

The sun's light was now beginning to make itself known and, coupled with the slowly lifting mist, Barry started cheering up. Any anxiety he had been feeling was also vanishing with that mist. Gradually, he could see further and further and the edges of this small wood were now revealed. As time passed, he could make out the houses across the road. Ian had told him that the police came checking up on them because someone from one of those properties had reported them as suspicious. He wondered which house it was, as he lit a cigarette and turned to walk to the other edge of the wood. All was peace and quiet and he was surprised at the warmth in the sun, so early in the morning. It looked like it was going to be another scorcher. He liked the sun so he was looking forward to it.

Chapter Twenty

Another Good Curry!

At around 9a.m. he thought it was time to wake Ian. He had only been asleep for about five hours but they really needed to make tracks. Barry put the kettle on for a brew and made a good start on breakfast. Ian was a little grumpy when he woke up but his mood improved when Barry put a hot mug of tea in his hands and announced breakfast would be served in five minutes.

'How was your stag, Barry? asked Ian.

'It was OK. It was easy for me. I was refreshed and had the pleasure of watching the mist go away and the sun come up. I didn't have any visit's from the police so I presume that means Bowler is still at large, unfortunately. I had a couple of brews, though and the time soon passed. I could do with my bandage changed after breakfast if you could manage that for me'

No problem. They showed me exactly what to do. It's not difficult, eh. Just tell me when.'

After a slight pause and with a smile on his face, Barry said, 'Breakfast is ready,' and handed Ian his plate.

'Oh, that looks good Barry and I'm ravenous!' said Ian, tucking in.

'Let's see if we can get all the way home today, Ian,' said Barry while eating. 'We should do. The route seems straight forward. Any wagons going North on the A6 are sure to be going to Penrith, the majority of them anyway.'

'Fingers crossed, Barry.'

They completed their breakfast, Barry had his bandage changed and started their packing routine, Barry, as usual, sorting the cooking gear and, when completed, gave Ian a hand with the tent. They made sure they strapped their short spears to their rucksacks and checked their camp for rubbish which they collected, ready to dispose of in any bin they came across.

Making their way out of the park, they turned up the road towards the A6. It was a hot day and there appeared to be a lot of traffic on the main road already. Still feeling cheerful, they turned onto the A6 and headed into the centre of Garstang. Because they were expecting uninterrupted sunshine for the day, they were wearing T-Shirts. They enjoyed the feel of the sun's rays on their bodies.

'If we are hoping to make it home today, we won't need to buy any more things in the local shops. A good job because I am nearly out of cash,' said Barry.

'I'm the same. Just a couple of quid left, aye, a couple of quid, that's all,' replied Ian.

They continued to walk through Garstang, not noticing the traffic, which was getting heavier and heavier and slowing to a crawl. As they reached the far end of the town they sat down for a minute,

Barry lighting his first cigarette for a while. They sat down on their rucksacks using them as seats. Barry took another drag of his cigarette and for the first time noticed how slow the traffic was moving. It was nose to tail with cars. He then realised what could be happening. Schools had only recently broken up for the Summer and the hot weather had sent families pouring out of the cities to head to holiday destinations including the Lakes. The M6 motorway was in the process of being built but was still some way off being completed so the A6 was still the main transport hub.

'Ian, look at this traffic! I don't think we are going to get a lift today, judging by all this! We can walk faster than they are moving!' he said.

'Bloody hell, Barry! What the hell are we going to do?'

'This hot weather must have brought them out and I think it will be the same for the next few days. Tomorrow is Friday and it's usually busy at the best of times. If this heat continues, I can't see the traffic getting any better!'

'Shit! What are we going to do, Barry? How are we gonna get anywhere today?

Barry thought for a moment. He put his cigarette out and said, 'Did you notice a phone box anywhere while we were walking through the town?'

'Yes,' said Ian. 'I think there is one back down the road a bit, opposite some hotel or other, aye, near a big hotel.'

'I tell you what. We are gonna have to give my Dad a ring. He was gonna have this week off work. He might come to pick us up.'

'Oh, right! Fingers crossed, Barry.'

They slung their rucksacks on their backs and started walking back down the road, passed the cars crawling along in the opposite direction, receiving some funny looks from some adult occupants and sniggers and rude signs from some of the children in the rear seats. Our heroes just ignored them. They were more concerned about how they were to progress today. The phone box was eventually sighted and Barry went inside after first taking his pack off and finding the required change. He rang his home number and after a couple of rings it was answered by his mother.

'Hiya mam, it's me, Barry.'

'Oh, hello son! Where are you and why haven't you been ringing us? We've had a policeman at the door. Something about you two being chased by a murderer! We've been really worried! Your Dad's rang the police station every day to see if there was any more news but they haven't been able to tell him anything.'

'Mam, mam, stop talking a minute and just listen. We are both OK and on our way home but we do have one tiny problem.'

'What's that, son? What's the matter?'

'We are in a place called Garstang, near Lancaster but the traffic is nose to tail and I think it will be like this all day. We can walk faster than the cars are moving! The sun has brought them out and I don't think it will be any different tomorrow or even at the weekend. Do you think Dad might be able to come for us? We're stuck otherwise and we are nearly out of money and food. We thought we would easily get home today but not now.'

'He's down at his allotment and won't be back until dinner time. Oh, just a minute, son.....'

Barry could hear his mother put the phone on the table and walk out of the room. She was talking to someone but he couldn't make out what she was saying. Eventually, he heard her come back in the room and pick up the phone.

'I've just sent Anne to the allotment to get him to come back. I'm sure he will come for you but leave it for another hour then ring me again just to make sure...'

Iris then went on to ask exactly what had been going on. Had there been a murder? Were they being followed? Was he still on the run? etc etc. Barry was running out of money so he told his mother that he would explain everything when he saw them. He said he would ring back in an hour and quickly put the phone down, not forgetting to say goodbye.

He left the phone box and told Ian the gist of the conversation.

'He's at his allotment, but I think he will come for us. We've just got to sit quiet for another hour before we know for sure.'

'Aye, I'm sure he will, Barry. He won't leave us stranded, especially knowing what has gone on.'

They moved over to the wide grass verge and lounged there, enjoying the warm sunshine.

'Guess what, I haven't seen one lorry go by! Apart from a couple of vans, it's all been cars, aye, just cars,' said Ian.

'You're right Ian. It's as if lorry drivers knew it would be busy today. Unless they are waiting until nighttime when it's sure to be quieter,' said Barry.

'That could be right. I suppose if the worst comes to the worst, we could hitch tonight, eh?'

'Let's hope we don't have to, Ian.'

'Aye, let's hope not.'

Barry dug out a bottle of water from his rucksack and handed it to Ian. It was a hot day and they needed some refreshment. The hour passed by with cars still crawling along. Barry thought that if his dad did come for them he would suffer the same fate and they would be no better off. He decided he had better let his dad know the traffic situation as he entered the phone box again.

'Hello,'

Barry recognised his dad's voice.

'Hiyah dad, it's me.'

'Hiya son. I believe you need me to rescue you,' said his dad, sounding jolly.

'Yes please, dad, but just one thing. The reason we need rescuing is because it is nose to tail slow moving traffic here. We can walk faster than cars can move at the moment. Maybe you should wait a while before setting off.'

'Don't worry, son. By the time I get sorted out it will be lunchtime so I won't set off until after I've had something to eat. I suggest you do the same. Hopefully by the time we get down there the traffic will have eased. If not, we will just have to take our time coming home. Nothing else we can do about it. I take it you're no longer in any danger from that madman?'

'No. I reckon we've lost him, dad, but you never know! I won't be happy until we know he has been caught. He's a nutter. I reckon he has flipped his lid. It just amazes me how he can keep evading capture!'

'He sounds a wily character. I better go now. Best keep yourself away from the roadside just in case. Oh, Where abouts in Garstang are you?'

'We are near the Crofters Hotel. You will see it. It's beside the A6 on the right hand side as you come in from Penrith. We will be near there and will keep an eye out for you. Just drive into their car park, dad, and we will meet you there.'

'OK, son. It will probably be mid afternoon as long as traffic isn't backed up on our way down as well.'

'Hopefully not. In Garstang, it's just the traffic going North that's tailed back. It's free flowing in the other direction.'

'Right, son. Take care. Bye for now.'

'Bye, dad.'

Barry put the phone down and exited the box. He informed his mate that his dad was going to pick them up and suggested that they find somewhere they could make something to eat. It would be their last cooked meal on their trip. Ian suggested a field just up from the hotel. There were a couple of trees which would shield them from the road and any prying eyes so they decided to prepare their last meal there. Barry got the stove going and rummaged in his rucksack for something to cook. He had a tin of stew they had acquired in the last shop, a few potatoes and an onion. He reached in again and got hold of the carton of curry powder.

'Hey, Ian, how to you fancy another of those curry's?'

'Aye, that's a good idea, Barry! I enjoyed the last one. Really tasty, aye, really tasty,' said Ian, licking his lips in anticipation.

'OK. Let's see if this one is as good. I will prepare it all. Just keep an eye out for Bowler, Ian, although I really think we have escaped him.'

'Yeh, I think your'e right, Barry, but I will keep a lookout just in case.'

Barry made sure all the food was prepared ready for cooking and lit the gas stove for what he hoped would be the last time on this trip. After the potatoes had boiled for a while, he put everything in one pan. It was easy enough to prepare. While it was cooking, he noticed Ian had fallen asleep on the warm grass. He didn't mind. Ian had stayed awake longer than he should have done to give Barry more time to recover from his injuries and it was easy enough to keep a watch for Bowler. The meal cooked itself, just requiring a stir now and then. He had a quick taste and decided more curry powder was required so another spoonful was stirred in. That should do it, he thought. He put the radio on, very quietly, hoping it wouldn't disturb Ian. He was hoping, probably beyond hope, that he may get news that Bowler had been apprehended but so far there was no mention of him. Time passed with Barry enjoying the sun while Ian continued to sleep. The food only needed an odd stir to make sure it wasn't sticking to the pan. After a while, it appeared ready to Barry, so he finally woke his pal.

'Here you are Ian, a curried stew, of sorts,' said Barry, with a grin.

'Oh, cheers, Barry. I'm ready for this!' said Ian, gratefully accepting his plate.

'Blimey! That's hot! The curry taste, I mean!' said Ian.

'It surely bloody is! I had a taste of it earlier but thought it needed some more so I put another big spoonful in. Nice though! Makes the stew more edible, I think!' laughed Barry.

'Very true! laughed Ian. 'I just need a hosepipe in case I burst into flames! Your curries should come with a health warning!'

The last of their water was soon used up but it did little to help ease the burning sensation caused by Barry's over-use of the curry powder. Nevertheless, they enjoyed the feast and were now firm curry lovers, although not quite as hot in future!

Barry once again took on the task of washing up and repacking, allowing Ian to lie back again and soak up the sun while they awaited the arrival of their transport home. He had a quick check of the hotel car park before rejoining his mate, having seen no sign of his father. He shouldn't be too long now, he thought. He sat down beside Ian, who was asleep again, and lit another cigarette, enjoying the warm, pleasant sunshine. He imagined how easy it would be to fall asleep as well but he was still alert to the possibility of Bowler interrupting such a pleasant afternoon and he needed to keep a watch for his dad. He looked at his surroundings. On one side of the trees there were open fields and he thought he could make out some cows in the distance but otherwise it was peace and quiet. Relaxing.

On the other side of the trees, he was looking back to the A6 and the still slow moving traffic, the occupants of the cars looking sweaty and frustrated by their lack of progress. Windows were open to allow some cooler air in but Barry guessed that all they would get would be more car fumes than fresh air.

Rather than risk falling asleep, Barry decided to have another walk to the hotel car park which he checked but there was still no sign of his father's car. He started to make his way back to the sleeping figure of Ian and was just entering the field when he heard the pip of a horn. He looked round and saw his father waving frantically at him. He gave him a wave back and shouted to him to make for the car park, before going to wake his mate up. They grabbed their rucksacks and made their way with a renewed spring in their step to the awaiting car.

'Hi Dad! Thanks for coming to pick us up. As you can see the road is manic. Maybe you should have left it until later!'

'Hi son, hi Ian. No, it's OK. We fancied a ride out anyway. We'll just have a break. Your mam wants the toilet. I'm sure they will let her use it in here,' said Ed.

Barry's mother was just getting out of the car. She walked over to the lads to say hello.

'Hello you two!'

'Hi mam' and 'Hi Mrs Davidson,' they replied.

When Iris reached them, she gave them each a hug and started to chuckle. 'I was just saying to your dad before we got out of the car, what good suntans you've both got, but it's not sun, is it! When's the last time you two had a decent wash, you're filthy?'

'Trust you, mam! We haven't had time for that sort of thing. Remember, we have been chased so we didn't really bother too much,' replied an embarrassed Barry.

'No, we had to keep moving, didn't we Barry,' said Ian, equally embarrassed.

'What excuses!' she said, trying to conceal a smile.

'Yes, well, anyway, nice to see you again, mam,' said Barry, giving his mother another hug.

Iris asked all sorts of questions. Were they OK? Who is this Bowler fella anyway? Was it true he killed his wife and why on earth was he after them? What had they done? The police had only told them so much. Barry and Ian replied to some of the questions but lied a little when they came to the reason for Bowler's obsessive interest in them, explaining that he was so jealous of his wife that when he heard she had taken them in and fed them, he believed that only one thing could have happened.

Barry asked if they had heard any more about him. Had he been arrested yet, but the answer was 'no', as far as they were aware.

While Barry's mother went into the hotel to use the toilet's, they stashed their rucksacks into the boot of the car and waited outside with George.

'I heard this Bowler fellow hurt one of you, is that true?' asked George.'

'Don't tell mam, but he attacked me with a knife and cut my arm a bit. It wasn't bad, though. Just needed a couple of stitches. I'm surprised mother hasn't noticed this bandage but I'm just gonna tell her I burnt it on the gas stove. I got a bang on the head as well, on two different occasions! But I'm OK. We armed ourselves with some spears Ian made. We've still got two with us.' They both continued to tell their tale to George and were just finishing when Iris returned. George tried to hide the concern on his face from her.

'I'll just have a cigarette,' she said. 'There's no rush anyway, looking at this tailback. Do you want one Barry?'

He accepted one and suggested they get away from the traffic and ushered them to the trees under which they had had their meal earlier. Iris did indeed notice the bandaged arm but his account of burning it on the stove was accepted. A few minutes later, their cigarettes finished, they made their way back to the car and attempted to join the traffic. A considerate driver allowed them to join the crawl through Garstang and their return to Penrith began.

'It's not as bad further on,' began George. 'The problem is some major roadworks, about another mile ahead. I think it's to do with the building of the motorway. As soon as it's built the better.'

'Pity it wasn't built now,' said Iris.

Chapter Twenty One

Endgame!

It seemed to take an age to get to the site of the roadworks but once they were through them the traffic did indeed begin to ease and George could pick up speed. A cheer went up from the occupants of the vehicle.

'At last! We'll soon be home! Who would have thought we would have such a memorable time away, aye, a memorable trip, eh, Barry?'

'Your right there, Ian. The concert was as good as we expected as well, mam!'

'Was it? I'm glad you enjoyed it after all the problems you had just to get there,' said Iris.

Barry and Ian then went on to tell them all about the concert and in particular the girl with 'Elvis Presley' stitched into her jeans. By the time they were finished they were just passing through Kendal and heading towards Shap on the A6. Traffic was now very light. Every now and then, Iris would ask a question about Bowler and the lads were careful with their replies. They didn't want to worry her unduly.

'I can't believe there is hardly any traffic now. Everyone seems to be going to the South Lakes. Only a couple of cars in front and one solitary wagon behind us. Just shows you it was those roadworks causing the problem at Garstang,' said George.

Barry turned round to have a look at the wagon. It was a green Foden flat-back. The sun was reflecting on the windscreen so he couldn't make out how many people were in the vehicle. He noticed that it wasn't carrying a load so he guessed it could be on its way to collect one.

The conversation continued with Iris telling the lads all that had happened in Penrith while they had been away. It didn't amount to a lot but it was interesting to Iris. She said that Bernie and Ada sent them their best wishes and hoped they had had a good time and Anne was very jealous of them. She would have loved to have gone with them if it had been possible. George wasn't in a hurry to get home so any cars on the road made their way passed. He was enjoying the ride out. Only the lorry failed to pass them, maintaining a healthy distance behind. They continued to make good progress towards Shap and the lorry was the only other vehicle they could see on the road.

As they were passing Wasdale Beck, the Foden seemed to increase speed. It was now right behind them, giving George the impression the driver was going to make an overtaking manoeuvre. Being courteous, and seeing there was no vehicle coming in the other direction, he slowed and indicated to the left, a signal to the lorry driver that the road was clear. Overtaking, however, was the last thing on the lorry driver's mind! He was now within inches of George's car and making no attempt to get passed!

'What the hell is he playing at?' said George, with a concerned frown on his face as he gestured behind him.

Iris and our heroes turned to look behind, just in time for the lorry to make contact with their car! They were all jolted back in their seats but George managed to keep control of the vehicle, the lorry falling back a few yards.

'What the hell was that for?' he shouted.

The lorry once again picked up speed and rammed George's car for a second time, this time a little harder!

'He's done it again George! He's done it again! What's he doing that for?' shouted Iris as fear started to grow.

Once again, George managed to maintain control and increased his speed.

'Oh my god! Mam! Dad!, that's Bowler!' yelled Barry. 'That's not his vehicle either! It says 'Lancashire Farms' on the front!'

'Yeh, Lancashire Farms' said Ian. 'Put your foot down and get away from him, Mr Davidson. I think he is trying to run us off the road!'

George was already doing just that but the lorry was still right behind them. His car didn't have enough power to put any distance between them. The road had some twists and turns but George remembered there was a lay-by on the other side of the road which he believed he was now nearing. It was quite a long lay-by on a slight bend and he estimated if he hit it at speed he could still bring the car to a halt before he reached the lay-by's end. By making a sudden change in direction, he hoped he would take the lorry driver by surprise forcing him to continue on the road. His next concern would be making sure he kept the car upright but he didn't worry his passengers about that. As long as he could get his vehicle into the lay-by on all four wheels was all he was concerned about at the moment. He didn't have time to think beyond that.

He put his foot to the floor and picked up speed. The lorry driver was doing the same but couldn't quite close the gap. The slight left hand bend appeared. George could see the lay-by.

'Hold on tight!'

All his driving skills and experience were needed as he swerved suddenly to the right, hitting the entrance to the lay-by perfectly. He slammed on his breaks as he feverishly turned the wheel to the left! He knew there was a wall separating the lay-by from a field. If he hit the wall it would have been certain disaster! Iris screamed in fright! She feared the worst. This affected George's concentration. He was on two wheels when the driver's side glanced off the first of two huge piles of sand which he wasn't expecting! The car came to a halt. It was nothing short of a miracle that his car was still upright!

He looked across at Iris and saw that she had banged her head on the side of the car. 'Iris! Iris!' cried George! He feared he had caused her a serious injury!

She moved.

'Oh my head,' she moaned.

As George hoped, Bowler went shooting by but they weren't out of danger yet. This was a particularly long lay-by. There was no traffic about and Bowler managed to cross the road. Although he had overshot the far end, he managed to reverse back and block the exit, just in case George was intending to drive straight through.

He got out of his vehicle and started to walk towards their car! In his hand he had what looked like a piece of metal piping! He obviously meant business! This would be the end, for them .... or him! It was their OK Corral!

There were no other vehicles in the lay-by which meant they could expect no immediate assistance. When Barry and Ian saw Bowler, they were both on the same wavelength. Barry shouted, 'Dad! You look after mam and we will deal with him!'

They got out of the vehicle and ran to the boot. They opened it and removed their spears from the rucksacks. They were only the shorter versions but it was all they had. Barry's dad stayed in the car to comfort Iris. She was still a bit dazed and he was worried for her.

Bowler was now getting closer!

Barry was closest to the roadside and Ian was next to the second pile of sand. This put Bowler between them, Ian being to Bowler's left and Barry to his right.

'You didn't expect me to be in that wagon, did yer! Ha! Well I'm here for the final retribution and I'm not just gonna get one of you, I'm gonna get both of you! And while I'm at it, I might as well get those others in that car!' he yelled. 'It will make me even more notorious!'

He's completely flipped thought Barry. He was shaking like a leaf and sweat was already building on his forehead. He was afraid of Bowler but determined to protect his parents if he could.

'You'll have to deal with us first!' shouted Ian, equally determined.

'Yeh. We've been more than a match for you before and we will be again! yelled Barry.

They were both sick of Bowler and were now filled with grim determination that this was going to be the last time they would be confronted by him, whatever the outcome. Their anger at everything he had put them through had added a little steel to them. They were also aware that they were all that stood between Bowler and Barry's parents.

One heroes kept their positions, realising this put Bowler in a predicament. For him to get any one of them he would have to turn, leaving his back exposed to the other. Bowler seemed to understand this as he contemplated what to do. Ian noticed what looked like blood on the metal pipe and wondered where that had come from.

While he worked out what to do, Bowler kept on talking. He was pleased with how easy it was for him to find them. 'I heard you had been dropped off at Garstang. CB's are a great thing, aren't they? So I made my way up there. I had to be careful, mind, because the coppers want me. Hahaha! Have I given them a run for their money or what! I stole this vehicle, well, hijacked it, really. You see, I struck lucky. I saw you get in this car at the hotel. I was further down the road at the time, looking for you on foot and this wagon was going by.'

He kept moving slowly towards the car hoping to provoke an action from the lads. Barry moved to stand in this way. Bowler halted.

He continued his monologue, 'The only wagon on the road at the time. It was going slow because of the traffic so I shouted at the driver and asked him for a lift. Hahahaha! I told him I was a lorry driver and needed to get back to my vehicle further up the road. He said get in, just as I saw you get in that car. There were a few others between you and me when you were waved in to join the traffic.' Bowler sounded deranged which worried Barry and Ian even more. This would make him even more dangerous! He wouldn't care what he did or what happened to himself!

While he was talking he kept turning to face first one then the other of our heroes but they kept moving as well, each trying to keep to their side of Bowler. They succeeded in keeping away from the car.

Suddenly Bowler made his move! He made a lurch towards Ian, with the metal piping raised high, ready to strike!

Ian was taken by surprise and stepped back. He found himself stumbling onto the second mound of sand! His right hand went out to steady himself but when he realised what it was, he grabbed a handful and threw it hard at Bowler's face. It was the last thing Bowler expected.

The sand hit him and a lot of it went into his eyes. He staggered backwards for a second.

Ian had time to drop his spear and grab another two handfuls. He threw them at Bowler, aiming for his face.

He was spitting and coughing up sand. He was looking through blurred eyes but this didn't stop the mad man from stepping one pace forward!

He swung the lead pipe at where he believed Ian was. Ian staggered back and once again ended up falling onto the mound of sand, but Bowler had missed!

Barry had been frozen to the spot while this was going on but now ran forward as Bowler was preparing to wield the metal pipe at Ian again.

He used all his force to jab his spear into Bowlers backside. He aimed as low as he could and hit his target with so much force that his spear snapped in two!

Bowler yelled out! He was in agony. He had forgotten about Barry. He turned round, lashing out at the same time. He didn't know exactly where Barry was. He didn't care. He waved the iron bar wherever he thought he was. His eyes were sore and the pain up his backside was excruciation. Barry had moved to one side. He was safe from Bowler's mad lurches.

Although in a mad rage, Bowler still had the sense to realise that the tables were quickly turning - yet again - so he ran in the direction of the wagon. He could hardly see. Everything was just a blur to him. He wielded the metal piping as he passed where he thought Barry was, screaming and swearing with every step.

He knew there was some bottled water in the cab. He intended to flush as much sand as he could out of his eyes so he could resume his attack and regain the advantage. He would be a bit more careful this time. He had to be quick though. A passing vehicle or even police car would notice the fracas and come to his enemy's aid.

Barry ran over to Ian and helped him out of the sand. They had both seen Bowler making for his vehicle.

'Quick, Ian. We can't let him get in there. He might try to ram dad's car again!'

They went headlong towards Bowler who had reached the cab and was opening the door!

He had dropped the iron bar as he approached the cab. He was climbing in as Barry reached him and grabbed his legs!

with a great effort he gave a great tug. Once more Bowler was taken by surprise! He almost fell on top of Barry who lost his grip!

Bowler was badly winded and Ian, who had been just a couple of steps behind Barry, grabbed one of Bowler's legs before he could recover and started dragging him along the ground! He didn't want to risk him gaining a purchase on anything.

Bowler was livid! He screamed and yelled and kicked out in his rage! Ian almost lost his grip but he held on tight!

Somehow, Barry managed to grab Bowler's other leg and joined Ian in dragging him around. It took

172

a superhuman effort to keep their hold. Bowler was cursing and swearing like the mad man he was, all the time.

Without realising it, their constant tugging of Bowler's legs meant they were getting closer to the car!

George had seen what was happening and, happy that Iris was going to be OK, he dashed to the boot and took out his tow rope. Running over to our struggling heroes, he jumped on Bowlers back with some force, winding Bowler yet again in the process.

Before he was able to shake off, George managed to loop the rope over Bowler's head. He pulled hard and forced his head back.

'Put your right arm behind you or I will break your fucking neck!' shouted George.

Bowler ignored him and kept kicking out, trying to free his legs! In his madness he still believed he would succeed in killing them all.

Barry and Ian struggled to maintain a hold!

'Fuck you!' swore Bowler. Now that he wasn't being dragged around, he was able to get his hands close to his body and readied himself for an attempt to turn over, which would force George off his back and help him to finally dislodge Ian and Barry.

George had other ideas and managed to place another loop over his neck and pulled even harder. He was now slowly strangling Bowler.

He tried to yell out but the rope was tight on his throat. There was nothing he could do. Even so, he wasn't planning on giving up and kept struggling.

His efforts started to get weaker as George's stranglehold was taking its toll. Bowler was slowly losing consciousness. George had to be careful he didn't kill him!

Ian understood what was happening and let Bowler's leg go. Instead, he grabbed his right arm, bringing it back to George who knotted the rope around it. He then grabbed the left arm and again passed it back to George who now tied both hands together.

There was still enough rope to tie a now silent Bowler's legs up as well.

Bowler was now almost unconscious. He seemed to be struggling to breath.

At last, the fight had gone out of him. There was nothing he could do. He was beaten.

Rather than have a death on his hands, George decided he better loosen the noose around the mad-man's neck and allow him to breathe. He wasn't going anywhere soon, trussed up like that!

'Bloody hell, dad! Brilliant! .....God, I'm knackered ..... how's mam?' shouted Barry.

'She'll be OK, son. She's awake and talking when I left her. No permanent damage I think,' said George, evidently out of breath. 'Well done you two! By the looks of him you faced up to a powerful man!'

'I tell you what, Mr Davidson. I'm surprised I haven't shit myself to be honest! Aye, shit myself,' said Ian, still shocked at what had occurred.'

They could now afford to laugh. Because of the circumstances, it was more laughter brought on by relief. To their surprise they had survived! At last, they had Bowler exactly where they wanted him! Not before time!

While they were getting their breath back and congratulating each other, a police car appeared from the Kendal direction. It entered the lay-by and two officers alighted.

When they saw Bowler tied up on the ground they removed their truncheons, not yet understanding the scene that greeted them.

'This is Tom Bowler. He is wanted for murdering his wife in Yorkshire and trying to murder us!' shouted Barry.

The officers looked at the distraught figure of Bowler, who, thankfully was breathing again. Beside him were our heroes who looked like they had just gone ten rounds with Cassius Clay. George was still holding onto the end of his tow rope. The officers had heard of Bowler. His disappearance and ability to evade the police from a number of forces had become legendary.

'OK, we will take it from here, sir. Apart from him, is anyone injured?' asked PC52.

'My wife has suffered a blow to the head. He was trying to run us off the road so I had to swerve in here to escape him. She is awake but shaken up.'

'Anybody else?'

Ian and Barry said they were fine, just a few bruises.

Turning to his colleague, PC52 said, 'John, radio this in please and call for an ambulance, mate.'

'Is that the vehicle he was using?' asked PC52, turning again to George while pointing in the direction of the Foden.

'Yes, it is. Come to think of it, he said he had hijacked it so it's not his. You better check inside, officer,' said George.

'And one more thing, officer,' said Barry, 'he tried to attack us with that piece of metal piping over there. He didn't hit any of us with it but isn't that blood on it?'

PC52 checked that Bowler was secure before going over to the metal piping. It did appear to be blood! What the hell was he going to find in the Foden?

He opened the drivers door and climbed inside. 'Oh god!' he muttered.

He got back out and ran to the other side. Opening the passenger door he looked inside. In the footwell was the body of what he presumed to be the owner of the vehicle. There was a horrendous gash to his head, his lifeless eyes staring into space! Leaving the vehicle, he went over to PC371 who was on the car radio back to base.

'John. This is a murder scene. There is a body in the passenger footwell of that Foden. I'm presuming it's the owner, judging by what these people are saying, so we will need the usual kit and caboodle up here for this one. I'll start taping off the lay-by.

'My god, did you hear what he just said? Another murder!' said Ian, 'aye, another murder!'

George had already gone back to check on Iris but he had heard what the officer had said. Barry was speechless. He found it hard to understand that people really did commit murder, and to be involved indirectly in two was hard to take in. If they hadn't gone into Bramham, none of this would have happened! He also realised how close they had been to suffering the same fate!

George believed his vehicle was still roadworthy but he was not allowed to move it because this was, as the officer had already said, a murder scene.

An ambulance arrived. Bowler was checked by the medics - he would survive - before taking Iris to Kendal hospital so that her head injury could be properly checked out. The officers allowed George to travel with her. They would get a statement from him later.

Tom Bowler was taken into custody and would receive any necessary treatment for his injuries which weren't as bad as the lads hoped. They knew he would be facing life behind bars anyway. Our heroes' journey home had to be delayed further as they were taken to Kendal police station for yet another statement.

Later that evening they were taken back to Penrith and arrived home just as George was on the phone to Barry's sister, Anne. He had explained to her what had happened and letting her know that Iris was staying in hospital overnight. The doctor had said it was only a precaution because she had lost consciousness for a while when she received her injury. He had given his statement to an officer while Iris was being assessed and he was to go back to the ward in the morning. All being well, she would be allowed home. His car was still in the lay-by. The police would let him know when he could retrieve it

Barry spent the evening explaining all that had occurred, to his siblings. Anne changed the dressing on his arm. The next day, Iris was allowed to leave the hospital. They returned to Penrith on the bus because George had another 24 hours to wait before he could collect his car.

In the days that followed, Bernie and Ada Nichol regained possession of their tent and equipment. Thankfully it was all in order. Ian went back to his job as a welder and renewed his relationship with Rosemary, while Barry, still without a girlfriend, resumed his job at WH Smith's, wondering when his luck in his relationships would change.. He told them everything that had occurred and it took a number of days before they finished questioning him. They looked at him in admiration. He seemed different - more mature. Joan was nice to him from thereon which pleased Barry. It was far better than her previous offhand manner.

Barry and Ian were 'flavour of the month' for a while in their neighbourhood, after which, normal service was resumed.

A few months later, they heard that while Bowler was awaiting his trial, he had hung himself in his prison cell. Our heroes would no longer need to appear in court and Ian, who was now engaged to Rosemary, agreed with Barry that it was the best end of him.

Another Monday morning and Barry could be found once more in the cellar at work. 'Yesss! The Elvis Monthly! I will take it home on my break so that Anne can have a good read before I finish work!

That evening, at home, his mother said to him, 'I've got a special treat for your tea tonight which I am sure you will like. Spaghetti Bolognese!"

THE END.

Printed in Great Britain
by Amazon